Sunflowers

Beneath

the Snow

To Iris & Friends,
May you always be
like the sunflower turning
toward the light!

♡ Teri MBlva

Sunflowers Beneath the Snow

TERI M. BROWN

atmosphere press

This book is dedicated to my sweet darling, my family, and my dear friends. Thank you for supporting me in my dream.

Part 1

IVANNA

Chapter 1

1973

Lyaksandro was aware of just three things. The slit of sun sneaking through the hurriedly closed curtains in an otherwise claustrophobic room. The air sucking into his lungs only to escape again in uneven gasps. And the unsympathetic, unyielding metal pressed against his temple awaiting his decision.

How had he gone from a simple man – Lyaksandro Hadeon Rosomakha – a university employee, a son, a father, and a husband – to a man facing a decision at the end of a gun? What had pulled him into a life littered with secret meetings, men with no names, and information passed in the hours between darkness and dawn?

Undoubtedly, the state police would slap an informant label on his forehead despite the mundane activities he was called upon to perform. His treachery was not the kind to find its way into the banned spy novels still wending their way through the eager hands of boys wanting to prove they were men. No, rather than the high-tension, clandestine meetings of books and movies, he merely passed along innocuous information on loose pages of lined notebook paper carefully taken from the university library that employed him.

Sometimes he was asked to provide a list of those visiting the library on any given day. Other times, he would be asked to provide the names of those who checked out certain books or inquired about specific topics. He'd even been asked to photocopy pages from manuals. He didn't know what they were looking for. The link between a man named Bodashka Kravets and an interest in 4th century Ukrainian history, for example, was never explained. Nor did he truly know who was asking. His place in the resistance machinery was minor at best, and deadly at worst.

In this moment, though not for the first time, he wondered if the information was actually worth dying for. He was simply a small gear in a huge network of informants. Yet, despite the inconsequential nature of the information he passed, he understood, if caught, he was unlikely to survive. Informants – spies – regardless of their importance, were not tolerated. At best, he might face permanent imprisonment in a psychiatric facility. At worst, he would be killed and unceremoniously dumped into the nearest ravine, never to be heard from again.

The cold metal pressed more urgently against his skull. Would he die here? The choice was his to make and his to live with or die from. Would he say yes? No? Beg for a different option, like a small child hoping to get a treat for lunch rather than carrots and beets?

Pictures from his life flashed into view, each one an arrow pointing toward the path leading him to this place, this time, this decision. Although he had no memory of his father choosing a strong name for a strong son, his naming had become a personal folktale with Lyaksandro as the hero. His father would hold his young son in his thick arms, smelling of sweat and freshly cut wood, explaining each part of his name in considerable detail.

"You, my son, are no ordinary boy, and you have been born into extraordinary times. I've given you a name to guide you – to show you what you are meant to be. You are Lyaksandro Hadeon Rosomakha.

"Lyaksandro. Defender of man. A protector and guardian of mankind.

"Hadeon. Warrior. But not merely any kind of warrior – impetuous warrior. I want you to be willing to complete your mission without concern for the consequences as you seek after your cause.

"Rosomakha. Wolverine. Ferocious and wild, yet intelligent. Connected to family. Willing to be alone but longing to be part of a community – preferably like-minded souls longing for something better in life."

By the time he entered school, he recognized who he was and what kind of man he would become. His name said it all.

A name, however, wasn't enough fuel to propel someone forward if they weren't willing to go. He was one Lyaksandro among many, and to his knowledge, they were all waking in their homes this morning while he drew in, what had the potential to be, his remaining breaths.

Although he had been born under communist reign,

his father never let the stories of the Ukraine he experienced as a boy die. In the same way he could recite the story of his name, Lyaksandro could narrate the stories of his home as it had once been before communism and the USSR. The community traditions, the dances, and the songs, even the acres and acres of sunflower fields fading into the horizon.

"Ah, the bechornytsi." This word would sigh from his father's lips turned upward into the closest thing Lyaksandro would ever see to a smile. "Once the crops were gathered and put up for the long winter to come, all the young people from the village would gather in a sparse building in the center of town erected specifically for occasions like these.

"Such singing and dancing, Leki! Young men performing the Gopack, alternating between standing and squatting while energetically flinging their legs and feet toward the giggling young women who shyly observed in hopes of being chosen from the crowd for more personal attention. Older women embroidering along the edge of the makeshift dance floor, keeping time with their feet. Older men telling tall tales and laughing too loudly at their rude jokes, secretly wishing they still had the ability to dance at the end of a long day to titillate the ladies.

"And the food. Oh, Lyaksandro, you have never seen such food. Varenyky, borscht, golubci, salo, papukhy. Everyone ate and talked and laughed long into the night. I met your mama at a celebration such as this."

In spite of never witnessing the glory for himself, he missed it with a fierceness as immeasurable as his father's – a man who died trying to gain back what had been forcefully taken away.

During the Shelest regime, Lyaksandro believed everything his father wanted for his beloved Ukraine was happening. He believed perhaps his father's death had not been in vain. Novelists, artists, and film directors created their art with few restrictions. Ukrainian pride – something quite apart from Party loyalty – flourished. Lyaksandro had found, courted, and married Ivanna, and the two of them had a darling daughter. What more did a man need to be content?

Except he had ignored the signs and pretended all was right with the world. He was blinded by the Politburo's permissiveness and flattery and was unable, or unwilling, to see the truth, until, without fanfare, and more importantly, with very little protest, years' worth of literature was ripped from the shelves. Any art deemed anti-Soviet or nationalist was burned. Dissidents, once tolerated with a mild slap of the hand, were incarcerated in corrective labor camps – ispravitelno-trudovye lageria, or insane asylums.

Then, one fateful day changed the course of his life and brought him here, a man on his knees, at a fork in the road which would change the trajectory of his life. He realized he could no longer be a bleating sheep, following along with a timid "as you wish" while the Party elite dined on stuffed pheasant. He could no longer tolerate a gradual reformation of society, when all around him, those he loved suffered.

Despite his mother's heroic efforts to keep him from taking up his father's sword, Lyaksandro would do no less – could do no less. It was for this cause he found himself with a choice to live or die.

His name. His father. His love. His country. Each

played a part that landed him in a dark alley – was it just last night? – instead of lying next to his wife of 12 years under a hand-stitched quilt, her soap-scented hair swirled on a pillow they shared. The pretense that all was well in his beloved country was over. This realization led him to seek out those who were actively making changes, while others only whispered about them, furtively looking around for Party finks. Ultimately, he had agreed to collect information to pass on to unknown carriers to squash communism and bring back the Ukraine his father had taught him to long for.

Last night had been the culmination of two long years' worth of effort. For months, he had been providing information through coded sentences in the still of the night, each time acutely aware that this could be the last time – each time lying to himself that this would be the last time. And yet, he ventured into various alleyways throughout the city on scheduled nights, again and again, delivering bits of information to further the cause despite these promises he made to himself while lurking in alleys in which he didn't belong.

Three hours ago, maybe four, he had been standing in a pitch-black alley, fear wrapping itself around Lyaksandro like a jaded lover's arms ready to administer another round of arsenic in the wine. Had he somehow known he would end up here, like this? His skin pricked on the back of his neck again, precisely as it had then, the small hairs standing at attention. He recalled the small sound, a distance away that had caused his breath to halt in his throat, fearing any sound might give him away. He had flattened himself against the doorway and listened intently, once again hearing the small but deafening noise.

Such a minuscule sound would have been swallowed up in the bustle of the day, but there, in the inky darkness, it became ominous and menacing. Though he had willed it to be his contact, his sense of foreboding suggested otherwise. Never had he heard the approach before. In fact, he was often disconcerted at how swiftly and silently the contact arrived, asking for a light before Lyaksandro fully comprehended someone was at hand.

The sound, like soft scraping of metal against stone, happened again. Then again. More regularly. And closer.

Lyaksandro carried no weapon, and though he was officially a spy, he had no training. Until this very moment, he had never considered what he would do if things didn't go as planned. Nonetheless, some instinct, or perhaps the hand of God, had him drop to his haunches, seconds before a bit of brick where his head had been moments earlier burst into fragments and rained shards into his hair.

Whether he yelled out or not, he did not know, but it wouldn't have mattered either way. A cacophony of noise instantaneously erupted in the once-silent night. Men's voices mixed with explosions and the tinkling sound of broken glass. Running footsteps. The squeal of tires. And then silence again.

This could not be happening. He wanted to help his country, to provide a place for his wife and child to thrive. Nothing more. Certainly not this. He wanted only to be home with his wife and child, and tears flooded his eyes as he crouched against the wall, immobilized by fear.

Before he comprehended what was happening, someone grabbed Lyaksandro under the arm and hauled him to his feet. He threw his arms wildly toward the hand that gripped him, desperate to get away. He wasn't a spy.

9

He was merely a man. "Please, please. I don't know what you want. I..." But before he uttered another word, a man in perfect Ukrainian said, "Come. Now. Quickly. We don't have much time. They followed you here, hoping to catch two birds with one stone, but ended up with nothing to show for their night's adventure, eh? Are you hurt? No? Come."

One foot quickly followed the other as the man, carefully concealed under a cap and scarf, weaved in and out of streets and alleys, bringing him to a fourth-floor flat in a run-down, nondescript building. He threw some clothes in Lyaksandro's direction. "Change. Quickly. No! Don't use the light. Hand me your things." Then, they were off again, this time, more slowly but not without purpose. Two more times, they ducked into buildings, changed clothes, and emerged again, the final time as others were beginning their morning routines.

Lyaksandro realized with a joyful clarity that, unlike his father, he had lived. His joy, however, was fleeting as the man who saved his life said, "Here. Enter here." As they moved inside, he gave Lyaksandro specific directions which seemed foreign and impossible to understand, consonants and vowels hobbled together but providing no meaning. "Sit here, in this chair so I can cut and dye your hair. We procured documents for you. We will have you in London by this time tomorrow."

"But..." Lyaksandro sat down heavily in the proffered chair, his mind reeling as he tried to take in the events over the past hour. Leaving his beloved Ukraine? Everything he did was to save this country, not leave it. And his family? What would Yevtsye think about leaving her homeland with a child in tow? It would make no sense to her. He needed to speak to her, to help her understand. "What about Ivanna? Yevtsye? When will they arrive? Where are their papers? They will be so frightened, so confused. I must explain everything to them."

The man's hand reached out and held Lyaksandro's shoulder. "мій друг, my friend, the deal is for you. You, alone."

Lyaksandro jerked away, wild eyes darting around the room. He would never leave his wife and child. They were the reason he did what he did. They were the reason for the risks he took. Without them, the midnight rendezvous made no sense. With a mixture of panic and resolve, he shouted, "No! No! They go, or I stay."

Bending at the waist, bringing his face level with Lyaksandro's, the nameless man who had saved his life hours before whispered slowly, as if speaking to a small child. "No. It is too late for ultimatums. We cannot get your wife and daughter. Your home is under surveillance. They watched you leave tonight. They followed you to the alley. They wanted to kill you. Your wife and daughter...they are...it is hard to say...where they might be?"

A wild, animal-like guttural groan escaped from Lyaksandro's throat. His beautiful Ivanna. His beautiful Yevtsye. He had killed them. He regarded his hands, realizing they were capable of both stroking his wife's cheek and effectively signing her death certificate. Had they started trembling in the alley, or only as he became aware of his new role as executioner?

More urgently, the man said, "Now. You must go now. We cannot permit you fall into your government's hands. Doing so would cause far too many problems for us. Get up. Now."

Mere seconds had passed. The man shifted his stance to stare directly into Lyaksandro's eyes, the two men merely a gun-length apart. "Are you going? Or are you dying here?"

Twenty-four hours later, a shattered man, stripped of his Ukrainian name and his family, landed at Heathrow.

Chapter 2

1990

Ivanna pushed her windblown strand of dark hair behind her ear for the umpteenth time since arriving this morning. Despite the long line and the West wind whipping directly down Vulytsya Artema – Artema Street – she was thankful for the break in the weather. Only last week, it had been minus 20 Centigrade, causing icicles to hang thickly from her nostrils whenever she ventured outdoors.

By pulling her heels upward and rocking on her toes, she finally spied the sign молоко above the door – milk. Her smile broadened. Today was a lucky day, indeed. One degree Centigrade and milk in under three hours. If her luck held out with the bread line, she would be home by noon and might get a short nap before her shift at the fishery. Real luck would allow her a moment or two with Yevtsye.

Her heart squeezed tightly in her chest as she thought of her daughter of nearly 27 years. She was a handsome woman with long, soft, chestnut hair and luminous brown eyes that gathered in the tiniest of details. More importantly, Yevt was intelligent, which had allowed them the luxury of moving to Novoazovsk to attend school after years of struggling in the tiny village of Prymors'ke.

Those had been grueling years. Rarely was there enough food to eat, and unlike here, there was no bread store and no milk store. There were no coupons guaranteeing something bordering on nutritious for the two of them to consume. The village water system rarely worked, and when it did miraculously spurt liquid into the kitchen sink, the smell of something akin to rotting flesh filled the air for hours. Scarcely anyone bothered to flip a light switch because no electricity had reached the village in years.

Yevt attended the local school with other children from the village, doing her sums and learning about the great Ukrainian Soviet Socialist Republic. Shortly before turning 14, a letter arrived from the State, commanding her to be in Novoazovsk on June 3rd for State tests to determine if she would continue in her education.

That letter, with the mighty state seal and the exacting signature of the education minister, changed the course of their lives. Few children got the privilege of continuing education and even fewer girls. Yevt had been preparing to end her schooling when she turned 14 and hoped to find one of the few jobs in the village or a husband to help care for her. But State testing meant she had a chance for a better life – something beyond the life her father had relegated them to five years earlier.

She took a deep breath, exhaling slowly in an effort to clear her thoughts. She rarely thought of him anymore and didn't plan to spend another moment of her lucky day on him now. Only one positive thing came from her relationship with that man – Yevt, for which she was beyond grateful. However, he was dead – and dead to her.

Yevt took her tests on the appointed day and, not surprisingly, did exceedingly well. Within days, Ivanna and her daughter were moved into modest quarters in Novoazovsk, where Ivanna was given work at the fishery, and Yevt became one of the youngest students at university, where she was now a cancer research assistant. Although she didn't know who had pointed out Yevt to officials, every night before falling asleep, she continued to thank this unknown benefactor.

Although she heard others grousing about the conditions in the city, she found nothing to grumble about. For a few hours each day, they had clean running water. Electric lightbulbs, when they could be found, illuminated their home during the darkness of long nights and oil heated their home during the frigid Ukrainian winters. And, as today's small victory proved, she procured food on most days by simply standing in a queue with a coupon provided by the State.

It wasn't that she didn't see the shortages or understand those with money could bribe others to receive better goods and services. She was not naïve and recognized the inequalities in the system. However, unlike those loud voices who pushed for some sort of revolution, she had experienced deprivation in a way completely different from most standing in this line. The five years of abject poverty prior to Yevt's schooling were indelibly etched into her mind. She perfectly understood the difference between hunger and cold versus starvation and dying of exposure. She would gladly take the former and all that came with it.

She was nearing the front of the line, and it appeared her fortune remained intact. The milk would not run out before her turn. She had chosen the milk line first today because a bit of bread remained uneaten from the day before. The milk, however, was a more pressing need, and she was thankful the State had, once again, furnished for her needs. Within minutes, she got her can of milk and quickly scurried to the store marked хліб, where she dutifully waited in line once more.

With Vulytsya Bryukhnova running from north to south, the buildings along the street shielded her from the wind which could no longer steal beneath her coat or tug relentlessly at her hair. However, the same buildings saving her from the westerly gusts also shaded her from the anemic winter sun, reducing both her warmth and her spirits.

Yevt's father popped unbidden into her mind once again. Why, she mused, must she be plagued with him today, a lucky day that might include a refreshing nap and a much-anticipated chat with her daughter about this man she had begun courting. Ivanna had been hoping Yevt would find someone to marry, but also secretly feared her daughter would meet with the same fate of an unfaithful husband who left her stranded with a child and nearly impossible survival odds.

Of course, she reasoned, Yevt had a promising career. Unlike Ivanna, she was never likely to find herself starving, relying on the kindness of others, who had nothing but kindness to offer, to help her rebuild some semblance of life. Her daughter was too accomplished to be hurt by a man the way she had been by Lyaksandro.

Leka. Still now, 17 years after his betrayal, her mind whirled in a myriad of responses from acrimony to despair to heartache. Despite his despicable actions, her love for him remained constant and steady, refusing to dim regardless of years of professed hate and disdain. This love for a man who deceived her, left her to fend for herself and care for their child in the worst of circumstances, caused her immense shame. Why did her heart go on pining for a man who snuck out of their bed on a midnight errand to lie with another woman?

She had rolled over that fateful morning, reaching out to touch the warmth of Leka to find, instead, cold, empty sheets. Sitting up sleepily, she wondered what prompted him to rise so early when he needn't be at work for several more hours. She listened intently for the sound of him preparing breakfast, but everything was still. Even Yevt, a child who rose early despite her mother's desire to snatch just a few more minutes of sleep, was still tucked neatly into bed.

Curious, but without any alarm, she had risen from bed, slipped on her house shoes, and walked expectantly into their living room. She imagined he had brought some tome home from the library and the desire to know the contents had kept him from a proper sleep. That was so like her Leka. He was always ready to learn something new, and this strong desire for knowledge had been passed down to their young daughter. It was a common occurance to find them sitting in a chair, faces bent together devouring a book borrowed from the university. However, she did not find him in the living room with a book. Nor did she find him in the kitchen or bathroom.

Inexplicable anxiety began to restrict her throat, a giant hand trying to squeeze the air out of a balloon. She had given herself a mental shake to rid herself of such foolish emotions. Leka was a good man. A kind man. If dawn broke without him home, there was a reasonable explanation. She would laugh with him later as she described the fear that tried to overtake her in the dim light of the morning. He would wipe the laughter from his eyes, kiss her long and hard, and assure her of his undying love and affection.

So, she waited.

When Yevt woke and wondered aloud where her father was, Ivanna brushed it off with a laugh that didn't reach her eyes and told the first of many lies that would leave her lips in hopes of easing her daughter's discomfort. "Papa had an unusually large project at work, so he left before the sun came up to get an early start." However, despite her cheerful countenance in the presence of the young girl, by the time Yevt went off to school, with still no word from Leka, Ivanna's anxiety had to work hard to exceed her building anger.

Images of KDB agents using exquisite torture devices on Leka moved across her vision followed closely by those of Leka staggering in a drunken stupor around the city streets like a participant in a State-sponsored parade, unable to find his way home. Neither image made any sense. Leka was a simple, honest, hardworking university employee. If the KDB needed information from him, they would ask, and he would surely tell them what they needed to know. As for drinking, she had only seen Leka intoxicated on one occasion – at his sister's wedding. And far from staggering around the city, he had merely laughed louder and danced more vigorously than he did when sober.

By the time the knock came at the door shortly before lunch, she expected only the worst of news. Moving as though her feet were encased in concrete slippers, she opened the door to a pair of uniformed officers. "Mrs. Lyaksandro Rosomakha? Ivanna Rosomakha?" they asked.

Barely nodding, and barely daring to breathe, she waited. "Mrs. Rosomakha, we are sorry to inform you that there has been an unfortunate accident. Your husband was killed this..."

This was where the memory ended. She had no explicit recall of transpiring events for the days and weeks that followed. However, at unbidden times such as these, she remembered phrases, authorative voices, glances, and tears, little fragments of information stabbing her mind, her heart, her love, making sure her death, like Lyaksandro's, was complete.

"...they were lovers..."

"...been going on for some time..."

"...how could you have missed him leaving the house..."

"...Oxanna...."

"...he found them together in bed..."

"...he set the whole house ablaze..."

"...nothing but ashes..."

"...this was found in the rubble..."

And then, a flash of a hand opening to reveal Leka's wedding band, the ring she had slipped on his finger the day they wed. The ring binding them together forever and making them one.

The bread sign, now meters away, blurred into obscurity as she tasted hot, salty tears moving across her lips on their way to fall unbidden to her shoulders.

Chapter 3

1990

"Somehow," Lyaksandro thought, "winter has returned yet again." This did not bring a smile to his face. He much preferred trees fully dressed in their green finery and puffy white clouds skittling across a blue sky to the dull, gray, lifelessness of winter. He contemplated the arrival of this most dreaded season as he wandered through the produce aisle, prodding and smelling fruits and vegetables before gently placing them in his cart.

It appeared, once again, the spring's endless rains had blossomed into a deliciously hot summer filled with humid air and sunshine. Then, as quickly as she came, summer faded into a gray winter, but only after a bedazzling display of reds, yellows, and oranges seeking to out-perform even the most spectacular sunset Mother Nature had to offer. Another relay race from winter to spring to summer to fall and back to winter again meant another year had come and gone. He made a mental tick with his forefinger, creating another tally mark. Seventeen.

He had trouble enjoying the beauty of autumn, with its crisp air and ever-changing colors. The beauty, though breathtaking, was as misleading as a billboard advertising an anti-aging cream containing nothing more than some poorly scented petroleum jelly. He didn't pay attention to the obvious signs of winter's arrival because autumn was simply the gateway to the frozen wasteland of winter, the longest months of the year that were always tainted with memories he'd prefer to keep hidden away. However, despite his best efforts, winter arrived each year with precision.

With the shopping complete, he stood in line, rechecking his list as he waited. He wasn't sure why it was in winter the memories came unbidden, creating a kaleidoscope of pictures, sounds, and even smells meant only for him. Maybe it was the long nights, devoid of the warmth and light needed to push away his despair. Or maybe it was simply that, despite moving on with his life, starting anew in another world with another name and another occupation, the sub-freezing temperatures and bitter winds reminded him of the home he abandoned.

Seventeen. The number came to his mind again. Quickly. Nimbly. Almost playfully. Lyaksandro's memories enjoyed playing a creative game of hide-and-seek with him as a reluctant partner. He never knew where they would be hiding or when they might jump out to surprise him as he stumbled across their secret lair. He might be doing something as mundane as washing dishes or climbing the stairs to his flat when a memory would catapult into full view and knock him to his knees.

When the memories came, they did so without the usual limitations created by age. They weren't slower and bent with advanced years. They weren't misshapen or sickly. They hadn't grown quieter, more mature. Despite the years as someone new, going through the motions, despite carefully wrapping each passing second around himself like a cocoon as a shield from his past, the memories stripped his meager armor away with the skills of a young warrior, leaving him raw and exposed.

This winter, seventeen long years after hurriedly leaving Ukraine by the cover of darkness, was to be, it seemed, no different than the rest. Mercifully, Lyaksandro made it home before the barrage, barely wriggling the key into the lock and thrusting the door open, spilling open one of the brown bags in the process. The image of his dear Ivanna crystalized in his mind as an apple rolled to a rest at the end of the carpet.

He saw Ivanna exactly as she had been on the day they wed. Dark hair. Dark eyes. A smile that took over her face each time something brought her joy. He would do anything to see her smile just one more time. He sat on the floor among the scattered fruits and vegetables and sobbed, remembering the last night that took him from her forever.

His Ivanna was a wonderful wife and mother. She cared for their daughter Yevtsye, made delicious meals, pungent thyme, sweet garlic, dill greeting him each day as he arrived from work, and loved him with a fervor that, once he began working with the rebellion, made him contend with his guilt. She was completely unaware he was gathering information and slipping from their bed to deliver it to unknown men from unknown places.

Lying to Ivanna was harder for Lyaksandro than anything else he had been asked to do. His love for her reached a depth he didn't know he possessed. He couldn't imagine his life before she became part of it. Together, they shared a home, a bed, a child, a life. She believed they shared everything, and he was certain that for her, it was true. She held nothing back, letting him see all her vulnerabilities and insecurities. He gave her everything of himself, but not the darkness.

Whenever he would consider telling her the truth, he would justify his silence by saying, "What good would it do? What could she possibly do with this information that would benefit anyone?" Despite the agony of withholding information from his wife, he resolutely rejected the idea of involving her any more than he was doing by simply being her husband. "She will be safe. My little Yevtsye will be safe. They cannot be hurt by information they do not know."

It always came down to that. He assured himself they would be safe because they were oblivious to his activities. He prayed this assurance wasn't merely a hollow promise he made with himself to cope with his decision.

He hadn't always been secretive with Ivanna. In the beginning, before the new KDB chief, before the book burnings and art smashings, before he was reminded of his father's legacy, he intended to honor his promise to be one with her. They had a child together. They lived in a comfortable flat. He had a decent job at a university. He was content with life.

But everything changed the day he watched the KDB in their gleaming uniforms march into the university library and wheel out thousands of volumes, depositing them in a colorful, almost festive, pile just feet from the door. From a place beyond the window's view, a man wielding a shiny metal can appeared and began to liberally douse the pile with a clear liquid. Then a tossed flame. Then a cheer that sounded more like a growl.

Lyaksandro stood at the window, unmoving, watching with horror as the books, their beautiful colors contorted and melded together to create a murky fuel for the yellow flames, eventually burning to ash. Lyaksandro, the defender of man, did nothing to stop them. He simply stood at the window and allowed these uniformed men to laugh while they burned everything his father stood for, until, finally, the pooling drops fell from his eyes. His superior ran to him as he pressed himself against the window, willing his anguish to be enough to put out the flames. "Please, Lyaksandro! Stop. You must stop before they see you." He grabbed Lyaksandro's arm, desperate to pull him from the view of those who had the power to punish them. "They will kill us if you do not stop."

Symon, though older and in a position of authority over Lyaksandro, was his friend. He understood Lyaksandro's need to learn and share. He mistakenly assumed Lyaksandro's emotional upheaval was due to the destruction of the books, unaware he was witnessing a transformation.

Lyaksandro had forgotten who he was. He had gotten soft and lazy. He took the lies he'd been fed and feasted on them with joy and thanksgiving. The humility and shame of these actions, this carelessness, caused him to sob, not the books. Like his father, he knew truth would prevail. The books would live on somehow. But what of himself? Could he redeem the slothful man he had become?

From that day until the day he left Ukraine, he took up his father's cross as his own. And that was why he lied to his wife, his lover, his best friend. Although not without guilt, he did so without apology. Lyaksandro Hadeon Rosomakha simply concluded he had no choice.

But that was then. Seventeen long years ago. Seventeen years to remember his wife and his daughter and wonder what might have been if only he had chosen his family over his reckless spirit. Instead, he was curled up on the floor of his flat, wishing he had had the foresight to take the bullet to his head rather than the plane to Heathrow.

Chapter 4

1990

Yevt peered intently through the microscope at the cells dancing sluggishly across the slide. Exasperated, she yanked the slide from view. She had been at this all day. For weeks, actually. And the results? Nothing. Agonizingly nothing.

Dr. Hryhorii's breakthrough appeared to be breaking apart instead. Over a year ago, he had discovered some unique cell formations after injecting rabbits with a new cancer treatment. Although he had run to her to share his findings, she hadn't understood what she was seeing. He had patiently explained the drug was mutating the cancer cells, leaving them without the ability to reproduce. Although the rabbits still had cancer, the cancer cells were rendered useless, unable to grow and divide.

Rightfully so, the medical community was in an uproar

over the findings. "Imagine," they exclaimed, "if the cure for cancer came from the Soviet Union? "

That particular sentiment bristled in some deep part of her soul which, until lately, had often been left unexplored. Yevt would have rather them said, "Imagine if the cure for cancer came from Ukraine." But, although Ukrainian nationalism was gaining some momentum among the younger generation, those older, like Dr. Hryhorii and his colleagues, had yet to catch the patriotic fever. And Yevt knew better than to voice those opinions out loud unless she'd rather work in a labor camp rather than as a researcher.

Unfortunately, in the past year, Dr. Hryhorii and his team had been unable to replicate his earlier findings. As the excitement over his 'new cure' waned, her boss pushed the team harder and harder, desperate to prove the new treatment had merit. In the Ukrainian SSR, failure wasn't tolerated. Dr. Hryhorii had already begun losing privileges at hospital and university. It wouldn't be long before he found himself as a clinician in a small town too close to Chernobyl for his liking.

So, Yevt and the other research assistants who still remained part of the team spent hours each day with diminishing hope, looking at slides to find the telltale cell formations that would vindicate him. Unfortunately, today was not going to be that day.

She glanced surreptitiously at the clock. Ten more minutes before she could put the case of slides away and think of anything other than cancer until morning. Reluctantly, she pulled out another slide, gently lifted the metal legs that held it in place, peered through the eyepiece, and carefully adjusted the focus. Nothing.

Heavy breath escaped from her lips as she pulled yet another slide for inspection. She was thankful she hadn't been promoted under Dr. Hryhorii. Of course, each time he passed her over to advance a man with less experience and far less intelligence, she had been incensed. But today, as a mere research assistant, she was not held accountable in any way for his failure to produce. Those who grasped at the glory and confetti trailing behind this once celebrated doctor, those she had once envied, were now either unemployed, or, in her opinion, worse off, having to take jobs far beneath their level of competence. She wasn't sure what she had done to be the recipient of such luck, but she was thankful, nonetheless. When she spoke to Danya about it, he had attributed it to providence, to the workings of an almighty God.

She smiled unconsciously as Danya's face floated into view. She met him in the cafeteria one day after an exceptionally long and difficult several hours in the lab. Dr. Hryhorii had been impossibly difficult, insisting that one of the members of his team find him the proof. Immediately. As though they had the ability to simply conjure up the needed cell formations and drop them on a slide via telekinesis.

Danya taught chemistry at university and rarely ate at this secluded cafeteria. However, on that day, he had taken his class to see a working lab. Rather than hike across the campus to eat with his colleagues, he grabbed a plate of pierogis, stuffed, though rather sparingly, with potatoes and onion. Food, even at university, was getting harder and harder to come by.

Because she was thinking exclusively about getting off her sore feet, she hadn't paid attention to her surroundings

29

and ran straight into him, nearly knocking his pierogis from the plate. Red-faced and apologetic, she had tried to excuse herself to a back corner of the room, but Danya invited her to sit down with him. And the rest was a foregone conclusion.

Although a handsome man, Yevt's interest focused on Danya's intellect. Rarely did she find someone to converse with who understood what she said, and more importantly, challenged it. Whenever she made what she asserted was a statement of fact, he demanded proof. When she couldn't provide any, he would say, "Ah, an assumption!" and was prone to quoting an American professor of biochemistry named Isaac Asimov whenever he wasn't in earshot of others. "Your assumptions are your windows on the world. Scrub them off every once in a while, or the light won't come in."

He had quoted Asimov on the day he suggested God was responsible for her fortunate circumstances at work. She had just taken a swallow of mineral water and nearly sprayed her companion as it spewed out her nose in response. "God? There is no such thing as God. Surely, you know that."

"Prove it," said Danya, gently. And, although she had tried, she couldn't seem to offer scientific evidence showing a God did NOT exist. On this day, when he quoted Asimov, Yevt figuratively began a thorough window cleaning. Now, two months later, and completely without her mother's knowledge, let alone consent, she had begun attending the Ukrainian Orthodox Church with Danya as occasion permitted.

Although not wholly convinced of the existence of a supreme, all-knowing being who was in charge of her life,

Yevt loved the sense of security that someone had a plan and wasn't relying on her. Of course, she also loved being in Danya's company and would have accompanied him to the driest chemistry lecture on earth if it meant sitting at his side with her small hand clasped in his much larger one.

Breaking out of her reverie, she quickly put her work materials away, made the appropriate remarks in her notes about finding nothing once again, and departed for home. Her mother explicitly asked her to come straight home from work today. As mothers are wont to do, she wanted more information about Yevt's love interest. And as long as Yevt could keep her from questioning his politics or religion, she was happy to oblige.

She enjoyed watching her mother's enthusiasm for the budding relationship. Although not an unhappy woman, Yevt rarely saw her mother express joy. For her mother, the act of existing and going through the daily motions was what life was all about. This did not bring her any kind of sadness, nor did it bring her happiness. Yevt found this existence quite depressing, especially since she still recalled her mother's disposition before her father had died.

That home had been filled with laughter, tenderness, and kisses. Her mother's smiles sent her off to school each day and greeted her when she came home. Yevt tried to remember the last time she had seen more than a fleeting show of teeth from her mother and couldn't come up with anything since she had gotten the grades to go to university 12 years ago.

Yevt promised herself again that she would not subject herself to a life as barren as the one lived by her mother.

Yes, it meant taking chances and suffering losses, but she had witnessed what a safe life looked like – dull, boring, uneventful, lackluster, mindless.

Danya was the antithesis of her mother's life. He poked and prodded, asked questions and demanded answers. He was not a blind follower as evidenced by his association with both the church and political dissidents who questioned the authority of the Politburo. His political leanings closely matched her own, though she had always kept those beliefs hidden in the dark corners of her mind, far away from those who could, with a dismissive wave of the hand, change the course of her life. She was keenly aware what might happen if one were too vocal against those seeking power.

Danya had no such fear. He was not ignorant of the potential consequences of his associations, but he was willing to live his convictions and take the medicine that followed. "This life," he told her, "is for learning, and then living, truth." Those words, those ideals, resonated within Yevt as deeply as if she had always comprehended them. Of course, this was nonsense. Her mother ate, slept, and repeated the Party lines...and lies...with no question and no expectation. Her mother would be horrified to know she didn't feel the same way and that Danya was helping her to solidify her political position and nationalistic leanings.

Of course, none of this would be mentioned in their short encounter before her mother left for the fishery. Her mother's banal questions about the etymology of Danya's surname, his mother's ability to cook, and his father's occupation would never lead to a substantial discussion concerning the existence of God or the limitations and weaknesses of communism. For this, Yevt was grateful.

As she approached her home, she gave herself a mental shake, carefully tucking away any signs of dysphoria. With the fear of losing her job over the failed research, her questions about the existence of God, and a rising sentiment of Ukranian nationalism carefully hidden from view, Yevt walked into her home looking, from the outside at least, precisely like the daughter her mother had always known.

"Mama! I'm home!"

Chapter 5

1990

Although never one to believe in fairy tales and happily-ever-afters, the months following her chance meeting with Danya were some of Yevt's happiest in recent memory. Despite the continued failure of Dr. Hryhorii's cancer research and his eventual termination from university, Yevt continued to work in the research department, gaining respect from her superiors for her dedication and hard work. Such demonstrative praise could be taken away as quickly as it had come, but she determined to enjoy the blessings while they lasted.

Then, when she hung up her lab coat at the end of her shift, she greeted Danya who waited outside the building for her to emerge, always with a smile and something of interest to discuss. He would take her by the hand as they strolled across the campus and out into the city, discussing the events of the day, both personal and global. She hadn't been this intellectually stimulated since her studies at university, and this, she conceded with a grin, was far more fun.

As March glided quickly toward April, the weather finally turned. Though still chilly and prone to overnight frost, their late afternoon and evening walks were often interrupted by Yevt spying yet another tender, green shoot pushing through the earth, ready to declare an official end to the long, harsh winter.

This was a habit she picked up from her father, one she knew better than to share with her mother who refused to allow anything in their home that reminded her of Lyaksandro. She had a memory of walking with her father, her thin arm raised upward to grasp his strong, warm hand, as they passed pile after pile of snow, now gray from the sooty air. He had stopped abruptly, swooped her into his arms and twirled her around and around, her feet waving in a circle around his shoulders. "Look, my darling, Yevt! Look!" He pointed excitedly at a thin, green stem, hardly visible in the space between the road and the mounds of snow. Excited but confused, Yevt had stared at the tiny green line, wondering how something so tiny could be cause for such immense joy. "It's the first plant of Spring, Yevt! Winter will surely blast his icy breath again before he skulks away, hiding from the warmth and sun, but this tiny plant is proof – PROOF! – that spring is nearly here."

She had been five years old, too young to comprehend how long Ukrainian winters were or how difficult it was for her parents to keep them fed and warm. She couldn't have understood how spring was a panacea for all the ills of a country ravaged by the policies of a communist regime. All she understood was this tiny green plant, this first sign of life after a long, lifeless winter, brought her father immense joy.

As she grew, she continued to search for these first signs, more so after her father's death – especially during those hard years when her mother became robotic and mechanical, rarely smiling, never laughing, and certainly never noticing the passage of seasons. By the time she was an adult, she saw springtime as a rebellious month, constantly chafing at winter's control. Rather than submit to frozen demands, Spring pushed the limits with blooming flowers and sunny days, despite Winter returning the volley with another round of snow. If people had the potential to be a season, she would be Spring, daring Winter to try to keep her from sprouting.

She brought up this idea one afternoon to Danya, suggesting Ukraine was the Spring battling against the Soviet Winter. Danya laughed heartily at the image, then pulled her into a long hug, his chin resting comfortably on the top of her head. She nestled in closer, listening to the steady pulse of his heart – constant and unchanging.

Without looking at her, he began to speak. "Yevtsye. I so enjoy our time together, watching you take in the world with fresh eyes. You see things I have failed to see for years. You possess insights that leave me awed and wide-eyed. You make me laugh. You make me think. You make me want to be a better man." He paused, trying to locate the perfect string of words to complete his thoughts. "I..." He hesitated once more, tilting her face to gaze into her eyes. "Yevtsye Rosomakha, will you do me the honor of becoming my wife?"

Yevt had known for weeks this day was coming. She was nothing, if not perceptive. But the question left her speechless, nonetheless. Danya was everything she had ever hoped for in a husband, but she had nearly given up on the idea of ever finding someone who would give her a life beyond endless bread lines and Party platitudes.

Still unable to speak, watching the question linger in his eyes, she nodded her assent. Taking a half step back, he stared at her again, locking eyes, making sure he understood her intent. This time, she nodded more vigorously as the "yes" previously unable to move beyond her thoughts came tumbling out of her mouth. "Yes. Yes! Oh, yes, with all my heart and soul, yes!"

With no warning, he grabbed her under the arms and whirled her around and around in a broad arc, just as her father had done when she was a small child. All the while, he laughed and chanted, "She said yes!"

It wasn't until they heard a smattering of applause that they became aware of others walking along the bulvar. With an elegant bow and cheery wave to the marriage proposal witnesses, Danya swept Yevt into his arms once again, but this time for a kiss, long and slow and definitely not meant for public consumption. Much to her embarrassment, the applause grew louder with a few whistles and cat calls thrown in for good measure.

With another wave to the growing crowd, Danya put his hand under her elbow, escorting her toward the restaurant he had chosen for dinner. With a wink, he said, "And that, soon-to-be Mrs. Petrushevych, is only the beginning."

Tired, and smelling of briny, bitter fish innards, Ivanna's heart leapt into her throat when she saw the lights on in the flat. Yevt was always asleep when she crept in after midnight. What was wrong? Who had died? Her thoughts often turned to death and dying when something was out of place and not following her prescribed plan. With resolution, she shoved Leka from her mind – once again.

Thankfully, her angst was short-lived. Before she had the chance to push the door open, a bubbly, bouncy, girl who very much resembled Yevt in appearance, if not in manner, threw herself in Ivanna's arms. "Oh, Mama! Danya has asked me to marry him. Isn't this the greatest of all news?"

Ivanna, beyond thankful that the news wasn't dreadful, smiled warmly. "Yes, yes, my lovey! How wonderful. Such amazing news."

Ivanna hugged her exuberant daughter, stroking her hair, wondering where the time had gone. Wasn't it mere moments ago that she held her tiny baby to her breast? And now? Yevt was a grown woman about to start her own family. Despite the happiness, nostalgia crept silently in and leaked from her eyes. Oh, how she would miss this child of hers. Thank goodness Danya had a job in the city. At least they wouldn't go far.

Swiping at the errant trickle before her melancholy had a chance to dampen Yevt's news, Ivanna asked of the upcoming plans. "So, what day will you register? Or are you planning a Komsomol?"

One simply uttered sentence brought with it the tension of two grown women pulling on a rope, each desperate to win the tug-of-war, but Ivanna didn't understand why. The question was not only simple but expected. Would her child and new husband register with the State, or would they choose, instead, to arrange a State-sponsored wedding – a Komsomol?

Either was certainly fine. Registering was quick and easy. Such a marriage took place in a matter of days. Although a Komsomol took more time to plan, the expenses would surely be picked up by their employers, as was the custom for State-sponsored ceremonies. Even the planning was relatively straightforward, what with the halls already decorated and the speeches already prepared. It was just a matter of purchasing a new dress and finding a date on the calendar.

Confused at how quickly her daughter's mood changed and how stiff she had become in her arms, Ivanna slowly released Yevt from her embrace, stepping back, perplexed. "Yevt? What is it? Why are you looking at me like that? I merely asked about your plans. Either way is fine with me. And I perfectly understand if you haven't come up with a plan yet. I mean, he only proposed today..."

Her voice trailed off as Yevt turned away, trying to hide...anger? Regret? She couldn't discern the emotions playing across her daughter's face and couldn't fathom the reason for anything resembling anger or regret on such a momentous day.

"любий, darling? What is it? Whatever is wrong?"

Yevt's next words collided with Ivanna's hard-shelled Party exterior, the joy-filled moment shattering into lethal shards around her feet. "Mama...we...we are to be married in the Orthodox Church."

Ivanna shook her head slightly, trying to rearrange the syllables coming out of Yevt's mouth into something recognizable – something that made logical sense. She had not taken Yevt to church in over 17 years. She never spoke with her about religion and never even used trite religious phrases like "Thank God" or "I pray it will be warmer tomorrow." Where had the notion of a church wedding come from?

Perhaps all the talk of romance had addled her brain, turning it into something akin to porridge? Perhaps the fairytales from her youth left her with expectations of ransoms, blessings, crownings, and feasts? She decided to firmly and rationally explain that the weddings of fairy tales didn't belong in today's society. Certainly, Yevt would understand such simple logic. She was a bright girl, afterall, even if falling in love had momentarily turned her into a simple village girl.

"Yevt, surely you cannot mean to participate in a church wedding. The State is opposed to such bourgeois relics of the past. If you want the ceremonial trappings of a wedding, we'll register you for a Komsomol. It will be lovely."

Now Ivanna easily read her daughter's face twisted with disgust and anger, as Yevt spat out, "Yes, we do 'surely mean to participate in' a church wedding. Danya and I have been attending regularly for several months now. I want a real Ukrainian marriage in the same manner that Ukrainians have married for centuries before the Party took it – and so much more - from us. I want Danya to pay his ransom to you and for you to demand more because I am your daughter and worth more. I want to receive blessings at the hands of you and his parents. I want to see who first steps on the rushnyk before taking our vows to know who will enjoy the final say during our marriage. I want to replace my single woman's floral wreath with the headdress of a married woman. I want a wedding celebration full of dancing, long toasts, and a feast. I want to sing the traditional songs 'Oy u vyshnevomu sadu' and 'Oy na hori dva dubky.'"

Each "I want" hit Ivanna like a boxer's punch meant to take down his opponent, making her weak and disoriented. Finally, upon hearing the names of the traditional wedding songs, her legs gave way, causing her to land heavily in a heap at Yevt's feet. With a bottomless sob choking her words, she said, "Yevt...please...no..." But Yevt simply turned away.

Quietly, from her place on the floor, Ivanna said, "I shall not be there to witness such a travesty against the State."

To which Yevt replied, "I didn't expect you would."

Part 2

YEVTSYE

Chapter 6

1990

The weeks before the wedding would be remembered with both nostalgia and angst. Acting the part of a bride-to-be made Yevt feel like a small girl playing make believe. Weddings, it appeared, had magical properties that turned back time and kept reality at bay – at least temporarily. Because she had said nothing about the wedding's venue to her peers at work, everyone simply assumed she would have a Komsomol. This assumption led everyone at work to glory in the romance with her. She recognized she should tell them the truth but hated to break the spell and create an atmosphere rivaling that found in her own home.

Although she still lived with her mother, everything had changed. They no longer dined together, talked with one another, or even acknowledged one another's presence. Yevt had tried smiling and chatting with her mother in their usual way, thinking with time, her mother would surely come around. She was, after all, the only child her mother ever bore. But this was not to be. Her mother, the woman who had cared for her every day of her life, who worked long shifts and rarely had a day off so she had the opportunity to go to university, who survived after her husband's tragic death because her daughter needed someone to care for her when others would have given up, had forsaken her.

Yevt was no longer a daughter. She was simply a dissident causing trouble for the Party. Despite their past, despite being mother and daughter by birth, her mother chose a suppressive, oppressive government experiment gone wrong over her own child. Her only concession to a bond that once existed was not turning them in to the authorities as troublemakers.

At first, Yevt let anger rule her emotional responses. Fine. Let her be that way. She didn't need her mother to be at her wedding with her sad face and pathetic life. She was better off knowing her mother's true feelings than continuing with the pretense that had been their relationship.

As time drew on, however, Yevt's anger dissipated, leaving behind deep sadness. Her mother, the only family she had, disowned her. The woman who had calmed her fears and encouraged her growth and independence, no longer claimed her as her own. How could a daughter live with the knowledge that her own mother no longer loved her?

The dichotomy between home and life outside the home couldn't have been any greater, and it often left Yevt exhausted. It seemed implausible to be simultaneously both so impossibly happy and so impossibly sad.

During these weeks of conflicting emotions, Danya's strength of character became more evident to Yevt, offering her a sense of stability and well-being. With Danya, she could be honest, and his responses were always kind, even when he disagreed with her reasoning or conclusions. Never, in all the weeks leading to their marriage, did he say something negative about his soon-to-be mother-in-law or her convictions. And despite his political leanings and rhetoric against State policies, he didn't condemn those who held strongly to those beliefs.

"Yevt," he would say. "Your mama has been through so much. The death of your father while you were so young. Trying to manage during some very challenging years with no way to earn a living and provide food for her child. Fearing every day she would find you dead from starvation or exposure. It is no wonder when the Party offered to put you through school that she jumped on the opportunity and accepted their way of life without question. Imagine if it had been you?"

The first time Danya reasoned with her in this way, she was still in her angry phase and wanted to do nothing more than rake the eyes out of his head for uttering such sheer nonsense. Now, with such deep regret at the way things were turning out, his wise words brought comfort and a bit of hope. Perhaps, with time, her mother would be able to forget the perceived trespasses of her daughter, and once again, they could be friends? One could only wish for the best.

A month before the scheduled ceremony, Danya quietly and calmly talked with her about her silence at work. He had patiently waited for her to be ready to declare the truth of their wedding plans at university. Because he worked there, too, he couldn't talk about his Orthodox wedding without creating problems for Yevt. But the time had come to be honest.

"Yevt, my love. Together, we decided to marry at the church. It was together, wasn't it? I didn't force you to agree to something that wasn't in your heart?"

She assured him that she wanted to marry at the church. She teased him that no one had ever been able to force her to do anything, to which he wryly had to agree.

"And yet, here we are, barely a month before the wedding, and only four people know of our plans. Me," he said, pointing one of his long fingers at this chest. Then he turned the finger to her, "You, your mother, and the priest." With a quick shrug of the shoulders, he let the assertion sink in, giving her time to see his point without actually having to make it.

Then he went on gently, "I know your mother did not take the news well. I also know the news isn't likely to go over well at work. But we have nothing to fear. Although the State encourages state sanctioned registration or weddings, no one in recent history has been taken into custody for marrying in a church, any more than anyone has been harmed for attending services on Sunday. You've been going with me now for months, and here we both are, still employed, still receiving our ration coupons, still walking freely through the city. What do you fear, and how may I help?"

Yevt realized how wise Danya was in his approach. He

offered no accusations to provide her with the fuel she'd need to respond with anger, blame, or excuses. He stated indisputable facts about the situation to help her see actuality rather than assumption. And finally, he asked for her reasoning without suggesting his own assumptions or biases – all while offering to do what she needed to move forward. Without a doubt, she was marrying a man who would live the definition of helpmeet.

Without stating it in so many words, his factual recap of their situation had touched on all her fears. Since childhood, she had feared the KDB – of being drug from her home, never to be seen again. She feared repercussions from those who held the strings of her life in their hands. She realized, with a start, that she was more like her mother than she had ever wanted to believe.

Yes, she believed in Ukranian nationalism. Yes, she had come to believe in God, not the Party. But only on the inside. On the outside, she marched to the tune of "Long Live USSR." She went to work each morning, always keeping her personal convictions hidden. She took the praise of her superiors knowing full well that if they grasped the depth of emotions in her heart, the praise would cease. She accepted the ration coupons as a way of life, letting her mother wait in long lines after an even longer shift at the fishery without any thought of doing otherwise. She went to church on a regular basis, but never mentioned God unless alone with Danya. Who was she to point an accusatory finger at her mother, when she, Yevt, was worse – a hypocrite?

With complete honesty, despite her humiliation at discovering the truth about herself, Yevt explained herself to her fiancé, eyes looking at the ground in shame. When she finished, she kept her eyes fixed to a spot on the floor, fearing the recrimination which would be evident on his face. His silence after her soliloquy only acted to confirm her fears, and she imagined her marriage slipping away before it had the chance to begin.

Finally, Danya coughed slightly to get her attention. "Yevt. Look at me."

She didn't raise her eyes. She didn't want to remember him with disappointment, or worse, disgust, in his eyes.

"Yevt. Look at me!" He gently took her chin in his hand, willing her to face him. Like a young rebellious child, she let him raise her chin, but kept her eyes closed against the sight.

"Yevt. Please..."

How could she deny this man something he wanted after everything he had given to her? Despite her misgivings, she slowly opened her eyes, not wanting to see the truth, but willing to give him the gift of his final request. To her surprise, his eyes held the same love, tenderness, and concern she had come to count on. Unaware that she was sobbing, she gasped as deep shuddering breaths wracked her body.

With intentional tenderness, he drew her to his chest, murmuring words of soothing endearment, much like a father comforting a child. At length, her breathing regained some normalcy, issuing only a sporadic hiccup or quiver.

With her still pressed against his chest, he said, "Oh, my love. My sweet, sweet love. You have been holding in so much hurt and fear all because of me. All you have been through is due to my failure to recognize your sensitivities. I shouldn't have pushed you so hard. You have only now begun to walk in faith and recognize the stirrings of rebellion in your soul. Someone with such tender roots cannot be expected to withstand cyclone winds, and I just kept beckoning the storm. Can you ever forgive me?"

Looking up into his eyes, she said, "It is I who need forgiving. My actions haven't lived up to my words. I say one thing yet do another. I fear you are going to spend your life unequally yoked. I love you too much to allow that to happen." With those words, she moved to extricate herself from his embrace.

Fear leapt into Danya's eyes as he tightened his arms around her. "No! Do not say that. We are well-suited, you and me. You possess all the qualities I lack. I have trouble seeing beauty and awe and wonder as a jaded man who has seen too much evil in the world – but you...you brought that back to me. What is that compared to anything I might possibly offer to you? It is you, my dear Yevt, who will be unequally yoked. But I love you too much to let you go."

With those words, he kissed her gently at first, and then more urgently, wanting to ease his fears and find proof that she wasn't going to run away. She responded in kind, knowing that whatever came, she could handle it with Danya by her side.

Pulling his lips away from hers, he said, "We will go register our marriage. Today, if possible. Then, we will secretly marry in the church." When she started to protest, he placed a finger against her lips. "No, it is better this way. It will heal things with your mother. It will allow us to both continue our association with university uninterrupted. There will come a time when such secrecy will no longer be needed, but for now, it is the right course of action. But I promise you this, someday, we will celebrate a Ukrainian wedding with all the trappings – and you will not be afraid to do so."

Chapter 7

1991

Ivanna shivered uncontrollably, her teeth clanking together loudly creating an uneven, fast-tempo beat a percussionist would have had trouble replicating. Her breath floated from her nostrils in puffs of white steam despite being indoors. The brutal Ukraine winter of 1991 had combined forces with the unfortunate economics of supply and demand, leaving many in the city without the necessities.

Today, for the third in a row, she had been unable to obtain bread or milk. Despite her ration coupon, the supply had run out long before the line. Her building suffered as well, having had no heat for a better part of the month. There was nothing left in her flat to burn. She supposed that was true of the entire city, so going out in search of fuel was futile, and potentially deadly, as thousands succumbed to hypothermia.

She had watched in horror, early this morning, as an elderly man standing in line collapsed into the snow. The sleight woman behind him reached out to help, but when he was unresponsive and showed no signs of a pulse, the concern for the man quickly changed to something akin to greed as she began pulling off his boots. Before Ivanna comprehended what was happening, several people followed her lead, jumping out of line to grab at the man's clothing – gloves, hat, scarf, even socks. One woman triumphantly held up the bread coupon he held clutched in his hand, laughing as though she had gotten the best prize of all, despite the unlikeliness of getting to use her own coupon, let alone his. Then everyone settled back into line again as if nothing had happened.

Ivanna closed her eyes against the memory of that poor, old dead man laying half-naked in the snow staring up at the overcast sky. She wondered about his family and whether they would find him or learn of his fate. She wondered how long it would take for someone to notice her own demise.

She thought of Yevt, who had been married now since late May. Ivanna had come home from work one evening to find a single sheet of paper laying on the table facedown, "Mama" scribbled on the back. She turned the paper over in her hands to discover a copy of Yevt and Danya's marriage registration. While her hands were deep in fish guts and scales, they had married, and as she soon discovered, taken Yevt's things.

Of course, she was satisfied they had not gone through with the church wedding but wondered at the suddenness of the new plans. Perhaps Yevt was with child? That could certainly explain her irrational behavior of late as well as the hasty registration.

She realized she didn't have Danya's address, and therefore, was unsure of where her daughter now resided. She supposed this was purposeful. The church nonsense had created a rift that would not easily heal, and despite the state marriage, she still expected an apology before she would bestow forgiveness on Yevt. Yes, she could reach her daughter at work, if need be, but unless an emergency dictated otherwise, she would wait for Yevt to express remorse and begin making reparations.

Shortly after the registration, Ivanna had been moved to a smaller flat, further from the town's center. This did not surprise her, as a single woman without a direct association with university didn't need such a spacious and convenient living arrangement. And rightfully, her rations were diminished to reflect her new status as a family of one. In her view, the efficiency and parity of the Party were to be congratulated.

That was eight months ago. As she sat in her frigid flat, she still had no news of Yevt, no idea if a grandchild was born, or any notion if they were still in the city. She steadfastly refused to make inquiries, determined that Yevt would have to take the first steps to repair the damage she'd created in this relationship, denying any personal responsibility. She did sometimes wonder if Yevt simply could not find her given her new address but convinced herself that an intelligent child like hers would have little trouble locating an old woman who still worked at the same fishery – never once considering Yevt had similar thoughts and feelings.

———————

Yevt found it difficult to adjust the microscope while wearing bulky gloves, but impossible to accomplish with numb hands. She also realized complaining wouldn't change her reality, so she alternated gloving and ungloving her hands, trying to take her mind off the cold.

"Surely," she thought, "Winter is almost over?" Each day on her way home from work, she looked in vain for the first signs of spring. However, the brave, green shoots were as elusive as a cure for cancer. She had even begun to wonder if winter finally won some battle and would now rule the weather with an iron fist of ice and snow in the same way the Party ruled her life with lines and shortages.

She tried to remember that she had it good compared to many. As an educated scientist married to another educated scientist, both working for a government-run institution, she was given her rations without having to wait in line. Although it was true the loaves were getting smaller and decidedly lacking in flavor, others had it much worse.

At night, while wrapped in Danya's arms, trying to find some semblance of warmth, they often talked about the economy and the politics that had brought Ukraine, indeed, the whole of the USSR, to this spot. She still listened in rapt amazement at his clear and concise explanations, developed through voracious reading.

For the last four years, under General Secretary Gorbachev's policy of glasnost, Western journals had made their way into Ukraine. As a university professor, Danya had almost limitless access to such writings. Having already formed dissident opinions long before glasnost, what he learned only strengthened his understanding and anti-Party positions.

After a lengthy explanation about a concept called capitalism, about which she had many questions, Yevt asked if capitalism was such a remarkable idea, then why was the new policy of perestroika, which sounded a lot like this Western capitalism to her ears, failing so miserably?

"Ah," said Danya. "That is a remarkably astute question. I see you have been listening to me and not just using my body to warm your own!"

Yevt laughed, despite the cold. "Don't believe for one second that I actually care about these things," she said slyly. "It's just my choice to learn is limited because you won't stop droning on and on!"

Banter was something new to Yevt. She and her mother often talked, but she had not encountered the quick back and forth of banter until Danya. Despite her late start, she had acquired quite a knack for it.

"Touché," laughed Danya. "And, to prove you right, I will answer your question with as many words as possible."

Yevt snuggled in closer, more interested than she'd ever admit in understanding capitalism, perestroika, and what separated the two.

"For years, as you know, the State had complete control of the economy. All industry – all farms – produced and grew exactly what they were told to produce. No more and no less. By the time General Secretary Gorbachev came to power, the economy was stagnant. Production was declining. People who had jobs were not putting in their best effort. More and more people were without employment and no new jobs were in sight."

He paused, saying, "Are you with me so far?"

She nodded into his chest, understanding how

students in his classes must feel as he lectured.

"Right, then. General Secretary Gorbachev determined there needed to be a change, so he instituted perestroika. Now, instead of one central entity controlling production, the different ministries across the nation determined what to produce. Plus, workers were now part-owners of the company and had the ability to demand better wages. This was instituted to increase their desire to work harder and produce more."

Before he could ask, Yevt nodded into his chest again. She understood, but still couldn't determine how this was not the capitalism he talked of earlier.

"The differences between perestroika and capitalism derive from the goals of the two programs."

"Good," she thought. "Now he's going to answer my question."

"You see, the goal of capitalism is to allow independent citizens the ability to produce goods and services for the best interests of society while at the same time making a profit for themselves. The goal of perestroika is to create an efficient socialism. So, although it looks kind of like capitalism from the outside, the goal was never to allow private citizens to make decisions or a profit. Gorbachev has no intention of ending a government-controlled economy."

She nodded slowly. Yes, she could see what he was saying, but still, why the failure? Why the shortages? As though he could read her mind, and she often accused him of doing just that, he continued.

"Now, instead of a well-run communist system, or a well-run capitalist system, we are experiencing the worst of both worlds. Do you know why we cannot find bread on the shelves?"

It made no sense to Yevt. She and Danya had picnicked on the edge of town during the final warm days of autumn. The golden stalks of grain whispered to one another in the gentle breeze. Before Christmas, on a rare Saturday of sunshine, she and Danya had again walked near the fields, only to find the grain had not been harvested but crushed beneath the snow and cold.

"Those fields at the edge of town were never harvested because workers from the city were not forced, as they had been during communist rule, to bring them in. To get even, those in charge of the agriculture ministries, likely the same leaders from before, are refusing to send the grain to bakeries in the city. The farmers don't care because they can't make money anyway. The city-dwellers won't harvest because it is no longer required. No one wins."

Yevt peeked out from under the covers. "So," she said brightly, "Perestroika and capitalism are kind of like the bread I brought home today."

Raised quizzical eyebrows and a concentrated frown etched Danya's face as he desperately tried to work out how bread fit into the equation.

Smiling at his stumped expression, she continued, "Unless you were to compare it to an old loaf, the new loaf would easily pass as bread. However, upon closer inspection, you'll find today's bread is far less substantial in both size and quality. It looks like bread, but it is actually just something to chew on."

Danya roared with delight. "Yes! I think you really do understand."

He rewarded her with a kiss, and then another. Soon, all thoughts of Gorbachevian economics, as well as the chill of the winter, vanished from her mind.

Chapter 8

1991

Only a fool could miss the signs of a revolution, leaving Danya to wryly observe that he associated with a lot of fools. Intelligent fools, but fools, nonetheless. This thought came following a staff meeting called after a massive demonstration on campus earlier in the week.

Hundreds of students crowded into the main dvoryk, the large courtyard nearest the administrative building. Hundreds more hung out of windows in adjacent buildings. All jeered and chanted, demanding change, real change. Better food. Better wages. Better life.

With orchestrated precision, the crowd opened, creating a small stage from which a student gave an impassioned speech, only to close again before the offender could be whisked away by authorities. Then, on the opposite side of the crowd, another hole would open to yet another student. Each speech was little more than a paragraph, but taken as a whole, these mini entreaties covered everything from freedom to nationalism to capitalism.

In the end, no one was arrested, and no one had claimed responsibility for the event's organization. Thus, a meeting was called, and professors were questioned as to who they thought might be behind the unrest. Danya resisted the urge to laugh when asked this question. Who? Who, indeed?

He couldn't name Gorbachev himself, though he was certainly a central figure spurring on the protests. And, in terms of students, it would have been easier to provide names of those who were most definitely not behind it.

Everywhere on campus, whether in the cafeteria, the library, or walking along the sidewalks between buildings, Danya overheard the whispered discontent often mingling with bold outbursts of envisioned anarchy. One didn't have to be looking hard to find those who were tired of eating what he and Yevt now called capitalistic bread. In fact, he was certain one had to be actively seeking not to discern the dissatisfaction.

He had dutifully considered the possibilities, then shook his head, giving the powers-that-be an honest assessment. "It really could have been anyone...but I didn't hear a peep concerning the demonstration until the students began gathering in the courtyard."

How the students had coordinated the largest demonstration the school had yet to experience without an inkling that something was afoot was a mystery to him. He was curious to determine how they managed it – not to seek punishment but to learn from their mastery. Such a skill may well come in handy in the future.

As the meeting broke up, he sought to joke with fellow colleagues about the absurdity of the line of questioning but met with blank stares. "Comrade Petrushevych, why did you find the questioning absurd? I think it is perfectly normal that we try to find the instigator of this crime," one professor stated.

Shocked by their assessment of the meeting, Danya had murmured, "Yes, yes, of course. But with such unrest among the students, picking out a name or two would be impossible, don't you think?"

Once again, they gaped at him as if he were speaking in Chinese rather than Ukranian. "Unrest? Here? Why, Comrade Petrushevych, the students in my classes seem quite content. Perhaps it is something you are doing wrong in your own classroom that causes such feelings?"

Danya conceded by nodding slightly and walking away, realizing either his peers were fools or pretending to be fools. He hoped the latter but assumed the former. He also realized that by opening his mouth, he was likely to be put on the internal watch list – names of those suspected of harboring ill-will toward the government. That list, like the potential organizer's list, in his opinion, would have been shorter in the negative.

The signs of rebellion didn't stop at the walls of the school. Protests popped up regularly throughout the city. Dissident pamphlets found their way into homes and businesses faster than they could be destroyed. The media, no longer bound to sugarcoat the truth, decried the inequalities between government officials and the regular citizens. And in outlying areas of the USSR, like Ukraine, the younger generation pushed against restrictions set by a central government that didn't appear to care who lived and who died, or who ate and who starved. Yet, despite all this evidence, so many people shuffled from one line to the next, not seeing what was before them.

That night, he asked Yevt's opinion on the matter. He was prone to harsh judgment of others and considered that he might need to wipe away a few assumptions to see more clearly. Yevt was always the perfect person to help him do a bit of window cleaning.

After explaining his day and seeking her input, he watched her thoughtfully mull over the information. She didn't rush into an immediate answer, instead considering the many factors presented. Her answer surprised him, though it shouldn't have – a student often turns their teacher's words back at them.

"Well, Danya, I certainly see your point and can completely understand your frustration, perhaps even your conclusion. However, a wise man once told me that sometimes people toe the Party line because they've known worse. The devil you know is often easier to deal with than the devil you don't."

He'd never used those precise phrases before, but he had indeed argued for his mother-in-law and others like her. Others like his colleagues.

"You win. You are right," he said, as he mimed wiping his window clean of the assumptions marring his view.

"Speaking of your mother...." He saw her stiffen and let the introductory phrase hang in mid-air.

She took a long breath in and blew it out slowly, before replying, "I don't believe anyone mentioned Mama. Is there something on your mind? Would you care to share?"

Her eyes belied her words, daring him to continue. But

he had started on the course and felt bound to continue. It was a subject he rarely broached but one that was often on his mind.

"Thank you for asking, because, yes, there is something I care to share."

Her eyes stabbed him with a thousand knives, but he continued. "It has been a year since you have seen your mother. I am aware she has moved, and I am aware you have learned of her new location. I was simply wondering what it was going to take for you to visit with her and start the process of forgiving."

There. The question was in full view rather than hiding in the middle of their relationship. Ivanna's reaction had hurt Yevt, but their estrangement continued to hurt her. He wasn't entirely sure if the breach was fixable. But this he did understand – the longer it took to begin repairs, the less likely it would be for the repairs to be enough.

With a softer voice, he said, "My love, it is time. Your mama is not getting any younger. I don't want you to grow to regret your decision to write her out of your life."

"ME? I didn't write her out of my life, Danya," she exploded. "You know that! She wrote me out. She treated me like a stranger. No, that's not true. She treated strangers better. She disowned her only child, and in all these months, hasn't reached out – not once. Why should I be the one to apologize? Why me?"

He simply answered her with, "Why not you?"

"Why not you?" floated in and out of her consciousness over the next several days. As she was prone to do, her initial reaction was anger. Anger at her mother for not understanding. Anger at Danya for bringing up the subject. Anger at the government for meddling in such things as weddings. But as always, when the anger finally abated, she was left only with a deepening ache of loneliness – a sadness born of missing her mother.

Danya knew her well and would not bring her mother up again – at least not in the near future. But he also knew if she could see past her fury, she would eventually come to a conclusion that not only made sense but held compassion for all involved.

She did miss her mother, even though she didn't fully understand her or her ways. She missed telling her about her day, even though those chats weren't nearly as stimulating as the ones she had with Danya. She missed the quiet hugs and the unconditional love. She wanted to recapture all that somehow, but how to begin?

Her mother was mulish. She knew that from experience. It was also a trait she herself had inherited. Two stubborn people in a room were not likely to find fence mending an easy chore. "No," she decided, "It just isn't going to work." Then, she replayed Danya's words again, "Why not you?"

Her mother would demand an apology. She still believed that elders were always right – never wrong. Elders were to be reverenced. Yevt had not only disregarded her mother but, in her mother's eyes, disgraced her as well.

The problem was Yevt was not sorry for wanting a church wedding and sometimes still regretted not going through with it. She was not sorry she told her mother she was a nationalist and didn't believe the propaganda from the Party. She didn't know how to get beyond the impasse.

That evening, she said, "Danya, I've been thinking about what you said...about Mama...I...I honestly don't know how to make amends. She will demand an apology, and quite frankly, I'm not sorry for the things I believe. I can't lie and say I am. I won't do it."

Danya held both of her hands in his and said, "I would never expect you to apologize for who you are. But let me ask you this. Is there anything about what happened that you are sorry for? Anything at all?"

She thought of many things – her anger, her tone, her disgust – and slowly discovered a path forward.

"Then, my darling, simply apologize for those."

Chapter 9

1991

Lyaksandro started, the book he was reading falling heedlessly to his lap. The sun was out, dressed in her best regalia, providing a momentary reprieve from the cold and lonesome winter. He had chosen to sit on the bench in the park not far from his flat to enjoy this rare treat. The sun, though high in the sky and strong enough to clear the frosty haze, did not provide much in the way of warmth. So, Lyaksandro had donned a black knit toboggan and thick gray scarf over his woolen jacket. His thick gloves had been shoved haphazardly into his pockets, empty fingers poking out at stray angles, because they hindered his ability to turn the pages. Each time he turned a page, he would trade which hand held the book and which hand would hide deep within a fold of his scarf for warmth.

He had been enjoying the book with its ability to whisk

him away to a far-off place where his personal problems couldn't follow until the spell had been broken. What had startled him to awareness?

He listened intently, trying to identify the sound that brought him crashing back to reality. Cars rushed to and fro, taking people into and out of the city. A siren pierced through the traffic noise, shouting to everyone within hearing distance that an emergency was at hand. Closer, and quieter, birds chirped in hopes that someone would drop a few crumbs and relieve them of their burden of finding food hidden beneath the snow.

But these sounds were comforting and familiar. They were the sounds Lyaksandro had grown accustomed to and brought him a semblance of peace, if not the real thing. So, what had pulled his attention away from his book?

Just then, a child's laughter silenced the traffic, the birds, and yes, even the siren's emergency, cutting through the snow and ice, racing past the trees and sidewalks, shoving passersby to one side, to hurtle around Lyaksandro, waiting impatiently for the memory to appear. Lyaksandro was helpless to do anything other than submit to the demand.

For months after his forced escape, Lyaksandro did little more than sleep. When he wasn't huddled beneath the rough blankets in his room made artificially dark by suspending one of those blankets from the flimsy metal rod like a curtain, he was blindly making his way through a new city, endlessly searching for the one thing he was never to experience again.

Had he been more aware, he would have noted others moving quickly to the opposite side of the street as he approached. His hair, now long and uneven, was tangled into ropes of greasy dirt and lint. His unkempt beard had begun to take on a similar twisted quality, mingling with his hair to create one never-ending frame around his thin, pale face. But more than the hair, his eyes were what sent others scurrying away from him, clutching at their handbags, pulling their children behind their legs, looking for the closest doorway through which to disappear.

His eyes had been simultaneously empty and crowded. Anyone merely looking his way could tell his empty eyes did not register the buildings or people of Brixton. Instead, the crowded, haunting memories caused his eyes to move about in an eerie, unnatural fashion, forming a noncommittal pattern of ups, downs, and sideways. Anyone caught by one of these unsteady movements would stop, gasping for air, fearing that, like a roe deer on the side of the road, they might dash into the path of this oncoming machine and meet their unfortunate demise.

The flight that brought him to London, and the short car ride to his tiny flat in Brixton passed in a haze of pain. He acknowledged instinctively that he was the worst kind of man, one who would forsake his wife and child, trading them for his own life.

But in the ensuing days, he had begun to hope that by leaving, they had been given a reprieve. That his absence ensured they had lived. Before he had been in England a fortnight, he was making surreptitious plans to go back to his homeland, rescue his wife and daughter from the gaping jaws of communism and sure death, and bring them here where they would start a new life.

This fantasy sustained him, as he worked with officials to solidify his new identity. He would acquiesce to their ministrations, allow them to create a new man, and, once he had his new identity fully reconstructed, he would turn his back on these self-important deliverers and find his family.

Someone, perhaps it was the man he knew as Oliver, the one whose job it was to help him assimilate into the culture of Brixton, became suspicious of his motives, though he couldn't be certain. He had been too eager, too willing to go along, only too happy to become who they wanted him to become. The change from the man sobbing at the airport to this man, the one easily 'fitting in' and forgetting his past life, was too drastic.

On a clear day, just one of a string that had been full of promise, Oliver showed him into a room with two metal chairs, a small table, and windows on three walls, through which others were looking on. He felt a momentary flicker of anxiety but let it pass. Whatever the hurdle, he would surmount it. It was purely another step toward Ivanna and Yevtsye. For them, he was willing to do anything.

Oliver gestured toward the seat facing the windows with his elbow, as he grabbed the other chair, turned it around, and straddled it like a horse. Addressing him by his new name, he began in an overtly friendly manner, masking an underlying tension.

"How are you getting along? It won't be much longer before you are 'released' as it were, from the program. You'll be ready to begin your new job and start a new life. The debriefing is almost to an end."

Lyaksandro did his best to hide the joy he found in these words. In a few short weeks, he would disappear from this tiny suburb of London and these men that brought him here. Once he successfully made the break, he would go to Ivanna, beg her forgiveness, and bring her back to the UK. The details – how he would get to Ukraine, how he would approach Ivanna without tipping off anyone watching their home, how he would get papers for his family to get across a communist border – didn't matter. He was Lyaksandro Hadeon Rosomakha – the impetuous warrior – who had lived when he should have died. His love for Ivanna and his daughter would be enough. He would cross each bridge as he came to it.

Without realizing how it happened, the interview took a shift in a different direction. Oliver's questions now had a distinct air of aggression. "What will you do once the assimilation is complete?"

When Lyaksandro said nothing, Oliver demanded, "What? What will you do? What are your plans?"

Then, before Lyaksandro could say another word, Oliver's tone changed yet again, throwing him off balance with their mocking tone and uncanny accuracy. "You are planning on returning to Ukraine? To retrieve your wife and child?"

Lyaksandro jerked, his eyes looking straight into Oliver's. "Come now, Lyaksandro." The use of his real name caused him to rock back once more. "Do you really think you can make such plans without us knowing? We perceive your thoughts before you've fully formed them. It's our job. It's what we do. It's why we're here."

Lyaksandro quickly realized that denying his intent was useless and potentially dangerous, so he tried to turn the interview into a conversation – one that would leave him with allies. Getting his wife and daughter back would be so much easier if he had the help of the men who were able to remove him safely.

"You are right. I am sorry. I should have told you of my plans. It was stupid of me to assume you wouldn't figure out my plan." He glanced up to gauge Oliver's reaction to his words. He needed to create sympathy for his plight.

"I miss her, you know. Ivanna. My daughter. I thought it was the right choice to come here alone. I did it to keep them alive. I reasoned that it would be better for them if I were gone. But now that I am here? ... I have realized they should be with me. I am nothing without them. So, yes, my plan is to go to Ukraine, and bring them back with me. Surely, now, after these long weeks, they are no longer in imminent danger. Surely now, you can meet with Ivanna and bring her to me. Surely?"

Was Oliver uncertain? Lyaksandro noted the glance toward the mirrored windows, questions hanging over his head. "What should I do? Can we help him?"

Oliver excused himself from the room, leaving Lyaksandro to nervously flit his eyes from one window to the next, silently begging for help. "Please. Please. I am not a spy. I am just a mere man caught up in something too big for me. I just want my wife and child. I'll do anything you ask. Anything." Those words spun in a loop through his mind, until the door pushed open, admitting Oliver once again.

His face, though grim, had an expectant quality. "We will see what we can do. No promises, mate. You understand that, right?"

Lyaksandro nodded vigorously. "In the meantime, let's

finish up some of our work. I've got our team working on a plan. When they determine what is possible, they will let us know."

Oliver had slipped into English, and Lyaksandro was pleased he understood the words. Based on these last few weeks, he had a knack for languages, and he hoped Ivanna would find it as easy to learn. Yevtsye would charge beyond him quickly. By the time she was grown, no one would ever suspect she had been born elsewhere – of this he was certain.

When it came time to end the session, Oliver continued. When Lyaksandro expressed a desire to go back to his flat, to end the day, Oliver insisted that they stay. "We are so close, so close to finishing. Let's press on."

It was now almost dawn. Lyaksandro had been awake for 24 hours and hadn't eaten anything since breakfast the day before. However, each time he suggested stopping, Oliver cut him short. Other than quick breaks to relieve himself, Oliver pressed on.

At noon, well past the edge of exhaustion, Lyaksandro saw a man he hadn't seen before coming into the room carrying a folder. Oliver got up, and Lyaksandro laid the entire upper half of his body on the table. He couldn't be bothered with the man and his folder. He just needed to sleep. He didn't understand the exhausting pace or the need to finish up everything now, today.

Whether it was minutes or hours, he didn't know, but he woke to the sound of Oliver murmuring in the hall. Lyaksandro caught snatches of words through a haze. "Both of them? ... How? ... Are you sure? ... There hasn't been some mistake? ..."

Lyaksandro straightened in his chair, straining to hear

the conversation. Were they talking about Ivanna and Yevtsye? Had they come up with a plan? And then he heard the words that darkened his world for months.

Dead.

Chapter 10

July 2, 1991

The cold had abated, but hunger was ever-present. Ivanna had taken to sneaking bits of fish skins and guts from the fishery while she worked. This was not easy to do undetected. Because of the food shortages, what used to be waste – skin, bones, and innards – was now turned into fish stew. Therefore, taking fish home, in any form, could easily lead to a stint in the labor camps. Stealing wasn't tolerated.

Ivanna did her best to be a Party loyalist at all costs, but she was terribly hungry, and more so because she handled food each day without the ability to partake of it. So, on days when obtaining bread or milk was impossible, she would press tiny bits of fish waste on her dress while skinning, fileting, and chopping in hopes some would fall into a pocket or wrinkle. Anything leaving the fishery with her must appear accidental, so even enormous efforts produced only the most miniscule results.

When she got home, she would carefully comb her clothing for every small morsel, not letting something as small as a single fish scale escape. Then, she'd add the collected oddments to some water, and boil them up into a colorless, and nearly tasteless, soup. It wasn't much, but it was better than boiling her leather shoes, which, based on the acrid fetor wafting in the alleys throughout the city, many comrades attempted.

Occasionally, she would wait in an alley behind one of the few remaining restaurants that served the leadership in hopes of obtaining a few scraps of uneaten food. However, her second-shift work meant she could not stake out the alley early in the day. By the time she got into the queue, there were dozens of people pressed close to the dumpster waiting impatiently for the remnants of someone's meal. She fared little better on her days off – the remains were barely more than she got from the fishery, and she had to fight hard to get them into her pockets and home without being mugged by others as hungry as she was – or hungrier.

Today began as any other – she had waited in line for bread and milk. As usual, of late, she came home empty-handed. It seemed a single, old lady whose only skills consisted of cutting up dead fish did not rate a front position in line. Of course, she was happy to concede her bread to the children and to those who would make the Party superior, but this knowledge didn't stop her intestines from contracting violently or cause the persistent diarrhea to subside.

Thankfully, she had always been a strong, muscular woman – not fat in any sense of the word but never one to be called slender. Once upon a time, she had envied women who had a slim, delicate build. But now? She had enough energy to work and find ways to survive, while their anemically thin, weakened bodies could do nothing more than lie down and, eventually, die.

She wondered how much longer it would be before her body, too, succumbed to something like scurvy or worse. She steadfastly refused to inspect her unclothed body in the mirror but knew she was getting leaner. Even the wire hangar in the closet rivaled her ability to fill out her dress. Such scrawniness meant only one thing – death was closer than it had been before.

Ivanna sighed. She had come to hate this time of day with several hours before work and nothing to do to fill her time. It was then that her mind would wander, either to imagining Yevt's life or to the stirring up of old memories, bringing to life ghosts she never managed to bury.

Today, she would focus on Yevt – her musings about Leka exhausted her more than her lack of food. Because she still held out hope for her relationship with Yevt, though saddened by her daydreams, their impact was far less substantial.

She often imagined Yevt with a baby, a strong healthy boy of about six months old. She would have given him a strong name, something with character and meaning. Perhaps Petro, a strong rock, or Andriy, courageous. He would be sitting on his own now, as well as scooting across the floor in search of something to put in his mouth, probably something he should not have. She smiled, remembering how Yevt would find the tiniest pieces of lint on the ground and attempt to eat them faster than they could get them from her tiny fingers.

Of course, being Danya and Yevt's child, he would be advanced, having words for food, milk, sleep, and book, when his peers struggled to say mama and papa. Like his mama, he would love books, and Yevt, who had worked out a schedule with the university to allow herself as much time as possible with her young son, would read to him for hours using different voices for the characters as she had learned from her own mama.

A timid knock on the door brought Ivanna, who had been in a living room on the other side of town playing with her unknown grandson, back to reality. As she pushed herself up from the chair, one of the few furnishings left after the frigid winter, she tried to imagine who would be calling at this time of day.

She kept mostly to herself and did her best not to bother her neighbors with her second-shift schedule. And, although she had nodded a few times and exchanged a greeting or two, she wasn't able to address anyone by name. Certainly, no one had come to borrow a cup of sugar? She suppressed a smile at the thought of borrowing sugar from a woman who ate fish soup made from fish scales scraped deliberately from her clothing.

Rampant crime was as much a part of the city as starvation, so Ivanna did not unbolt the door, but instead, called in the gruffest voice she could muster, "Yes? Who is it? What do you want?"

Ivanna fell against the door with a whimper as she heard Yevt, her dear, sweet daughter say, "Mama?"

Her mother's apartment was small and barren. Though her rooms were spotless, a rank odor permeated the entire building, a combination of death and sickness, fish and urine. That would have been enough to inspire Yevt's next moves, but her mother's appearance was the catalyst for swift, decisive action.

Within hours of seeing her mother for the first time in over a year, and once the hugs, kisses, and "I love you's" had diminished in frequency, Yevt had taken leave of her mother and spoken with Danya. Together, they went to the Housing Ministry, requesting a family allowance increase that would now include Ivanna Rosomakha, Danya's mother-in-law.

Because of their positions with the university, permission was granted for the move, though, currently, there were no two-bedroom units, and they would be placed on the waiting list. A bespectacled older woman with a mouth pinched so tight it appeared her lips were held together with elastic bands informed them that Ivanna could remain in her apartment until such time as a new unit became available.

Jabbing his finger forcefully on the counter that separated them, Danya stated unequivocally that Ivanna would move in immediately. Shrugging, as if to say their cramped discomfort would not speed along the process in any way, she produced the proper paperwork to be taken to the food ministry two blocks over, as well as the paperwork needed to release Ivanna's quarters back into the system. "Comrade Rosmakha's quarters must be vacated within 72 hours, at which time new tenants will take possession." Expecting no response, she pushed the papers with the official party stamp across the counter into Danya's waiting hands and called the next person in line.

As they entered the next building, an official at the door asked to see identification to determine which line they would be required to join. Once again, their university positions sped along the food allocation process, allowing them to hopscotch ahead of many who appeared to have been there long enough to now be part of the decor.

Yevt tried not to gape at the gaunt faces they passed on the way to the processing office as she realized just how bad off so many were. Most everyone here looked more like her mother than not, and few, in fact, only two, she and Danya, appeared to still be vibrant and healthy. With the paperwork from the housing ministry, a copy of their marriage registration, and their current coupon vouchers, they were able to add Ivanna as an occupant of their household in moments. So, with the Party's official approval in hand, they hurried to bring Ivanna home.

Yevt was stunned to find her mother was not waiting for them, but instead, had gone to work, the apartment locked up tightly against, what? "I cannot begin to imagine why she would lock the door. What is there to steal? A chair? Her second set of fish-stained clothes? She doesn't even have a bed to sleep on, Danya!"

"Your mother is a creature of habit, my love. She has locked the door on the way to work for years, and my bet is she will continue to do so for many more."

Yevt turned her frustration on her husband. "Fine. Make light if you want. But here we are, ready to take her home, and she's cutting up stinky fish and won't be home until after midnight. What was she thinking?"

Danya, who after a year of marriage was used to Yevt's occasional emotional outbursts, stated the obvious. "I am not making light of anything, Yevt. I am merely stating facts. As to why she went to work? Why wouldn't she? You said you were going to move her into our home, but nothing happens quickly for your mama, and it hasn't happened quickly for years. You saw those lines at the ministries – the eyes of those who have been waiting. Some of those poor souls have likely stood in that same line for days, hoping today would be the day they make it to the front before the office closes. How was your mother to know we would accomplish in one afternoon what most cannot accomplish in a year?"

He let that sink in and continued. "This is not a great area of town, so we cannot wait here at her door until she comes home. And I don't think coming back in the dark of the night and whisking her away to our home after her shift makes sense either. Let's slip a note under her door explaining we will be by to collect her first thing in the morning."

Yevt's face fell. She didn't want her mother to be in this wretched apartment for one more night. Her obstinacy had already caused so much damage, and now that she knew the results, Yevt didn't want to live with the knowledge without having done something to rectify the situation.

However, she realized Danya was right. Spending the evening in the hallway or moving her mother and her meager possessions in the wee hours of the morning made no sense. She quickly penned a letter to her mother, signed it to include the words "I love you" and slipped it under the door.

"We may not be able to bring Mama home until

morning," she said with determination, "but we can make our home ready to receive her." With that, she turned on her heel, her mind already rearranging their living spaces.

Chapter 11

August 22, 1991

Now, six weeks after Mama had moved in, Yevt could laugh a little at the process of getting her here and settled. At the time, however, she didn't find it the least amusing, feeling her mama was being unreasonable, ungrateful, and doing her best to push her daughter's buttons.

After a full evening of arranging, rearranging, and arranging yet again, Yevt found a way to provide some privacy for her mama while still maintaining a semblance of a living room. Satisfied that they could live like this for months if needed, she had gone to bed, planning to be at her mama's house by eight the next morning.

Despite her best efforts, sleep was unattainable. Visions of her mother's emaciated body and hollowed out cheeks converged with those she saw standing in line at the ministries. She wondered what had brought them there and whether their needs would ever be met. When she did finally sleep, she did so fitfully, the covers bunching up around her feet and twisting into knots.

She finally fell into a deep sleep around daylight, and before she knew it, it was nearly time to be at her mother's. She had scolded Danya for not waking her and rushed to get out the door as quickly as possible. When she and Danya finally arrived at the apartment, there was no sign of her mama, and the door, once again, had been locked against any intruders.

Exasperated, she had cried out, "Now what? We don't even know if she's been home!"

Danya, sensing her frustration level was far beyond teasing, pointed down to the floor. "She's been here. Yesterday, this floor was spotless. This morning, I can see the prints from her fish-covered shoes."

Knowing she had not somehow died in the night did help alleviate some of Yevt's anxiety, but not her frustration. "But where did she go?"

Danya's reasoning hit her hard. "I suspect she's gone to stand in a food line, Yevt. Isn't that what she always did? Work, sleep a few hours, send you to school or work, stand in line, sleep a bit more, and work again?"

Mama wasn't used to someone taking care of her. She had no such expectations. She would have never guessed they didn't need her to stand in line.

Slumping against the doorframe, she said, "I guess we'll have to wait."

Three hours later, Ivanna shuffled into the hallway with a quarter loaf of bread and a triumphant smile. "Look! Look at my luck today!"

Yevt simply couldn't fathom the deprivations experienced by her mother that would garner such enthusiasm over a small piece of capitalism bread. Tears stung at her eyes, the evidence that she had been a miserable daughter piling up before her.

With a bright smile that belied her true emotions, Yevt congratulated her mama and said, "Let's get your things. Here's all the paperwork, so you can move in with us today." Her intent was to have her mother ensconced in their home before noon meal and spend the rest of the day helping her to settle in. Her mama, it appeared, didn't understand or care about that intent.

"Where are the papers? I want to see them," Ivanna had demanded. Although they had the papers with them the evening before, having just come from ministry, Yevt had not brought them today. Despite assuring her mama that everything was in order and that she could spend all afternoon reading them once they got her home, Ivanna refused to budge. She had vehemently declared that she would not vacate her home until she knew of a certainty the Party had sanctioned the move. With that declaration, she dropped into her chair with arms tightly folded against her chest.

Danya, not daring to leave his wife and mother alone together, sent Yevt back home for the required paperwork. Once back, Ivanna had read every word – twice. She then held the paper up to the light coming through the window as if to inspect whether the seal on the bottom of each page was actually provided by the State or a fake. Finally, she was ready to pack.

With so few possessions, the process should have been quick and painless. But their university positions didn't hold the same sway over Mama that they did over the various ministries.

Danya had scored two small boxes from work the day before and gave them to Mama to fill with her things. She began in the bedroom, shaking out, looking at, and then refolding each piece of clothing before placing it into the box. Then, she meticulously folded her threadbare blanket despite their insistence that they had a better one for her use at home.

She had no toiletries except a comb and a small bar of soap. These were placed into the second box so as to not dirty her clothing items. The only thing in the living room was the chair, and since it wouldn't fit in the box, she moved quickly to the kitchen. It was here that Yevt's patience strained and quivered, waiting for just the right reason to snap in half.

Instead of simply filling the box with the kitchen's contents, her mama would hold each item and recount a little story: where she found it, who used it, her favorite meal with it, or something as banal as when she last used it.

Asking her to hurry, as Yevt discovered, only made it worse. She would put the item down, consider her daughter in the same way a principal would consider an errant pupil, and deliver nothing short of a sermon about memories and their importance. Then, she would pick the item up once again, continuing where she left off.

When the last spoon was in the box, Yevt snatched the box from the floor, handed it to her husband, and said, "You carry this one. I'll get the one with the clothing. Mama, just follow us home."

But her mama stood there looking dumbfounded. "Leave? With the house looking like this? I have never once left a home for good in disarray, and I can assure you that I will not begin today."

Yevt, with a heavy sigh, put down her box. The cleaning, which wasn't much of a clean because her mama had no soap, took over an hour. She wiped down every wall, every ledge, and every drawer. Yevt doubted there was an inch left untouched.

Finally, her mother said, "Now, how are we getting the chair home?"

Yevt, her patience long since gone, roared, "We have no room for the chair. It is not going home. It is going to stay right here. Period."

Her mother, completely unperturbed by the outburst, said, "I will check if someone in the building can use it." And marched out the door.

Yevt wanted to smash the chair and throw it piece by piece at her mother's retreating back, but simply sat down and put her head in her hands. Had her mother always been this difficult, or was this just part of her punishment for being an ungrateful daughter over the last year?

In the end, a family from the top floor was happy to take the chair, and Ivanna was finally ready to leave her home. As they walked the two miles laden with boxes, Mama pulled out her bread and began to eat, stating it was well past time for the noon meal.

———————

As difficult as it had been getting Mama home, Danya felt she had settled in well with only a few bumps. The biggest problem had been her work. Living several miles from the fishery at her age, in her health, and at that time of night, was a problem that needing solving immediately.

After unloading her things into their home, she had

immediately changed into her work dress, put on her odiferous shoes, and walked out the door. Stunned, Danya trotted out the door to catch up with her.

"Mama Ivanna? Where are you going?"

Regarding him as if he were daft, she stated, "To work. Where else would I be going?"

"But Mama Ivanna, you don't have to go to work anymore. Yevt and I both work. We can provide what we need for all of us."

Without breaking her pace, she responded, "I work an allocated job at the fishery every day from 4:00 to midnight where I use my skills to create food for the people of the Soviet Union. My labors are necessary for the good of this great land. To withhold my labors would be an insult to all the Party has done for me and my family. I am grateful for your hospitality, but that does not excuse me from my duties as a citizen."

Danya, who was having difficulty matching her steps which had increased in speed with her patriotic speech, gaped at his mother-in-law. Even now, after near starvation, she believed in the Party. Though he had easily labeled his colleagues fools for a similar view, he couldn't do that to her. She was many things, but not a fool.

He tugged at her sleeve, stopping her forward momentum, and said, "In which case, Mama Ivanna, may your journey to work and back again be safe."

The following day, he made some discreet inquiries at the university. Working here provided a tremendous number of privileges even to those simply cleaning toilets, so jobs not requiring specialized education often went to those with connections. Danya's connections were limited, and his reputation was a bit cloudy, but he determined that asking and receiving a 'no' was better than not asking at all.

The Department Head, Ivan Strotovi, though not a friend, was certainly not an enemy. As a 10-year employee, Danya knew him well. Rapping on the door with the back of his hand, Danya was ushered in with a, "Ah, Dr. Petrushevych, it is good to see you. What is it that I can do for you today?"

He had decided to be honest and forthright – there was no need for embellishments. Of course, he would not share her prior deplorable living conditions or what he believed to be the root cause of these conditions, but the rest of the story would be enough.

"My mother-in-law has recently come to live with us. She works at the fishery seven miles from our home on the second shift. Due to her age and the time of day, both my wife and I are concerned for her. We have suggested she stop working, but Mama Ivanna is a Comrade and very loyal to the Party. She believes her skills are most necessary for the advancement of this great country. We, of course, do not wish to dissuade her from these views. However, we were hoping to find her something a bit closer to home."

He stopped talking. He was not asking Dr. Strotovi to help him find a job for his mother-in-law. He merely stated his situation and waited for his boss to offer suggestions. He observed Dr. Strotovi's eyes looking up and to the right. He had once read one could determine what a person was thinking by where they moved their eyes, and this movement meant he was accessing a visual memory.

Then, with the practiced mastery of someone who could read minds, he said, "I am remembering something

I read the other day while with the Dean. Because of the heightened tensions," he let that phrase sit quietly for a moment before going on, "We are in need of more eyes on the students." His expectant gaze focused on Danya. "I believe if you would be willing to add yourself to the Faculty Solutions list, such a position could be found here for your Mama Ivanna."

Danya understood what he was being asked to do – listen in on and turn in students who were non-conformists. Until now, he had generally been able to stay out of the university politics. He knew he was being carefully watched due to his statements and his selection of reading materials, but he was cautious not to do more than talk to his peers and read. Both were well within the purview of a professor and could be attributed to keeping abreast.

Now, however, he had been asked directly to participate. Even if he withdrew his unstated request for Ivanna, the offer to be part of Faculty Solutions stood. Saying no would be political suicide. If it were just him, he would walk away without question, proceed to his office, and pack up his desk before they had time to throw him out. But he had Yevt and Mama Ivanna to consider.

He wasn't sure how he would manage to appear to be doing his job without actually doing his job, but the only answer to Dr. Strotovi was yes. With a smile he hoped hid the truth, he accepted the offer. Mama Ivanna got an official letter the following week and began working at the university as a dishwasher in the kitchen.

In the ensuing weeks, Danya had listened carefully to his students, going as far as taking notes. His hope was they would recognize him as a member of the Snoop

Team, as they called it, and stop talking boldly around him. One time, when he heard others bandying about a name they would be turning in that day, he turned in the same name with them, assuring himself that this student would be brought in for questioning or dismissed from his studies either way. During committee meetings, he echoed the concerns of other professors, always careful never to add something new.

None of these activities pleased him, but he understood it was merely a game of survival. Thankfully, he didn't feel the game would go on much longer. Just the day before, Latvia was the second country in as many days to declare independence from the Soviet Union, doubling dissenting countries to four. Surely, Ukraine was not far behind, and no Faculty Solution was going to change that.

Chapter 12

August 25, 1991

Ivanna was quite satisfied with the recent turn of events in her life. Imagine, having the Party write to her personally to ask that she use her skills at the university! Of course, she gladly would have remained at the fishery if that was where her talents were needed, but they had assessed her abilities and found a more suitable placement.

How fortunate her hours nearly mirrored those of her daughter and son-in-law! She and Yevt walked to work each morning, leaving before the sun rose, clocking in at six in the morning. On good days, she would see her daughter eating lunch in the cafeteria. The research shift was eight hours, allowing Yevt to walk to the market, and then home to fix an evening meal. Danya's first class began at 8:00 and his last was at 4:00. But if he had faculty meetings, which was often the case, he walked her home when her shift ended at 6:00 p.m.

At first, she had a bit of trouble adjusting to the schedule. After a second-shift position for so many years, retiring to bed and rising early seemed strange. Even more disconcerting were the weekends. She could not remember the last time she had two days in a row without work, and now, it was a regular occurrence.

Yevt and Danya used the weekend to sleep in, talk about any number of things, most of which she didn't care to understand, and take long walks through the city and down by the sea. The first weekend, she had wandered through the house haphazardly, like a ship pulled loose from its mooring.

Yevt suggested she try taking a walk, but she walked every morning and evening going to and from work. Walking without a purpose was absurd.

"What about reading? We have access to all the reading material you can imagine from the university library," she offered. But that, too, felt illogical. Ivanna had all the information she needed for her new job and was not in need of special skills. The Western journals – propaganda – on their shelves was of no interest to her. And fiction? Why should she waste her time with a story that was not real, or worse, not plausible?

Ivanna watched her daughter's jaw tighten as a little whoosh of air escaped from between her compressed lips. She didn't mean to exasperate Yevt but found she did – quite regularly. "Well, Mama, what do you enjoy doing? I'm sure we can accommodate your wishes if you'll just let us know what they are."

And that was how she came to spend her weekends cleaning. She derived great pleasure pulling things from shelves, ridding them of dust, and putting everything back again, neater than it was before. Her day began long before Yevt and Danya emerged from their room, but she was careful to be quiet in her endeavors until they had risen for the day.

Just yesterday, Yevt wondered aloud how her mama could find so much to clean in such a small space after so many weekends. Ivanna hardly understood the question. Cleaning wasn't about mess, it was about cleanliness, which was a never-ending process. The minute one turned their back after dusting a shelf or mopping a floor, the surface once again longed for its more natural state of squalor.

A shelf didn't get dirty all at once, but one small speck at a time over seconds, minutes, hours, and days. So, even if she dusted in the morning, she could do so again in the afternoon and again in the evening, each time thwarting the universe's desire to be filthy.

Her daughter considered her to be a simpleton, but Ivanna often reflected on life's lessons, like cleaning, for instance. Two weeks earlier, when talking to some Party stalwarts during a break, she compared cleaning to the Party's role in their lives. Left to their own devices, people thought and did things that were contrary to cleanliness or purity. That was why having the Party determine behavior made so much sense. Without the guidance of the leaders, the whole country would disintegrate into a wretched quagmire.

Yevt and Danya agreed with these new policies of glasnost and perestroika brought under Gorbachev. And mind you, she was not one to criticize a Party leader and would follow him until told to do otherwise, but she considered the rampant confusion and rebellion of the people as a natural outcropping of such policies.

With no consideration that their job came from the government they derided, many of the kitchen staff grumbled about conditions and freedoms and independence. These ideas came from outside the Party because the Party had not only failed to continuously clean the country but had actually encouraged the filth to come in and take up residence.

She had concluded her analogy with this statement: "The time is at hand to perform a spring cleaning. Once rid of these inane ideas, we can get back to the business of eliminating inequality and suffering." She was pleased by the smattering of applause and hoped she might find a way to help the Party progress with these skills as well as with her function of washing dishes.

As she quietly removed the dishware from the shelves, she slowly became aware of a sound she couldn't readily identify. Cocking her head to one side, she tried to analyze the sound and determine its source. The rhythmic, muffled thudding? Footsteps – running? At least moving quickly, and more than just one or two people. The humming buzz? Whispers, perhaps? Someone talking at a distance?

She moved stealthily to the front window, hoping the noise outside had not disturbed her children. As she moved the curtain to one side, she watched a young man slip quickly past the house, and then another and another. Soon, they were passing in groups of two and three. And within minutes, it felt like the entire city's population was on the move.

She jumped slightly as Danya, who obviously couldn't

sleep through the stampede, took hold of the curtain above her own hand, and held it back further, hoping that doing so would somehow make the mysterious behavior clearer. Yevt joined them momentarily, having quickly donned a dress but neglecting to comb the sleep from her hair.

Danya, telling the women to lower the curtain and stay inside, feared some sort of riot. He slipped out the backdoor to see what he could learn to best keep his family safe. In less than a minute, he was back in the door, a broad grin on his face.

"We did it," he announced joyfully. "Ukraine has seceded from the Soviet Union and claimed its independence!" Then, he grabbed up Yevt and let out a long whoop as he twirled her around the living room. They were both so busy rejoicing they didn't notice Ivanna lamenting in the corner.

Work the next day was fraught with emotion. Those who wanted independence were ecstatic. Those who believed in the Party were split into two groups: furious and disheartened. The furious ones stayed busy writing down the names of every individual who celebrated the news. The disheartened ones sat quietly in small groups, commiserating about what was going to happen to them now.

Ivanna vacillated between the two, at times so despondent she could barely work, and at others, so fiery mad she wanted to punish the offenders herself. Yevt and Danya's disgusting display eventually dried up her sobs, as her stomach clenched, and bile rose in her throat.

"Stop that! Stop that this instant! Have you two gone

entirely mad? How can you watch the slow dismantling of a great nation with cheers and shouts of joy?"

Yevt and Danya stopped twirling, mouths hanging open, eyes wide in surprise. She wasn't sure if it was her tone or her words that shocked them most.

Although the two had tried to help her see the reasoning behind Ukraine's decision, she would have none of it. "I am loyal to the Party and will remain so until my last breath. Mark my words, someday, you will regret what you've said here today. Thankfully for you, I am the only witness." With that, she had turned her back on them, marched to her partitioned-off sleeping quarters, and remained unmoving for the rest of the day, letting the despair of the moment wash over her. This morning, she walked herself to work to avoid making niceties with her daughter.

Although she was aware that many had talked of rebellion, she was stunned at the number of those who publically displayed their lack of Party loyalty, as though they honestly believed there would be no repercussions. She patently avoided these shortsighted fools and trusted her daughter and son-in-law would have enough sense to keep their anti-Party thoughts out of the workplace.

By noon, six hours after arriving at work, the frenetic movements and sounds from excited students had gotten the best of her. She began a slow slide into depression and sat along the wall with others, who, like her, didn't have the energy to work. Not that there was any work to do – not a single person had eaten at the cafeteria since it opened.

She closed her eyes and massaged her temples when she heard a subtle humming. The tune, though hushed, was immediately recognizable. Someone had begun first whispering, then singing the State anthem. She stood, as did others in the room, as the words grew louder and louder. Joining in on the chorus, Ivanna sang with her heart full of emotion:

Славься, Отечество наше свободное,
Дружбы народов надёжный оплот!
Знамя Советское, знамя народное
Пусть от победы к победе ведёт!

Be glorious, our free Fatherland, a reliable stronghold of the peoples' friendship! Banner of the Soviets, banner of the people, may it lead from victory to victory!

Chapter 13

December 26, 1991

Yevt's concern for her mother grew larger with each passing monumental decision. Although the Ukrainian government stated its desire to be independent of the Soviet Union at the end of August, the vote by the people didn't come until the first of December. The ensuing weeks were filled with debate and impassioned pleas from both sides of the controversy.

During this period, Yevt saw a side of her mother she had not witnessed before. She had always assumed her mama was simply a sheep, moving along with the herd with no real understanding of where she was going or why. But, to her astonishment, her mother was able to hold her own in conversations that often turned to debate on topics Yevt would have wagered her mama knew nothing about.

When talking of the new government, Ivanna had boldly asked, "Who is it, Danya, that will lead this great nation of ours? You? Me? Who has had experience in such matters? Only the Party, which means despite your ideals of democracy and capitalism, it will be the Party that recreates Ukraine. This independence you seek will come at the expense of your friends and neighbors and family." She pointedly regarded her daughter, before she continued. "Instead of relying on a strong central government backed by millions of workers, new Ukrainian leaders who are not actually new at all will create the same government they always knew but on a smaller scale. And it will fail. One of the Union's greatest strengths is its size."

Despite disagreeing on the merits of size, Danya later told Yevt that Mama made some very valid points about the leadership. It appeared those vying to lead the nation were, in fact, the very same people who were part of the Party establishment. They both marveled at the older woman's insight, and Yevt realized her assumptions about her mother, like so many she'd made throughout her life, had no merit. Once again, she found herself cleaning the windows of her mind to achieve a clearer view.

At the end of November, shortly before the vote, Gorbachev gave a televised interview. In it, he gave an impassioned plea to the people of Ukraine, begging them not to secede. He talked of his own heritage with a grandmother from Ukraine. He even read a poem penned by a 19th century Ukrainian poet. Whether his weeping was real was uncertain, but Yevt presumed he was sincere, though misguided. Her mama cried through the entire speech.

The following day, all her friends and acquaintances

went to the polls to determine if they would secede and, if so, who would be the new leader. Her mama was certain, despite data showing a majority of Ukrainians supported succession, that after such a heartfelt expression of love and concern for the people of Ukraine, the whole idea of independence would be easily defeated. Rather than walk with Yevt and Danya, she determined to go with those of like-mind and celebrate with them, too, when the final votes were counted.

The win, or loss, depending on who one asked, was overwhelming. In the end, over 90 percent of those who voted approved the declaration of independence. By a smaller margin, Leonid Kravchuk became the first President of Ukraine. In one of his first addresses to the newly independent nation, he declared, "A new Ukraine has been born. A great historical event has occurred which will not only change the history of Ukraine but the history of the world."

It was a day that marked the beginning of Ukraine's statehood. Gorbachev sent a note congratulating President Kravchuk and hoped for cooperation between them. For this, her mama never forgave him.

A week after the elections, President Kravchuk met with the leaders of other former Soviet nations which had declared independence and signed the Belavezha Accords – an official declaration that the Soviet Union ceased to exist. Her mama cried bitterly, and for the first time in her life, refused to get up the next day to work. "What's the purpose? The Party is dead. I am the Party. I, too, shall die."

That was two weeks ago, and each day, her mama's tiny frame became smaller and less capable. She rarely spoke. She never smiled. She simply stared at the ceiling and only ate when prompted, rather forcefully, by Danya. The Party had been her life. She believed she had nothing left.

Although today was a Thursday, Yevt had taken a day off work. She had plans to force her mother out of bed and into the sunshine. Despite the winter weather approaching, the days still warmed up, and her mother's pallor was alarming. She needed to talk some sense into her. She needed to help her find a reason to live.

Ivanna did not want to be coaxed out of bed. She had no reason left to live. Her daughter and son-in-law were traitors to the Party – what was left of it. Her job, her gift to the people of her nation, was now nothing more than the earning of poor wages for cleaning other people's dirt. Her Leka had been gone for almost two decades. Even those she had befriended over their mutual admiration of the Party had been swayed to wave the Ukrainian freedom banner. Everything she loved was truly ruined or absent.

However, her daughter had the persistence of a gnat intent on flying into one's eyes or nostrils. No matter how many times she swatted her away, she just kept coming back for more. In the end, it was easier to dress than it was to remain prone with her arms folded over her chest.

"Fine, Yevt. Fine. I will get out of bed. What good you think it will do, I am not sure. How you, a woman with a degree in a medical field, can believe a 'bit of sunshine' in the company of a traitor can cure my ills makes no sense." She had hoped this last bit would cause Yevt to abandon her designs, but she had no such luck. If possible, her Yevt was even more stubborn than she was short-tempered.

Yevt wanted to go for a walk, but Ivanna refused, adamant that she would not submit any further. "I am out of bed, as you wished. I am dressed, as you wished. I am outdoors, as you wished. I will not walk." She sat down on the stoop and refused to move.

With a sigh, Yevt sat down, too. "Mama..." She said nothing else for such a long time that Ivanna wondered if she had forgotten what she wanted to say. Looking surreptitiously over at her daughter, she was surprised to discover she was silently crying.

"Mama," she said again. "It is true that the life you've been living is over. But...each day we live, the life we knew changes. One day, Daddy was with us, then he was gone." Ivanna flinched at the mention of Leka. She hadn't heard Yevt refer to him since she was a small child. "We lived in the small village and then we moved. I was going to stop school and then got chosen for university. I was going to remain single and then met Danya. We were estranged and now you live here with me, and I am blessed to see you every day."

With this statement, Yevt caught her eye and smiled weakly. "Now, the Party is gone, and a new government is being put in its place. Not all change is good, but not all change is bad, Mama. One thing is certain, though, change will always come."

Ivanna wondered when her daughter had grown so wise. Yevt was nearing 30, and wisdom did come with age, but surely, she herself had not been so discerning.

She realized, with a start, that Yevt was the same age she had been when Leka died. "You are wise, my child. Do you realize that by your age, I had been married over a decade, had a child, lost a husband, and struggled to make ends meet?"

Yevt nodded absently.

Her daughter, because of the sacrifices she'd made all these years, had it far easier, for which she was grateful. It was her role as mother to do that for her child. She'd do it again. But she wondered how Yevt's life would turn out without a child. All that wisdom would go to waste if she only spent it on her stubborn mother.

"I've been wondering," Ivanna said with the first hint of a smile in weeks, "when are you and Danya going to become parents?"

Her question was meant to remove the target from her chest and place it squarely on Yevt. It was also an honest question and something she had worried over ever since realizing their quick marriage was not in response to a pregnancy.

With a small laugh, Yevt said, "That's an interesting way to change the subject, Mama. The answer is quite simple. I'm waiting for the day you decide to live. I can't imagine bringing a child into this world without my mama here to greet her."

Yevt rested her head on her mother's shoulder, and Ivanna leaned back. She was right. Change happened. She didn't have to like it, but it was going to happen anyway. "Then you need to get started right away."

Ironically, later that day, Ivanna learned the Soviet flag failed to rise over the Kremlin. The Soviet Union officially dissolved on the day she officially decided to live.

Chapter 14

December 1993

Pleased she had been able to purchase six eggs at the store that morning, Yevt donned her apron and began chopping potatoes to make deruny, potato pancakes, for her family for their evening meal. It was hard to believe Mama had been living with them for over two years, now. Although it felt like only yesterday, she could also barely recall a time when they weren't cramped into the tiny home – a home that would soon feel significantly smaller.

She absently rubbed the ever-expanding bulge, now hidden by the red and white striped smock, which announced the coming of their first child. She was due in barely six weeks, and the hopes of finding larger accommodations were negligible. Mama still occupied a corner of the living room, and the baby, at least for now, would be in their room.

This temporary solution would work until the baby began toddling about, after which she wasn't sure what they would do. As she fretted, she heard Danya's gentle voice in her mind, "Yetti, stop! Things will work out. They always do, yes? Yes! Indeed, they always do. Why fret over something so far in the future over which you cannot control?"

She smiled. He was not one to sit back and let the forces-that-be run roughshod over his life. On the other hand, he had a knack for knowing when to choose patience over action. He was right, of course. Even with a much larger home, the baby would naturally spend its first months close to them. This proximity wouldn't be an issue for a year – or more.

She took in a deep breath, as deep as possible given she had a baby pressing into her lungs. Since becoming pregnant, she noted that fretting had become her go-to emotion. Sure, she could still summon up a good head of angry steam, but she was far more likely to wring her hands and weep. She wondered if it was a maternal instinct or simply the strain of growing a child. She hoped the latter, as bouts of sobbing and constant worry didn't suit her.

When she first learned she was with child, she and Danya were ecstatic. However, for Yevt, elation had quickly turned to fear. They had been hoping for a baby for three very long years. Each time they made love, she firmly believed it would produce the baby they longed for. Unfortunately, her cycle stayed regular and marked with finality, the end of that belief.

With each passing month, she had gotten more discouraged, feeling that maybe she would never be able to bear children. Danya remained upbeat in front of her, but she was certain he was equally as despondent about the lack of children as she was, having told her he had always dreamed of having four strapping sons and at least two fetching daughters.

So, when she finally did conceive, she began to fear that she would lose the baby. Everything frightened her. Take food, for instance. Eating terrified her. What foods should she eat so the baby would continue to grow and be healthy? Would the food they could locate be nutritious enough? Had the dairy been exposed to room temperature too long as it sat on the table?

Unfortunately, not eating also terrified her. During those early days, when her stomach often sat in her mouth, threatening to violently evacuate the premises, nothing sounded tasty. What's more, the smell of certain foods would cause her to gag and run to the toilet. On those days, when eating a bland cracker was an accomplishment, she worried that she was going to starve her unborn baby to death.

Those first weeks were agony as Yevt contemplated whether each mundane activity in her life – walking, sleeping, cleaning – might affect the baby and how. Thankfully, her mother understood the fear and helped her get a better grasp on reality.

"Yevt, sweetheart. Babies have been born since the beginning of time and in far worse conditions than this. Imagine when women lived in caves and dined on raw bear meat. And yet, their children survived. We know this because we are here to talk about it," she said with a chuckle.

The thought of raw meat had sent Yevt scurrying to

the bathroom, but her mother's reasoning was sound. Food was not as plentiful as they had hoped when campaigning for independence, but she was not starving. She had shelter over her head and the ability to stay warm as winter approached.

She determined to keep her fears in check and was successful a respectable amount of time. Occasionally, some stray insecurity would push past the barriers, leaving her a pile of blubbering apprehension. She had come to count on both Danya and her mother during these regrettable debacles to gather up the quivering mass they knew as wife and daughter and help her to, once again, find the strong, competent scientist hidden deep inside.

She squinted as a bump, a foot perhaps, rolled from left to right and back again. This child of hers was strong and active. She, Yevt had an intuition she was carrying a girl and thought of the baby as a she without conscious thought, would be a survivor. An ideal trait for the times.

Ukrainian independence, it seemed, much to her chagrin and her mother's triumphant satisfaction, was not the solution to all the ills from years of Soviet repression. As her mother had predicted, political turmoil was typical as past players jockeyed for power in the new system. Instead of working to privatize businesses, greedy politicians grouped together to create policies that gave them money and power. Yevt was sure her mother had to refrain daily from saying, "I told you so."

Unfortunately, the reformists most likely to advance the cause of democracy and capitalism were patently against cooperating with anyone who had participated in the communist regime. So, when Leonid Kravchuk, once the third in command in Ukraine's Communist Party of the Soviet Union, became president, leaders of the People's Movement who were instrumental in moving Ukraine toward independence refused to participate in the new government.

Danya, incredulous at the news, came home one evening to inform her that Viacheslav Chornovil, refused the prime-minister position. "Can you believe it, Yetti? What an idealistic fool! Here's a man who has spent his entire life fighting for the independence of Ukraine, willing to go to prison for his beliefs as well as be exiled, and when he finally gets what he has been seeking, he refuses to accept the position of prime minister and the right to appoint his own Cabinet. And why? Because he wants nothing to do with a communist! Doesn't he realize if he doesn't take the position, someone else will? Someone most likely with a communist background?" As if on cue, the first prime minister appointed by President Kravchuck was indeed a man who discovered wealth building machines under the equalization of the Soviet regime.

Despite their leader's communist connections, Ukrainians waited expectantly for monumental economic and social changes to occur. Just as small children who believe in the "and they lived happily ever after" in fairytales, the fall of the Soviet Union left the citizens entertaining ideas of riches and free markets despite such evidence as continued food and fuel shortages. It was not uncommon to hear people suggesting that in less than a year everyone would be driving a Jaguar, owning a mansion, and vacationing in the Mediterranean, preferably on their own yacht.

Danya scoffed at such dreams and often talked late into the night with her about what would have to happen for

Ukraine's new government to be successful.

"Everyone acts as if changing from Soviet control to independence is as easy as flying a new flag over the capital," he said with a heavy sigh, his right hand rubbing at this temple. "But it will require so much more than a new flag and national symbol. We will have to create a democracy with all the appropriate checks and balances and determine how to move from the command economy to capitalism, all while getting other nations to accept that we are now an independent state. If we don't do all three, we are doomed to fail."

Each, he told her, would require a lot of hard work supplemented by time and money. He felt the leaders, even those who once embraced communism, were sincere and willing to work hard, but time was not on their side and money was in short supply. Although he wanted to see an independent Ukraine and had, without restraint, voted for one, he was worried the fairytale of instantaneous wealth for all tossed out to the average citizen by those seeking political positions and popularized by the media was making the job impossible for the new leaders.

"Our new president is focusing all his attentions on building statehood, and I applaud his efforts. Nearly every nation now recognizes us as a sovereign state. We have our own army and a central bank. We have strong relations with other Eastern European nations. He is working to solidify our borders and refuses to hand over our land to the greedy Russians."

She fully expected him to spit as he said Russians, which she found both funny and concerning. Danya was typically even keeled and could find the virtue and honor in anyone. But when it came to Russians? Let's just say

Yevt realized she was more pragmatic about early pregnancy.

He continued, "He has done all of that, but at what cost? He has barely touched on democracy and economic reform. What he has managed to do, he has failed to follow through on. And the corruption." He stopped, slapping his hand on the table for emphasis. "The corruption is endemic."

It was true. Over the last two years, despite all the strides President Kravchuk was making internationally, Ukraine was suffering from food shortages, escalating costs of everyday necessities like lightbulbs and soap, scarce housing, and a financial crisis the likes of which the nation had never seen. When one added in the crime resulting from this privation, life in an independent Ukraine was no better than life as part of the Soviet Union.

She had to admit that compared to many, they were doing well, firmly entrenched in the new middle-class, but that didn't mean they weren't affected by the failing economic policies. Even for Danya, an educated man with a job at a still-thriving university, choices were extremely limited.

During weekly shopping excursions, finding fresh fruit was nearly impossible, and although grateful not to be starving, Yevt was positively sick of potatoes, onions, cabbage, turnips, carrots, and radishes. Oh, how she would love to dine on vegetables exposed to the sun, turning their skins and pods red, green, and yellow instead of those that always smelled musty and left traces of dirt between her teeth. And meat? They had trouble affording bread and roots – meat was a rare treat indeed.

Just last month, the local store had butter, and

everyone went crazy, including Yevt. As soon as she heard the news, she waddled, as quickly as her girth allowed, to the store, getting in a line that rivaled the bread lines of the 80s. She, like many others, were disappointed to learn the butter was, indeed, available but only to war veterans and disabled elderly shoppers. She had trouble swallowing the bread smeared with lard that evening at supper knowing how close she had come to real butter.

Other household goods were easier to find, but their exorbitant costs made the average citizen unable to purchase them. Danya had used the term hyperinflation. "From the beginning of time, I suppose, prices have gone up, but people's wages did, too. When the two go up in a balanced way, everything is fine. However, when prices increase faster than wages, then we have something called inflation. Do you see what I'm saying?"

Yevt nodded thoughtfully as she rubbed her belly. "You're saying that despite being paid a bit more for your teaching position, the price of items at the store, like pork" – the word pork had a dreamy quality as it left Yevt's lips – "have gone up faster."

Danya nodded enthusiastically. "Yes. Exactly. So, the money I make can't buy as much as it used to. Inflation also happens in America," he said with a sigh. "But what's happening here is worse. It is hyperinflation. The imbalance between what I earn and what it can buy is enormous. You've seen it with your own eyes. Would you ever have thought you'd be forced to take a bag of money just to buy the essential groceries?"

Yevt had been unnerved by the amount of money needed to buy bread, milk, and the most basic vegetables, often wondering if what she took to the store would be enough to buy what was needed. Last week, she watched a skinny woman struggling with an oversized, cloth bag stuffed with money walk by the house. The wind had snatched several bills from the mouth of the sack and before they could flutter to the ground, others had raced to add them to their own pockets. The same woman, less than an hour later, returned with nothing more than two loaves of bread and a sack of potatoes.

Of course, hauling money to the store was only possible for those lucky enough to get paid. Yevt's research job was eliminated shortly after she learned of her pregnancy. Mama's job had disappeared months before that. Both women sometimes found day work cleaning, but Yevt was rarely chosen now that her size was an encumbrance, and her mother, looking a bit more stooped despite being only 50 years old, was often passed over for much younger and more able bodies.

Thankfully, Danya still had a job. More importantly, he had a job which paid actual wages. She knew of many who worked day in and day out, only to receive a frozen chicken as payment, or worse yet, an IOU. The family next door hadn't seen a paycheck in a year and had no idea when, if ever, they would see the money. She couldn't fathom how they found food, knowing the stores wouldn't accept an IOU that would likely never be paid.

Danya continued, "In such an environment, people become willing to do just about anything to reduce their deprivations, and the greedy are willing to do just about anything to help them do so, as long as it includes making obscene amounts of money."

Yevt knew the black market, often referred to as the shadow economy to lend it a more genteel air by those involved in it, was alive and well in Ukraine. For the right price, she could buy nearly anything, as long as she didn't mind haggling with criminals.

But Yevt did mind. The local nightly news, filled with gang shootings and likely mafia hits, assured that she purchased all her goods in legitimate retail establishments, even without Danya's dire warnings about getting mixed up in this underground society. She also spent some of their hard-earned money on two locks, one for each door of their home and refrained from going out at night. She supposed the locks were not as helpful as she imagined, but the price was worth a decent night's sleep and helped her keep her anxieties at bay.

As she thought about Danya's lesson in economics while mixing the potatoes and onions into the bowl and cracking two of the eggs into the mixture, she reflected that today was a good day, despite the state of life outside her over-crowded but happy home. She had a husband and mother who loved her, enough money to purchase food for her growing child, and eggs for deruny. Today, at least, she would simply enjoy her life within this new, free Ukraine.

Chapter 15

January 7, 1994

She was a stubborn old woman and freely admitted she was unwilling to actively seek out new experiences. In her life, she'd seen more change than she cared to recount. Only a fool, and she was no fool, would purposefully seek to throw an already unsteady world into a tailspin.

That being said, despite still firmly holding to her atheist beliefs, Ivanna enjoyed this year's Christmas celebration. When Yevt was a child, before the death of her father, they celebrated the New Year, the Soviet substitute for Christmas. When it was just the two of them, celebrations were rare. Even when Yevt was studying at the university, Ivanna's work hours rarely left any time for holiday exploits and money was scarce enough that Ded Moroz, Father Frost, and his snow maiden, Snihurónka, could not make an appearance.

She gazed at the tree they put up the night before. Covered in red, green, silver, and gold ribbons which Yevt carefully saved from year to year, as well as delicate paper snowflakes and folded stars she cut from scraps of paper, the tree, first wrapped in lights, was charming in its simplicity. She anticipated the dark of the evening, when Yevt turned off the lights, and they ate by the light of the festive twinkling tree.

Because she was not-so-patiently awaiting the arrival of her first child, Yevt, in Ivanna's opinion, had been a little heavy handed with the paper snowflakes. Not only did they adorn the tree, but they graced all the windows and even hung from the ceiling. Neither she nor Danya said a word, both recognizing that to mention the overabundance of snowflakes would likely lead to hurt feelings and another round of weeping.

Today was the Orthodox Christmas Eve, and Ivanna was looking forward to the celebration with the anticipation of a small child. Although they were not exchanging gifts, they had scrimped and saved to create Sviata Vecheria, a feast with 12 courses, one for each of Christ's disciples. Ivanna knew little of these men or why they mattered, but thoroughly enjoyed the traditional Ukrainian dishes that reminded her of her mama so many years ago.

She had assumed all the dishes were lacking meat, eggs, and dairy because of the difficulty of obtaining such extravagances. This year, however, she asked if they might be able to find enough meat to add to the cabbage rolls and Yevt gaped at her with surprise.

"But Mama! One never eats meat on Christmas Eve! It goes against all tradition!"

"What foresight this Jesus must have had to create a Christmas celebration that could happen despite a food shortage," thought Ivanna.

For most of the dishes, ingredients had been easy to find. Weeks ago, they began stocking up for red borscht, pierogi, holophchi, and sauerkraut. However, with honey, raisins, poppy seeds, and walnuts almost impossible to find, making kutia, the main dish of the evening, took much more effort.

Many neighbors, even those who steadfastly refused to do so at other times of the year, found what they needed on the black market. Although she tried to persuade Yevt to do the same, her daughter would not hear of it.

"Absolutely not, Mama. There is no way I want to put my baby" – she laid her hand protectively across her stomach – "into harm's way. Those people have no scruples. They are just as likely to hurt me as to help me. And, even if I weren't afraid, I refuse to be part of the problem. Buying and selling on the Black Market only encourages people to take advantage of one another. It can do nothing but make the situation worse."

Despite Ivanna not seeing how one small purchase would made the economy worse, Yevt's mind was firmly set, so she gave up trying to persuade her.

In the end, several stores carried small quantities of everything except the nuts. The local store owners were both benevolent and merciless. Understanding how many people wanted these items and how disappointed they would be if they couldn't create the traditional meals, as well as wanting to be able to charge as much as possible for what they sold, the hardest-to-find supplies were rationed according to family size.

After a final shopping trip, Yevt came home jubilant. "I finally purchased enough of what I need. I think with a bit of creativity and some imagination on your parts, I can concoct something that will closely resemble kutia."

This traditional porridge simmered on the stove, filling the small space with a delicious aroma despite its weakened state. Of course, the aroma was only heightened by Ivanna's hunger. As tradition dictated, she had not eaten a bite since the meal the night before. The feast would not begin until the first star rose in the night sky. Once again, this had something to do with Jesus and how he was found as a baby, but Ivanna simply loved the idea of going outside at dusk and trying to be the first one to find a star.

As the sun began to set, she rushed out the door, pulling on her coat as she went. Danya laughed and joined her outside, determined to be the winner this year. Due to her swollen feet that were made worse by all the kitchen preparations, Yevt elected to sit indoors and watch them through the living room window.

Ivanna scanned the sky, one hand shielding her eyes to help eliminate the fading light from view. Although there was no prize at being the first one, she had so thoroughly enjoyed finding a star before Danya last year that she very much wanted the honor once again. She may be getting older, she thought, but her eyesight was still as keen as ever.

"There!" she shouted, pointing her finger toward the night sky.

Danya squinted his eyes. "I think you are trying to pull one over on me, Mama Ivanna. I don't see anything."

Mildly irritated that Danya would think she cheated,

she retorted, "Well, then you need to get your eyes checked. The star is right there and bright enough to read by!"

Danya squinted in that direction again, and then, he, too, saw the star. Heaving a deep sigh, but delighted to be able to start the feast, he said, "You are the winner again, Mama Ivanna. Next year will be my year."

She snorted as she pushed past him and into the kitchen. "Not likely, my son-in-law. Not likely."

───────────────

Yevt was happy to see her mother enjoying herself and tried her best to capture the spirit of the day, but simply could not get comfortable. The meal she had slaved over for days was delicious, but she had so little room in her stomach for food, what with the baby compressing everything from her pelvic bone to her ribs. When she did manage to eat, she would lie awake for hours with indigestion.

At her last appointment, Yevt's doctor merely smiled as she detailed her many discomforts. In addition to not being able to eat, she also did not sleep more than an hour or two at any time, spent entirely too much time going back and forth to the bathroom, and could no longer wear any of her own shoes, opting for her husband's slippers.

Instead of helping her with these issues, her doctor simply stated it would still be days before she delivered. She couldn't imagine feeling like this for hours, let alone days. She was ready for the baby to make an entrance into the world, even though it meant the pain of childbirth.

Labor scared her. She wasn't a sissy by nature and had endured many privations in life. She had grown accustomed to working hard, eating little, and surviving despite the cold. But, based on what she'd been told and the books she'd read, what she would soon experience would make everything else pale in comparison.

Unfortunately, she had heard many stories. It seemed that women who had been through the experience enjoyed talking about it in vivid detail, each successive story trying to outdo the one before. Most of these stories had terrible plot turns involving the tearing in places that should never tear, babies showing their feet before their head, and days of labor instead of hours. She wished she could magically wave a wand to skip this part, and simply snuggle her baby, but had determined the discomfort in these final days was what was needed so a woman would relish the idea of labor rather than deal one more moment with another human taking up residence in their mid-section.

At the conclusion of the feast, Yevt simply wanted to lie down on the bed and rest, but that wasn't an option. Christmas came just once a year. If she didn't take the time to enjoy all the festivities, she would be sorry long before the holiday came around again.

So, she went into her bedroom, grabbed the coat Danya found that had enough material to cover the enormity of her body, and readied herself to walk door to door. It was time for singing koliadky with her neighbors, going door to door and singing the traditional hymns of the season. Yevt loved this old tradition, made new again now that Ukraine was independent.

In addition to the beauty of the songs, Yevt enjoyed the idea of rebelling. Of course, it was no longer banned, but many still cast their eyes about in confusion as people came to their door singing about Christ.

Her mama participated in almost all things Christmas

but chose not to carol and not to attend church where they would study the displays and listen to the retelling of the story of Christ's birth. She would have loved for her mama to come with them but understood she simply couldn't let go of the old beliefs. Finally, when the services were over, they would walk home, and then she would rest.

Despite her awkward size, and the difficulty getting enough air to hold out the notes, she loved singing, and the lovely music lifted her spirits. They were in the middle of the chorus of Shchedryk, a very fast song that took more breath than she could muster, when she felt a whoosh of warmth below her protruding belly.

With eyes rounding in surprise, and a clear understanding that the doctor's assessment was incorrect, she tugged on Danya's sleeve and said, "How do you feel about exchanging gifts, after all?"

Laughing at his puzzled expression, she put his hand on her belly. "Danya, it's time. Our baby wants to join us for Christmas."

Chapter 16

1994

If she turned her head to the right, just slightly, she could see a small sliver of sky turning pink in the sunrise. These moments before dawn, before anyone else was awake, had become her favorite part of the day. Silent. Peaceful. Relaxing. Such words didn't exist once the day began. Such was the life of a mother with a small baby.

She dared not move too quickly, or the baby would awaken, hungry and demanding. Her breasts tingled at the thought of the cries, ready to let down her milk supply at the slightest noise. From the moment her daughter woke until she finally went down for the night, Yevt never had a free moment to herself. So, she soaked up the silence and the solitude, filling herself with the energy she'd need for the day.

She loved being a mother and all it entailed. Now. But

those first few months? A shuddering sigh involuntarily escaped from her lips. Eyes darting quickly toward the crib, she was relieved to see the noise had not disturbed her sleeping child, and she fell back to her thoughts of the recent past.

Her birthing story had no twists and turns like those thrown at unsuspecting women pregnant for the first time. Apparently, her daughter had read the same manual Yevt read, and only six hours after her water broke, and four hours into Christmas, she delivered a healthy, 7-pound 6-ounce girl with a head of dark hair.

Danya had insisted he be with her and had convinced her doctor of this fact weeks before. It was a western thing, the husband coaching his wife through labor. The idea was new to Ukraine, and the nurse on duty was positively against the practice. She muttered about men being in the way and useless.

For her part, she was thankful to have had him there. His presence reassured her. He helped her remember that she could do hard things and leant his strength when hers lagged. His exclamation, "I can see the head! Oh, darling, you're doing it. She's almost here," had provided the incentive to push just one more time until...her daughter was laid against her chest.

She marveled at her tiny fingers and toes and the lips that puckered into a tiny circle. Her eyes were round and wide, soaking in her surroundings, despite being so fresh from the womb. Still wet from birth, with splotchy red skin, and an elongated head, Yevt thought she was the most beautiful baby she had ever seen. Danya, speechless, simply rubbed his daughter's tiny hand and wept.

They had been talking about names without any

success. Danya, despite Yevt's absolute conviction that she was carrying their daughter, believed they were having a "fine, strapping boy" and fixated on several boy names. Whenever she had interjected with a "fine, strapping girl" name, he waved it off like an annoying fly at a picnic.

She believed strongly that the right name was important. She had a vague recollection that her father had always been proud of his name, and he had chosen her name specifically because of its meaning – life. When she asked her mother to tell her the story of her naming, she had gotten few details. Any memory involving her father caused immense pain for her mother, so she didn't push it any further.

She had settled on Anichka Sofiya – grace and wisdom – both traits she wanted for her daughter. But now, with her child having the same birthdate as the Savior, she reconsidered.

"Danya, her name? I don't think Anichka is right. I want to acknowledge her Christmas birth in some way. What do you think? Perhaps a Biblical name? I recall a Rebekka and Sara. Do either of these suit her?"

They studied her intently, almost willing her name to appear to them, but nothing materialized. Nonetheless, they both knew without a doubt that she was not Anichka, Rebekka, or Sara. "Do not let it trouble you," Danya had told her gently. "It is late. You've been through a lot. We have plenty of time to name our child. Just rest, now."

Though tempted to flip through the baby name book she brought from home, she realized how tired she was. The nurse took the baby to the nursery, and she urged Danya to go with the baby. Within moments, she had fallen asleep.

She wasn't sure how long she slept, but when she woke, Danya was asleep in the chair by her side. The baby, clean and wrapped in a blanket, was in a small bassinet, a red bow in her hair, resembling a Christmas tree ornament. The nurse, one much younger and friendlier than the one from the night before, peeked through the door to see how everyone was doing.

When she saw Yevt was awake, she smiled and asked, "How is that sweet Noel doing?" Before Yevt could answer, the nurse busied herself over the baby, giving Yevt a chance to make a face without hurting her feelings. Although Noel was a cute name, it was too Christmassy. She didn't want her daughter to be a walking cliché along with every other girl born during the Christmas season.

As soon as the nurse left the room, Yevt grabbed the book, desperate to find the right name before Noel stuck. She chose this book for one specific reason. The names were not listed alphabetically, but by meaning, which, in her opinion, made finding the right name much easier.

She was born on Christ's birthday, so maybe some Christ-like traits? Love. Peace. Kindness. Giving. Pure. She flipped to each trait, hoping to find a name that fit her little girl. "Lyudmyla." She let the name roll around her tongue. "No. It is such a big name for such a tiny girl." She flipped pages. "Orynko." No. That name seemed to stick to the roof of her mouth. "Katrya. Pure." She wrote it down as a possibility.

By the time Danya woke, she had 14 names but was still of the opinion that she hadn't found the right one. He removed a few from the list. He once knew a 'Solomiya.' Because he was not fond of her, he was not fond of the name. Two others were eliminated because he didn't like the way they sounded with their last name.

When her mother arrived later in the morning, the baby still had no name, but that didn't seem to matter much to her mama. She was enchanted with the baby and was so proud of her daughter. She turned to Yevt, holding her face in her hands. "Oh, my sweet, precious girl. You did so well. I am so proud of you." The connection between them grew stronger now that Yevt had bore a child – the rite of passage of true womanhood.

Her mama scooped the baby from the bassinet with a practiced ease and began to sing softly. Although Yevt couldn't recall the words, the tune was familiar and cozy, bringing back memories of the days long before her father died. "Mama? What is that song? I feel like I've heard it before."

Mama smiled. "You have. A long time ago. My mama sang it to me, and her mother before her. And probably her mama before her." She went back to her gentle singing.

When the song ended, Yevt was startled to see tears streaming down her mother's face. "What is it, Mama? Is the baby okay?" She stole an anxious glance toward her child, afraid her mother saw some problem her inexperienced eyes hadn't yet recognized.

Her mother smiled, swiping at her weeping eyes. "She's fine. She's perfect. It is not the baby but the song causing the tears. All these years I've listened to this song, sung this song, and I only just now considered the words. 'A child, a child, such is a gift from above.'" She shifted her gaze from daughter to granddaughter and back again. "A child is God's gift, Yetti. I think I must have always known it."

God's gift. That was it! She watched her mother cry softly, realizing the importance of her declaration. Not once had Yevt ever witnessed her mother attribute anything to God. Her tiny baby brought the gift of belief to her babusya.

She opened the book to Gift of God and began scanning the names listed there. There, among dozens of names, standing out against the page as though in bold, was her own mother's name. Ivanna, Gift from God. She pulled in a deep breath, a tiny miracle unfolding before her eyes. God had been with her mother since birth, and God's grace was surely in this moment.

Before leaving the hospital, they settled on Ionna Khrystyna – Gift of God and Follower of Christ. They couldn't imagine a more fitting name.

Those first few days were beautiful and magical, then came the debilitating anxiety and sadness. For reasons she could not comprehend, looking after Ionna was overwhelming, and she found herself crying for no reason in particular.

She worried about her daughter dying in her sleep or that she wouldn't hear her if she woke, so she held the baby in her arms through the night while sitting uncomfortably in the overstuffed living room chair. She didn't want Danya to help at night because he had to work. She wouldn't have been able to live with herself if he lost his job because he was too tired from helping her.

The lack of sleep only heightened her anxiety, as she tried to figure out how to fit in nursing and changing the baby, while taking care of the house and attending to her personal needs. Things in the latter group suffered considerably. She rarely found time to shower and did nothing with her hair except pull it into a ponytail. She didn't believe she should take time for herself – not with a child to care for.

It wasn't that Ionna was a difficult baby. Her mother kept on and on about how good she was. And it was true that Ionna wasn't fussy most of the time, but for several hours each evening, she would cry inconsolably. Yevt tried rocking, holding, walking, bouncing, and nursing, but nothing would calm her. During these hours, she wouldn't even latch on to nurse.

Compounding the problem was that she could hardly stand the sight of her husband and mother. Everything they did or said sounded like criticism, as though she didn't have a clue how to hold, soothe, or feed her child. When they would offer to take Ionna, especially during those difficult hours, she would bristle and insist on doing it herself. Yet, when they left her alone, she experienced despondency, as through no one cared.

She began to read everything she could find and talk to every mother in her neighborhood to determine the 'right way' to do things. But with each piece of advice, she found something that contradicted the last one. "If your baby has colic, consider trying formula," one mother suggested. Could her milk be the issue? Was she harming her baby?

Yet the neighbor on the other side was adamant that breastmilk was the best thing for colicky babies. "And by all means, don't give the baby formula! That is the surest way to give little Ionna colic." But Ionna was breastfed and did have colic. If this was true, what did the baby's fussiness say about Yevt?

These mothers had opinions about everything from how often to nurse to how long to hold the baby each day, and the articles she read even suggested the types of sounds the baby needed to experience to develop appropriate speech. She began to worry uncontrollably about all the horrible things that would happen to Ionna if she made a mistake.

When Ionna turned two weeks old, Yevt cried the entire day. "My little one will never be this little again. It is all going by so fast," she mourned. Despite the ever-hastening time, the last two weeks also had felt more like years. She began to think they'd made an enormous mistake deciding to have a baby.

On the day she began thinking about leaving – her home, her husband, the baby, her life – she understood what a terrible person she must be. She had a wonderful husband who loved her and a beautiful daughter who she thought she'd never have. Only a horrible person would want to leave. And that thought made her more sure she had to go. Her baby would be better off without having to deal with someone as despicable as she was.

While the baby was asleep in the bassinet and her mother was at the market, Yevt put on her heavy coat and walked out of the house. She walked for hours, having no real idea where she would go or what she would do. As the sun met the horizon, the cold winter day turned into a frigid winter night. But rather than seek shelter, she chose to keep walking. It would be fitting to die on a night like tonight, cold and alone.

She assumed Danya would miss her, but she assured herself this condition wouldn't last too long. As a smart, educated, handsome man, he would find someone else who was fit to raise a child. Ionna would never know her, so she would never miss her. And her mama?

She started to cry as she thought about her mama and all the wonderful things she had done for Yevt over the years. She had hoped to be as good of a mama to Ionna, but that wasn't to be. The part inside that was supposed to instinctively figure out motherhood was broken or missing or damaged. Maybe it was losing her father at a young age. Maybe it was all the hardships. Maybe it was God's punishment for not believing in Him all those years.

Not that the cause mattered. Regardless, her ability to be a loving, kind, generous mom was sorely lacking, and she didn't want to pin that on her precious daughter. She crouched down against a building and cried a little harder as she thought of Ionna. She loved her so much – so much that she would leave to protect her.

Suddenly, a pair of black boots with a fake fur trim appeared, and an older woman cleared her throat. "Are you okay? Do you need some help? It's too cold out here. Come, let me help you up."

Yevt looked up with a tear-stained face, small icicles forming on her chin where the droplets pooled before falling to the ground. Before she could protest, the woman had her under the arms and helped her to her feet. "What is your name? Where do you live?" Yevt, stiff and mute, gazed down the darkening street without seeming to hear her.

"Fine. It doesn't matter. I'll call you Sophia. My name is Katrina. I live close by. Let's get you warmed up." And Katrina led her by the hand as if she were a small child, and like such a child, Yevt followed.

It wasn't until she was filled with warm soup that she realized how cold she had gotten or how far she had walked. No longer in Novoazovsk, she learned as Katrina chatted that she was in one of the smaller villages on the outskirts, several miles from her home.

Katrina didn't pry. She seemed to instinctively understand that something was desperately wrong but that Yevt, whom she called Sophia, wasn't ready or able to discuss it yet. Upon arriving at the simple home, Katrina had warmed up a bowl of soup, put a blanket around Yevt's shoulders, and began rubbing her feet. Although she had worn her coat, she had not changed from her house shoes, and her feet were past feeling.

As she thawed, sensations began pricking at her toes and fingers, and her cheeks stung with a thousand tiny pricks of a razor. But despite the pain, she was so tired that all she wanted to do was sleep. Katrina, as kind and loving as she had been, grew stern.

"No, Sophia. I can't let you sleep right now. You are suffering from exposure. I need to keep you awake, at least for a little while."

Yevt groaned. "So tired. So very tired." Those were the first words she uttered since being found, and her benefactor smiled.

"So, you do speak, and with a lovely voice, I might add." She nodded toward Yevt, "Let's chat a bit while I keep an eye on your health. Once I'm convinced you are recovering, you can sleep. I promise."

Then Katrina began chatting about her life. She had three children, all grown. Her husband passed away several years ago. Things had been tough, but, as she said, "Who hasn't had it tough, right?" Her pragmatism, however, came in second place to her optimism. "Life has a way of turning out the right way. I always say that everything turns out okay in the end. If it isn't okay, it isn't the end."

Yevt considered that statement. At first pass, she was absolutely opposed to the concept. All kinds of things ended poorly. Her father died when she was a mere child. The country she loved had been enslaved for years, and now? It was worse than before.

Then, in her mind, her husband's words echoed, "Prove it."

"Absolutely," she thought. "My father is dead. That was not okay. The end was not okay. Not for him. Not for me. Not for my mom." She was certain that would be the end of the argument, but Danya's voice echoed again. "Is death really the end, Yetti?"

She paused in her thoughts. He was right, of course. Death was an end, but not 'the end.' So, in terms of her father, his end was heaven, and that, indeed, would be okay. And for her mother? That was more difficult. Her mother remained sad to this day. Yet, even with the sadness, her mother had survived and now thrived as part of a little family. Ivanna would likely say she was okay. No, not at first, but in the end.

And herself? Her father's death had been difficult, made worse by her mother's mourning and the ensuing economic struggles. Nonetheless, she had gotten an education and found a wonderful man to marry. In the end, she was okay as well.

Yevt realized that Katrina had moved on and was now

discussing some family recipe. She should listen, out of respect, but her mind wouldn't focus on the words. She wanted to guide her back to the idea of 'okay in the end,' but she couldn't form words. Her head was so heavy, and her thoughts began running together into a blurry sludge of Danya's words, ingredients for vegetable stew, and the mantra 'okay in the end.'

When she woke, the sun was streaming in the window. Her mind was fuzzy, like she had celebrated with too much vodka on her birthday. Her tongue felt swollen, and her body ached all over. She rolled cautiously to one side, to discover that Katrina was softly padding about. When she realized Yevt was awake, she said softly, "There she is. I figured you'd wake up eventually. How are you feeling this morning? Can I bring you a cup of warm broth?"

Then, as if by magic, she was sitting with a blanket around her shoulders, sipping broth. She didn't recollect getting up, and her thoughts were very disjointed. Where was she and why was she here? Who was this woman? Where was her mama?

Slowly, she remembered. Cold. She had been very cold. This kind stranger took her in. But Mama? Why had Mama let her get so cold? But it wasn't Mama's fault. It was her own. She left the house without telling anyone. Then, out loud, she said, "Oh my God, I left the baby!"

Startled to hear more words from Yevt's lips, Katrina turned to her. "Shhh, shhh now." Yevt realized she was sobbing. "It's alright. Everything is alright," she soothed, as she sat down next to her, holding her close and swaying to and fro. "We will figure everything out."

When Yevt finally stopped crying, Katrina stated simply, "You've been crying out in your sleep about your baby. Did you lose a child? Is that what is troubling you?"

"No, no, no," escaped from Yevt's lips as the wailing started anew. "It is so much worse than that." And without even knowing why, she began to tell this stranger about Ionna's birth, how long she had waited for a child, but now that she was here, she realized she could never be the mother her child deserved. "So, I left her at home. She needs so much more than me."

Yevt's heart squeezed tight at the thought of her daughter. She loved her so much it hurt. Why would she be given such a loving heart and not the ability to mother? Why would God play such cruel joke? It made no sense.

She hadn't realized she was talking out loud until Katrina answered her. "He wouldn't. He didn't. If you love Ionna like you say you do" – she glanced at Yevt to see her nodding fervently – "then, you have the ability to mother."

Now, Yevt shook her head vigorously from side to side. "No, I don't. She cries. I don't know what to do. I'm going to cause her irreparable harm. She's better off without me."

Katrina took Yevt's face between her hands, gently but with a firmness suggesting she would not tolerate nonsense. "Sophia..."

Yevt interrupted. "My name is Yevtsye. You may call me Yevt or Yetti."

Katrina smiled warmly, "It is nice to finally know your name, Yetti. Thank you." Then, she turned Yevt to face her. "I want you to listen carefully to what I'm saying. I have been a midwife for years. I've helped hundreds of women, those who couldn't go to the hospital, bring their children into this world. And I've seen many women suffering as you are. You are not a bad mother, Yetti. You are suffering from what your mama would call the baby blues, but doctors now call Post-Partum Depression. It's a chemical imbalance. Your body has been through so much and is having trouble adjusting."

Her piercing gaze held Yevt's eyes. "Do you hear me, Yetti? You are not a bad mother. You are just ill. Some good rest, eating right, and some herbs will help get you back on the right track. I know exactly what to do. Will you let me help you?"

Yevt nodded, though not thoroughly convinced.

"Good! That's good. But first, we need to let your family know you are safe. Can we do that, Yetti? Will you let me contact your husband? I'm sure he is worried sick."

That had been almost three months ago. Katrina's assessment of Danya's concern was correct. He had spent the better part of the day and well into the night searching for his wife, assuming the worst. He just held her and cried when he was reunited with her. "My darling, oh my darling. I knew you were having a hard time but didn't understand what to do. I love you so much." He had even begged to be forgiven for failing her, but she believed she needed forgiving far more.

Danya, though he wanted to bring her home right away, let Katrina convince him that she needed more time. She desperately needed to sleep. She helped Yetti pump her breasts and suggested how to feed Ionna if the milk wasn't enough. Danya came by each day, to collect the milk and check on his wife.

Yevt's progress was slow but steady. She carefully followed Katrina's guidance, eating healthy meals each day, walking around the block for a bit of sun and some gentle exercise, and beginning a regimen of herbs to help her body heal.

"So many doctors ignore signs of depression after childbirth, assuming that what is going on is to be expected. But just because something is expected doesn't mean a woman should just have to cope. Yet, they offer nothing to help ease the symptoms or allow a woman's body to find the strength to return to a more normalized state. Thankfully," she said with a grin, "you didn't sit on a sidewalk near a doctor's house!"

From an old, brown leather satchel, Katrina had pulled out several bottles of dried leaves, stems, and powders, plant parts that appeared more withered than beneficial. Despite their appearance, Katrina's eyes lit up when looking at the different bottles, selecting some, and putting others back into the bag. Then, with a flourish, she said, "To help with your mood, that horrible feeling that you just aren't good enough and that you are incapable of being a good mom, I give you this."

She showcased three bottles lined up on the table, dramatically pointing with one hand as if they were prizes on a TV gameshow. "These first two, mint and yarrow, can be made into a tea. I recommend drinking the tea twice a day until little Ionna is at least three months old. But," she said firmly, "don't be afraid to continue drinking the tea until you are your old self again.

"The mint is easy to grow in your own home, right on the window ledge." She pointed to her own kitchen window where dozens of pots contained leafy green plants of various sizes. "I'll furnish you with some starts before you leave. You'll love the mint. You can even add it to some of your favorite meals. Unfortunately, the yarrow is a bit harder to find in these winter months, so I'll give you plenty to last you until you can hunt down your own."

Yevt had an image of her out scouring the countryside with a magnifying glass and a tiny shovel looking for some obscure plant. "I honestly don't know anything about plants. I don't see myself out among the trees looking for yarrow."

Katrina hooted with laughter. "You won't be among the trees, Yevt. You'll find yarrow growing along the sidewalk in town as you take Ionna on walks. I'm sure you've seen it before. They are those delicate white flowers with the tiny cluster in the center. Do you know what I mean?"

Yevt nodded. She had seen them all her life and never considered them to be more than a prettier-than-average weed.

She handed both the mint and yarrow to Yevt, saying, "If you run out before you have the chance to dry your own, just come back to me. Okay? I have sources for getting more."

Yevt wondered vaguely if her sources consisted of the black market, but she was still too tired to care too much and figured if Katrina dealt in the black market, it was her own business – she wouldn't ask.

"This third one is carline thistle. It also grows along the side of the road, mistaken for a common weed with no redeeming qualities. Put a spoonful of the petals in your bath."

Yevt's eyes danced in amusement. "Are you telling me that one of my 'medicines' is to bathe with skinny, white flower petals? I'm never going to get Danya to believe a luxurious, scented bath is necessary for my mental health!" She laughed ruefully.

Katrina, however, put down the bottle, and with complete sincerity said, "Your mental health is more than the ability to perform daily tasks for your child and husband. It is about taking care of yourself, finding ways to decrease your stress, and looking for joy. Your husband knows how lucky he is to have you. He'll be more than happy for you to bathe in flower petals. He'd be willing to build you a tub on a pedestal and find fresh river water every day if I told him it was needed so you would be well again."

Yevt wasn't so sure about that but had to admit that Danya seemed willing to do almost anything to get her back home. Katrina had moved on, providing her with several more herbs that, according to her, would help her body heal from the hardships of growing a child. "I recommend you take these," she handed her bottles labeled birch, stoneseed, cowberry, and guelder rose, "until your menstrual cycle starts again."

"Finally," she said, "We need to talk about the topic of nutrition. Naturally, the best way to help your body heal is to give it all the vitamins and minerals you need. Unfortunately, that isn't possible on a diet consisting mostly of potatoes and grains. But there are things you can do."

She reached into her satchel again and pulled out a bag stuffed with sunflower seeds. "Thankfully, despite the wretched economy, sunflower seeds are easy to find. And, as an added bonus, if you grow a few in your yard, you'll have something lovely to look at!"

The thought of cheery sunflowers growing along the side of her house made her smile. She would ask her mother to plant them for her once the weather turned warm.

"So, what do you think?" Katrina asked.

"Everything sounds easy enough. Drink some tea. Take some herbs like vitamins. Bathe in flowers. I think I can manage it," said Yevt, feeling lighter than she had in days.

"That's excellent because I have one more little tidbit I want you to consider, and I saved it for last." With one final dive into her satchel, she pulled up a bag with dark green leaves. "Green algae," she said triumphantly.

Yevt gagged at the thought. "Algae? Are you really suggesting I dine on the slimy green plants growing along the edge of the sea?"

Katrina laughed at her expression, "Dine is probably the wrong word, but yes, eating two to three cups of algae each week would do wonders. It's not so bad. You ate some earlier today and didn't even realize it."

Yevt thought back to today's meals. She was certain her hostess was trying to see how gullible Yevt was. "I don't believe you," she said firmly. "Everything you've made tasted perfectly delightful, and there is no way I'd say that about eating algae."

"But, my dear, you are so very wrong. The cabbage in your holubtsi was more than just cabbage. Didn't you wonder at its lovely shade of green? And the strong flavor of borscht is an easy way to hide nearly anything you'd prefer not to eat. Finally, the filling for the varenyky was more than dandelion greens. Today alone, you ate about one cup of algae, and I think I see a difference already!" With that proclamation and the astonishment it brought to Yevt's face, Katrina laughed loudly, until finally, reluctantly, Yevt joined in, too.

She was so thankful that this woman was willing to

share all her knowledge and help her to get well. But even more important to Yevt was their budding friendship. Katrina spent hours each day talking and listening, providing insights into Yevt's issue, and simply letting her talk all the poison out of her.

"I wish women talked about their feelings after birth as much as they talked about labor," Yevt had lamented to Katrina. "I didn't even know this condition existed, but I could recite every gory detail about breech birth. If I had known..." Her voice trailed off as she quietly berated herself for her failure as a mother again.

Katrina would have none of it. "Of course, you didn't know. How could you? For reasons beyond my comprehension, this type of chemical imbalance is completely taboo. It is hidden behind closed bedroom doors and women suffer needlessly. I think you'd be surprised to learn how many women who give birth suffer just as you have suffered. Not only do women suffer from depression after birth, but they also deal with anxiety in those first weeks of pregnancy."

Yevt took in a quick breath. "Anxiety in early pregnancy? You mean, things like worrying about food and exercise and sleeping in the wrong position? Are you telling me I was suffering from a chemical imbalance then, too?"

Katrina nodded. "If you were worried about which way you were sleeping, then I'd have to say you were experiencing anxiety. If that is not the way you typically handle things" – she cut her eyes to Yevt, who was shaking her head no – "then it was likely a chemical imbalance. It's not so surprising. I've found that most women who suffer from depression after birth usually experience some degree of anxiety beforehand."

Knowing she was not alone, and that what was happening inside her brain was not her fault, helped Yevt feel more settled. She wasn't a failure as a mom, she was simply suffering from over-reactive hormones. With time, rest, and love, she would be fine. She would be strong. She would be a good mother to her darling Ionna. By the end of the week, Yevt was ready to go home.

Danya came for his wife and was thoughtful enough to bring some his mother-in-law's stew and a loaf of bread still warm from the oven.

"Thank you," said Danya as he gave a slight bow toward Katrina. "From the bottom of my heart, I thank you. I cannot imagine my life without my Yetti."

Katrina waved her hand, brushing aside his comments. "Your wife is strong, physically and emotionally. Even without me, she would have figured it out."

But Yevt knew better, and in time, so did Danya, as she described those feelings she had and her desire to die cold and alone. Now, three months later, she still had to be gentle with herself, but she was much better. And each night, as she got in bed, she and Danya thanked God for Katrina's wisdom and His guiding hand.

Hearing a slight sound, Yevt turned to find Ionna staring at her. When she caught her mother's eye, the baby smiled. Yevt's morning solitude was over, but she didn't mind. She was learning to love being a mother and was beginning to understand for herself that everything turns out okay in the end.

Chapter 17

1995

Yevt watched as her daughter grabbed at the edge of the sofa with both hands and then pulled until she was standing, legs wide, one arm letting go of its anchor to wave excitedly around her head. Then, with a stillness, eyes focused directly in front of her, the tip of her tiny tongue poking out between her thin pink lips, both hands were free, and she was hanging in midair where she would stay until she shifted her eyes toward her mother and landed on the floor with a padded thud. Up. Balance. Thud. Up. Balance. Thud. Up. Balance. Thud. Little Ionna's perseverance would likely turn her into a walker before she turned a year old.

Yevt glanced out the window to see a thin layer of white forming on the lawn outside. The snows had come early this year, blanketing the mid-October morning with stillness. "And cold," thought Yevt wryly. She wondered if an early winter also meant a cold one.

She hoped not. Last winter had been brutal and getting the needed heating oil difficult. She had neighbors who burned their furniture to keep warm, and she couldn't help but remember the state of her mother before they brought her home. And the news was rife with stories about older, poor Ukranians found outdoors, frozen in place, dying while performing some mundane task. Only last week, neighbors found a man standing in his front yard, holding onto a shovel. It was only after he stood motionless most of the afternoon that they realized he was dead. Once again, she felt blessed. All a difficult winter meant to her was wearing an extra layer or two and putting a hot water bottle in bed with the baby for the night.

For Yevt, last winter had not been difficult because of the cold, or even the economy. Her difficulties had come in the form of motherhood and figuring out her new body while simultaneously learning about her new baby. She tried hard not to dwell on those early weeks when the depression had been so overwhelming that she almost let the weather take her life like those too poor to have a choice. She wasn't proud of her decisions during that time, though she worked hard to remember she was sick and not fully responsible for her behaviors.

Once she came home, things were so much better, but they were still difficult. In another world, one in which she hadn't considered freezing to death in the snow to save her daughter from having such a rotten mother, she would have said those months were the most difficult she'd ever been through. But difficulty, she had learned, was a subjective experience.

Although her mother swore that Ionna was an easy baby, as far as Yevt could tell, this was only something said to make her ashamed of herself. If Ionna was so easy, then why was she having such a hard time with her? Why did the crying never stop? Why did she never sleep? Why was she always hungry, eager to suck not only milk, but the very life, from her mother?

Ionna had been born with an opinion. She only liked to nurse on the right side and had to be tricked into nursing from the left breast by starting her on the preferred side and switching to the other side without changing her position. She only wanted to be held facing out, rather than snuggling into her mother's shoulder as Yevt had seen other mothers' babies do. She didn't want to be swaddled, screaming unless her hands were free but screaming louder each time her startle reflex sent her arms flying outward in an uncontrolled burst of energy.

Eventually, her daughter had gotten the hang of nursing, and Yevt had gotten the hang of cradling her belly against one arm, leaving Ionna's hands free and giving her a view of the world. But rather than grow content now that she had gotten her own way in the world, she simply gained more opinions.

What toy she wanted to thrust into her slobbery mouth. Her hatred of socks and footed pajamas. Her preference for bouncing rather than rocking. Her need for Daddy's singing voice rather than her mother's. Her distaste for the stroller, preferring to be strapped high on her mother's back holding tightly to hair on either side of her mother's head.

Learning these distinct likes and dislikes was not easy. It wasn't as if Ionna had the vocabulary to say, "Mother, I would prefer you give me the yellow, pretzel-shaped chew toy instead of this set that looks like a ring of multi-color keys." Instead, she would pucker up her face and suck in an enormous breath before letting out a piercing scream, followed closely by silence as she pulled in another breath, continuing this Morse code of piercing screams followed by equally long silences – continuing even after the offending problem had been solved.

For Ionna, timing was everything. She let her needs be known, and then Yevt had less than five seconds to make things right or the screaming would begin. Once started, Ionna would scream until she ran out of energy to do so. And so, the day would go, from one outburst to the next. It was not uncommon for Danya to come home from work to find his mother-in-law mumbling in the kitchen and his wife crying on the couch while nursing a hot, sweaty child finally calm enough to eat.

Ionna never napped alone. From the moment she woke in the morning until she went to bed at night, she had to be touching someone, preferably her mother. When she would fall asleep nursing, Yevt would sit as still as possible, letting the child rest. The smallest movement often woke the baby, who would immediately want to nurse again, and Yevt barely produced enough milk for the every-two-hour feedings without adding feedings in between.

Whenever circumstances allowed, Yevt read everything she could find about being a mother. The newest, most up-to-date advice came from the West, and she tried to follow these tips as carefully as possible, much to her mother's annoyance.

"Yevt, stop reading those articles. Just do what you believe is right. That's what mothers have been doing for generations. I never read one article when you were a baby. Not one. Nonetheless, here you are. Perfectly fine. Just do what seems natural."

But for Yevt, there was nothing natural about being a mother and nothing natural about Ionna's behaviors. Everything she read said Ionna should be sleeping on her own, feeding less often, and relying more on self-stimulation. Ionna wasn't reading the same articles.

However, her baby girl was healthy. She was taller, heavier, and stronger than other children her age and met all the milestone markers on time, if not early. At two months old, her gaze tracked her mother's movements across the room. At three months, she rolled from front to back. At four months, she got razor-sharp teeth on the bottom...and top.

It was in the fourth month that the sleep deprivation, the physical requirements of two-hour nursings, and the appearance of four teeth in a matter of two weeks, almost sent Yevt scurrying back to the calm and quiet of Katrina's home rather than deal with her daughter.

Everything she read said babies did not need to eat solid foods until they were six months old. Their bellies were not prepared to digest the food, so introducing rice and semolina might cause allergies and other irreparable issues for the growing infant. So, despite her mother's insistence that she began feeding Yevt solid foods in a bottle mixed with breast milk almost from birth, Yevt steadfastly refused to feed her daughter solids of any kind.

However, now with teeth, Ionna had begun biting at her breasts during feedings, making the every-two-hour events even less inviting than they had been before. Yevt was sore. And tired. The thought of feeding Ionna nothing but breast milk every two hours for the next two months was unbearable – unbearable enough that she contemplated running away and letting her mother and husband deal with the inconsolable child.

That feeling of wanting to run scared her. She had been there before and didn't want to be there again. This time, rather than hide her fears and insecurities, she threw the words at Danya as soon as he opened the door.

"I can't do it. I can't keep doing this," she cried, holding tightly to her daughter. "She eats all the time. Every two hours all day and all night. I just can't keep doing this until she's six months old. I just can't."

Danya sat down next to his wife and pulled her close, letting Ionna rest her head on his lap while her lower half rested on her mother. Giving Yevt a decisive solution might have appeared to be an ultimatum, and therefore, would have been useless. He knew this from experience, having given her a sensible answer to a dilemma only to have her take the opposite side despite it being the answer she didn't want. So, he had done the very best thing possible – understood her predicament and given her choices.

"I can see how tired you are. And I understand how difficult it must be to be the only one who can feed Ionna. The way I see it, you have several choices. One, you can keep doing what you are doing until she turns six months old." Yevt started to cry, and Danya rubbed her back as he continued.

"Two, you can stop nursing, and we'll start giving Ionna formula. That way, you aren't the only one in charge of feeding the baby." Yevt waggled her head vigorously. "No. I want to breastfeed. It is best for her. And I'd be worried all the time that we couldn't find the formula we need without buying on the Black Market." Now, she was crying harder.

"Shhh. Shhhh, now. Let's keep looking at your options. Shhhh." He waited until her crying had turned to quiet sniffles.

"Three, you can continue nursing and supplement that with formula so you can create some space between feedings." Yevt considered this, thinking it may work. Potentially.

"And finally, four, you can continue nursing and add some solids into Ionna's diet, so she isn't as hungry."

She heard her mother's snort of approval from the kitchen, and said, "But the doctors in the west say..."

Before she had a chance to continue, Danya said, "The doctors in the west don't live in our house with our child. She is big for her age. And you are just not able to produce all that she needs unless she eats every two hours. I agree that feeding a baby solid foods too early could be problematic, but our Ionna is the size of the typical six-month old. She eats enough to be the average six-month old. And our family, despite being fed solids early on, has never experienced any allergies. I think it may be an answer. But Yevt, it is up to you. What do you think is best?"

That discussion did not lead to an immediate solution, but within the week, they had purchased some rice cereal prepared especially for babies and mixed it with some of Yevt's milk. Then, because Ionna was so young and not coordinated enough to eat from a spoon, they pilfered a syringe ordinarily used by Danya's students to inject liquids into chromatographs and plunged a minute amount into her mouth.

Ionna's delight was instantaneous, a broad smile breaking across her face, feet kicking and hands waving, as she quickly turned as much of her body as possible in the direction of the syringe with the open mouth of a baby bird waiting for a worm.

Now, at almost ten months old, Ionna ate mostly squashed up table food and a sippy cup of water, supplemented by morning and evening breastmilk. She was happy, healthy, and apparently allergy-free as she worked to perfect her balance.

Yevt realized that somewhere in the last weeks and months, she had become settled and happy, no longer as harried, tired, worried, or sad. And yes, even ready for another winter, one in which her daughter would be toddling all over the house, getting into things that had once been safely out of her reach.

Chapter 18

1996

A wry smile graced his lips as he watched his daughter move about the room. His Ionna never stopped moving unless she was asleep or strapped into a chair to eat. She flitted from chair to toy to couch to book in much the same way bees gathered nectar from flowers. On them, he reflected, it looked far less frenzied.

He couldn't believe she was already two years old. The time had flown by, and except for Yetti's troubles immediately after birth, the two years had been quite predictable. Ionna rolled, scooted, crawled, and began using words when the small library of child rearing books they had amassed said she would. He secretly wondered if she got up in the night while they slept and read the books to determine just what she should be doing next.

Despite the ordinariness of it all, he found everything

his daughter did captivating. From growing teeth to potty training, the capacity to grow and learn was astounding. He wished his university students came to class with the same kind of eagerness and curiosity for knowledge his young child possessed. He sighed deeply, running his left hand through his hair. Somewhere along the way, such a fondness for the new and different disappeared, leaving his students and everyone who affected his life, dull and unchanging.

Take the political state, for instance. Danya had to clench his mouth tight when this topic arose to keep his disgust from exploding into the world. Instead, it just seeped between his teeth leaving a bad taste in his mouth.

He and Yetti had spent weeks studying the various candidates for President, especially as they came to understand the necessary changes that had not been addressed. He recalled a conversation he and Yetti had shortly after they had begun dealing with her postpartum depression. He had worried about whether politics was too much for her, but it appeared to produce the opposite effect, almost as if having a focus beyond the baby was good medicine.

It was an early evening, and he had been researching candidates. "Yetti, our government just can't keep going on this way. We have been recognized as a free country, and yet...there doesn't seem to be much free about it."

Both he and Yetti glanced toward the partitioned area that was Momma Ivanna's bedroom when they heard a slight snort. Ivanna never said "I told you so" outright, but those words broadcasted from her simplest noises whenever they were talking politics.

"I know, darling. Finding what we need at the store is

truly beyond reason. I'm getting tired of choosing between potatoes and turnips. I long for something red or yellow! And we are the lucky ones. The economy must be the next focus, don't you think?"

Danya had started off believing the focus must be three-pronged. Although he firmly believed this was the recipe needed for ultimate success, the economy was topmost in his mind. He had told Yetti as much.

"I reluctantly agree. Without a doubt, getting our leaders to really embrace democracy is essential, but if this economy isn't straightened out soon, I'm afraid the people are going to see the whole thing as a failed experiment and beg to create a Soviet Union replica again. Which is why, I think I will vote for Volodymyr Lanovyi. He is a relative unknown in the Soviet regime, so he is more likely to be ready to accept democratic principles. And his passion for making Ukraine an economically sound nation is inspiring. I think he may be the one to move us forward."

Although Yevt enjoyed these talks about politics, she had little time for extracurricular reading or outside events. Ionna was an intense child who already had an opinion at weeks old. When she wanted something – her mother's breast or to be snuggled – she wanted it immediately. If someone didn't catch on fast enough, then Ionna would become inconsolable, screaming for 20 to 30 minutes at a time. Danya believed that she would eventually grow into her opinions once she had the words to express herself, but in the meantime, his Yetti had too much to do to worry about the next president.

As a university employee, Danya was prohibited from actively campaigning for a candidate on campus. In fact, he studiously avoided mentioning politics, which wasn't too difficult as he lectured about atomic structures and chemical bonds. However, he did spend an inordinate amount of time each week after work pushing his candidate's agenda to anyone who would listen from someone in line at a store to the neighbor man enjoying a brisk evening walk to Katrina, who had become a regular visitor to their home.

On the day of the election, he had been optimistic that his candidate would win. He and Yetti had bundled up Ionna and gone to cast their ballot. Mama Ivanna insisted on going alone, still not wanting to be part of their misguided political leanings. After casting his ballot, he had said to Yetti, "Tonight, my love, will be the beginning of something new!"

Unfortunately, his optimism was misguided, and his time would have been better spent finding a way to stockpile hard-to-find goods rather than promoting change. He had wanted to give the newly elected government a chance to succeed and honestly prayed that they would, but all changes appeared to be moving backward to a more Soviet-style government instead of embracing democracy and capitalism. Now, two years into the presidency, President Leonid Kuchma, who started out strong and placated the masses with all the right sentiments, seemed far more satisfied with the status quo than someone who claimed to be a reformer should.

And to make matters worse, although Kuchma continued to build relations with the West, he had also consented to build them with Russia.

"Russia of all countries!" he exploded, throwing the paper to the ground and grinding his fist on his knee. "Why would he tie Ukraine to the Commonwealth of

Independent States? What possible explanation could he have? It is ludicrous. No. No it is more than that. It is dangerous. Mark my words."

It was so clear to him that he could not begin to comprehend how anyone saw things differently. Participation in the CIS meant Ukraine and Russia would be linked economically, militarily, and politically. Why, after all Ukraine had been through at the hands of the Communist Party, would their government consent to being subject, once again, to the same leaders brandishing different banners?

He continued to marvel at his mother-in-law's insight when independence was first declared. Yet, he bristled when others were so short-sighted. Yetti tried to help him examine things from a different perspective, but when it came to the Russians, his windows remained cloudy, and likely always would.

It wasn't that Yevt wanted Ukraine to cozy up to the Russians, but she did point out that having one's closest neighbors as allies certainly couldn't be a bad idea. He had retorted about "sleeping with snakes," and she let the topic drop, understanding that there were no words that could easily pierce his dissatisfaction, nor could words erase the actuality of the situation.

Although Danya enjoyed being right, relished it in most cases, he hated the consequences of his 'rightness' in this situation. He inspected his home. Nearly everything purchased since declaring independence had come from Russia. The bedsheets on his mother-in-law's bed. The baby's bowl and spoon. The shirt he wore to work. Even the food in their kitchen was mostly imported from Russia. And if that weren't bad enough, he also understood that if a man in Russia took inventory around his house, he would find nothing purchased from Ukraine. The balance between the two countries was terribly lopsided, with Ukraine on the wrong side of the scale.

He had tried explaining this imbalance to a colleague now that he was no longer seen as a rebel for wanting a free Ukraine. "Our citizens are using three times the energy we can produce. If it weren't for Russian gas and oil, we would have a shortage." But rather than recognize how such a reliance on Russian goods would lead to the downfall of the fledgling nation, Fedir had said, jovially, "Thank God for Russia!"

He ran into that sentiment more frequently than not. His countrymen were enamored with Russia because the Russians provided them with the goods they wanted. Why should they worry about producing their own when the Russians would provide? Why, indeed.

As with everything in life, nothing was all good or all bad. The Ukrainian parliament had just ratified a new democratic constitution. Once again, Ukraine had a guarantee of free speech and, according to the document, he and Yevt could own their own home. Of course, that was merely on paper. The reality was, that despite the constitution and his job, they were still crowded into the one-bedroom house they were "allotted" when they first married.

Abruptly, he turned his thoughts back to Ionna. He longed for a way to provide her with more space to play and learn and grow. He often felt her whirlwindedness was due as much to the limited space as it was to her inquisitive nature. Regardless, she would be much less underfoot if they had a separate space for her to play.

Who was he to complain? Throughout the years, both as part of the USSR and now as an independent nation, Danya had a job which allowed him to use his mind and interact with others and, though the university was not perfect, his job was far better than a majority of those throughout the country. And what of his living arrangements? He personally knew several people who would give just about anything for their "cramped" quarters where four people, one of them quite small, were living in a 3-room house rather than an entire extended family trying to do likewise, or in some cases, in significantly smaller spaces.

His eyes followed Ionna, buzzing about the room, laughing with glee over her books and toys. Yevt appeared at the door to the kitchen, wiping her hands on a towel while speaking gently to their daughter. Shortly, the two were bent low, hovering over a book, smiling, and chatting, notwithstanding Ionna's limited vocabulary.

He stood in awe of Yetti and her natural abilities with their child. Despite having the brains of a scientist, she happily stayed home each day to care for him, their daughter, and her mother – all without complaint – except perhaps when the market didn't carry the basics. Even then, she complained with humor.

Although the pregnancy and delivery had been hard on Yevt's mental health, she had bounced back once the hormones had settled. In fact, Danya felt that having a child had left her more grounded and given her a greater sense of wonder, if that were even possible. He was a lucky man.

He was startled to note that tears were threatening to fall over his lower lids for his family to witness. "I'm getting soft in my old age," he concluded, and brushing at his eyes with the back of his hand, he went to join his wife and daughter and their discussion of *Kotyk i Pivnyk* – The Cat and the Rooster – about a crafty fox who steals a rooster and how the rooster is saved by his friend, the cat.

Chapter 19

July 2000

Ivanna had spent the morning cleaning the bookshelves. Ever since Danya had purchased this three-bedroom home with a study, she had noted the books found their way into the house but rarely found their way back out. One entire wall of the study from floor to ceiling was stuffed with books. Thick volumes explaining chemical properties far beyond Ivanna's understanding. Thin, poorly bound political essays on democracy and capitalism. Colorful paperbacks with covers promising some happily-ever-after. Each book jammed on the shelf in such close proximity to its neighbor that Ivanna felt they should simply join together and become one.

Eventually, this bookshelf, the one that nearly sold the house on its own merits, had begun spitting books into small piles around the den, simply unable to hold a single chapter, let alone another a complete title. So, Danya had purchased first one, then two, and finally three smaller shelves which stood in cramped spaces behind chairs and under windows.

By the time Ionna had started school, these three smaller bookshelves had multiplied as well, with six more shelves finding permanent homes in the living room, two more in the master bedroom, and three, filled completely with children's literature, in Ionna's room.

Ivanna had initially considered the books to be nothing more than dust collectors and grumbled each time she had to remove the books to dust. Over the years, however, she had come to love the job, though she tried not to let on to Danya and Yetti. She didn't want them to think she was growing soft in her old age.

For months, she would pull the books off the shelves and speculate about what wonders might be inside. Finally, without realizing what she was doing, she had begun opening the covers and flipping through the pages, until finally, she found herself sitting down with a book and reading it from the first page to the last. She quickly realized the chemistry and biology books brought home to keep her children abreast of their field of interest were too advanced. And, quite frankly, too boring. The political books made her angry, though she did like learning things to use in her arguments with Danya.

It was the day she opened a novel, a quirky little book called *Perverzion* about a poet in Venice, that changed everything. The book was clever and full of word choices which made Ivanna laugh out loud. And amazingly, it wasn't real. Here was a piece of fiction that removed her from her life for a time and nothing perverse came from it.

Ever since that day in late 1998, she had been secretly reading for pleasure. She no longer gravitated toward nonfiction books with their equations and facts, but focused on abandoned novels that, once read by Yevt, became no more than another spot of color on the shelf. Now, when she cleaned the bookshelves, she did so for two reasons – to rid them of dust and to find her next adventure.

Today, her fingers traced the title *Double Leon*, by Yuriy Izdryk, an author Ivanna did not recognize. This book was not yet a castaway. Instead, Ivanna found it sitting on Yetti's bedside table as she dusted the cases in their room. She only read the first chapter, careful to keep the pages pristine. She did not want her daughter to suspect she had been reading. It would ruin her little game, the one in which she was merely a piece of furniture with the occasional intellectual insight that stunned her family into silence. She enjoyed their stunned reactions, though she often wondered why they never made the connection that Yetti, her smart scientist, was biologically her child. The DNA for her intelligence had to come from somewhere.

The only time the family saw her read was to Ionna. Children's books did not conjure up an intellectual image, so reading storybooks to her granddaughter did nothing to damage her reputation. It merely suggested she loved the child, and Ivanna's love for Ionna was something she didn't mind everyone knowing.

Having a grandchild was the best thing that had ever happened to her. She had loved being a mother, but so many of those years were fraught with hardships and entwined with memories she would rather forget. Once

Leka had died, Yevt had been Ivanna's only source of joy. Unfortunately, that joy showed itself only in sporadic flashes like the pulse of light from the Vorontsov Lighthouse amid an arctic cyclone.

But with Ionna? Joy was something that came every day, often in waves that lasted hours. Something as simple as a dimpled smile caused Ivanna's heart to fill her chest. She never tired of watching her granddaughter – how she moved, what she said, the tilt of her head as she learned some new concept.

She and Ionna had been 'talking' together since she was an infant. Babusya, according to her daughter, had a knack for getting the baby to babble. She would pick up the baby, gaze deep into her eyes, and the two of them would chat, first one, then the other. As Ionna grew, these 'conversations' grew as well. Now, the two of them spent hours with their heads together discussing the things of importance to the child: books, bugs, baking, bubbles. Any topic of interest to Ionna easily became a half-hour discussion excluding anyone else in the room.

With a start, she realized she had been daydreaming, a pile of books on the floor around her feet, and the duster hanging limply from her hand. She had been doing that a lot more lately – finding herself lost in a world inside her mind rather than dealing with the world firmly under her feet. She attributed it to old age. Though she was only 57, middle-aged by western standards, the years fending for herself without Leka, the long hours at the fishery, and even now, years with limited fruits and vegetables, had taken their toll.

She closed the lid tightly on these depressing thoughts before glancing at the clock. Ionna would be home from school in less than an hour. Ivanna hurriedly put the books back on the shelf and disappeared into the kitchen to make bublik to snack on while they talked of her day and made Holuntsi – of course, without the pork, a luxury they rarely experienced despite their freedom from 'oppression' – for their evening meal.

Ionna loved everything about school, from walking to the building each morning holding tightly to her mama's hand, to the broad smile of her teacher, to her friends Liliya and Myroslava, to the letters and numbers that unlocked the mysterious books tucked on shelves around her home. Unlike some of the children who insisted on going home because of a stomachache or watched dully out the window instead of bending over their work, Ionna soaked up her surroundings with enthusiasm, asking questions and challenging everything she heard.

Most of the time, Ionna was considered the perfect student, although there was the time her parents had been called to school because of her questions. She didn't understand why her teacher with the warm smile was so upset. She had just been trying to understand the story, but the teacher told her tatusyu that she was being insolent.

"Tatusyu," she had asked earnestly after the parental meeting, "what is insolent?"

Her father squatted down to meet her gaze. "The teacher believes your questions were rude. She felt you were trying to be disrespectful to her."

Ionna didn't know what to make of this word. She had not been rude. She merely wanted to know more. When her teacher was telling them a story about a shopkeeper and how he didn't have any bread to sell to his customers, Ionna had asked whether the shopkeeper lived in Ukraine. Her teacher nodded, but before she could move on with the story, Ionna had asked, "Is this story from now or was this story from a long time ago?"

Confused, her teacher said, "I'm not sure, Ionna. It doesn't matter, really."

Ionna chewed on that answer for just a moment, interrupting the story for the third time. "But, Mrs. Zlenko, it *does* matter. If it is about now, when the shopkeeper owned his own store, then I wonder why he couldn't buy the things he wanted. My tatusyu says that shouldn't happen in a caspultalic ... capsulitic...castulolic country like Ukraine. Why didn't the storekeeper have any bread to sell?"

The teacher had ignored her, continuing on with the book that had something to do with all the villagers making stew, and then her parents had been brought in to discuss her behavior.

Her tatusyu had gently explained, "Sometimes, young one, a story is just a story. I'm glad you are curious. Just do your best to listen to your teacher and be polite. But no matter what, don't stop asking questions."

Ionna still asked a lot of questions, but she tried not to ask questions about stories. Instead, she would bring those questions home to her parents and to her babusya. It didn't take her long to discover her tatusyu and babusya didn't always agree, and that sometimes her questions would cause the two of them to get loud, on occasion leading him to pound his fist and her to slam the door to her room. But by the time Ionna was ready for bed, everyone was talking again, so she decided not to worry too much about what she now thought of as their insolent behavior.

Today had been an excellent day at school. She walked along with Liliya and her mother as she did every afternoon. They lived right across the street from Ionna and dropped her off with her babusya after school. The girls chatted about the new jump rope song they had learned during recess that day and how many jumps they had achieved. "After red hot peppers," Liliya had announced with pleasure, "I jumped six whole times."

Ionna had gotten to seven, but she knew saying so would make Liliya sad. Liliya liked to be better at things than Ionna, and Ionna didn't mind letting her win in jump rope. "That's very good," said Ionna. "Maybe tomorrow, you can go even higher!"

Then, she was at her own door, and gave a quick wave to her friend. Before Babusya could even say hello, Ionna shouted, "Guess what? I learned a new jump rope song, and after we said red hot peppers, I jumped seven whole times!"

As she knew would happen, her babusya smiled, wrapped her thin arms around her waist, and dropped her easily on the counter. "Wonderful! What would you say to a bite of bublik while we talk about your day? And if we are lucky, we'll have time to continue reading in the storybook we started yesterday."

Chapter 20

2006

Ionna rushed home from school as she had been doing for as long as she could remember. However, the rushing was more urgent now, as if every moment counted. She would stare at the hour hand slowly creeping from 8 to 9, then from 9 to 10, eventually reaching the top of the mountain at noon. She always wished those hours going back down would go faster, that somehow gravity would catch the tiny arm and hurry the tiny mechanism on its way. If anything, the distance between those final two hours seemed substantially longer.

When the hour hand finally reached 1 o'clock, she would focus her attention on the minute hand, noticing each stutter step forward, willing the minutes to dare going by twos and threes. Finally, at 1:55, she would concentrate on the second hand sweeping around the clock – no variance, these final seconds no more important to the timekeeper than any others.

When the bell rang, Ionna would leap out of her seat, pulling her backpack to her shoulders as she pushed past students in the hot, crowded hallway until she finally burst into the cool, fresh air. Her friends no longer called to her, having determined that Ionna's flight toward home had no room for detours or distractions. Several weeks of terse "I don't have time's" and "I need to go's" had helped them gain this clarity.

Those hours stuck in school were a complete waste of time – time she wouldn't get back. Ionna was not a poor student. She was top of her class – in everything. Depite only half-listening and spending far too much time focusing on the clock going around in endless circles, she made high marks.

She had begged her parents to let her stay home with Babusya, "I need to stay home and be with Babusya. She is happiest when I am with her. If I'm here, she will get better. School can wait. I could miss weeks and catch up in an afternoon. Please!"

The discussion ended with, "Babusya needs rest. The doctors say there is nothing left to do, Ionna. Sitting with her won't make her well. Missing school won't accomplish anything." They were firmly in the 'absolutely not' camp, and nothing Ionna said would change their minds.

Ionna was not prone to believing fairy tales, though her life had always been one of happily ever afters. In her world, things worked out exactly as she intended them to work out. It was simply a matter of knowing what was wanted and asking God to make sure it happened. Like the time she wanted a bicycle and her parents said it would be impossible to find in the store so she shouldn't get her hopes up. But she had prayed earnestly for that bicycle for several nights in a row. Then, one day, her father came home from work pushing the very bicycle she had envisioned in her mind – bright yellow with shiny streamers blowing gently from the handlebars and a small, white wicker basket perched on the handlebars expectantly waiting for Ionna's treasures.

This experience had only been one of many which helped her learn how the world worked – want something, pray earnestly, get the wanted thing. Life was as easy as multiplying fractions or making deruny. One simply had to precisely follow the steps.

So, of course, she had been doing just that about her grandmother's illness. Each night before she went to sleep, and again in the morning before she even brushed her teeth, Ionna would pray for her grandmother's recovery. "Dear God, It's me, Ionna. I hope you are doing okay today. I wanted to thank you for letting me have a good day. And for all my stuff. I don't have time to list everything because I want to be sure I have time to ask you about Babusya. She is still sick. Mama and Papa are worried. I keep telling them it will be okay because I am praying, but they worry anyway. I'm not worried. Well, not really worried, though it would be nice if you could go ahead and let her get well soon. I miss the lunches she used to pack and the little notes I would find inside. So, anyway, please help her get well. Soon. Thank you. Amen."

Her parents talked with her regularly about Babusya's health and her age. How Babusya had lived a hard life during some hard years. How she spent many years without enough to eat but having to work long, hard hours anyway. How all this had stripped away her health. How she was not going to regain her strength.

Ionna understood that Babusya was old. She knew all about communism and how bad things had been in Ukraine from her papa, who never tired of telling her the stories which always started with "Back when I was your age." She even understood that living that way must have been bad for her babusya and her health. But their conclusion that she was not going to be healthy again was flawed, and she steadfastly refused to believe it. "No. Do not say that. Do. Not. Say. That. Babusya is going to be fine. I'm praying about it." Then she would go into Babusya's room to hold her hand or read another chapter of a book they were enjoying or spoon some warm broth into her dry mouth.

Ionna hurried to be with her babusya, not because she feared her death, but because she just feared...what? She wasn't sure. Whatever it was floated through her like a cold fog. She tried to grab it, to inspect it, to determine what it was that made her feel like something was slipping through her fingers, but she didn't have the dexterity to capture the feeling.

Today, as she moved deftly around a mother and her toddler moving slowly and taking up the entire width of the sidewalk as the child discovered tiny ants skirting along the cracks, pebbles, bits of paper, and the purple blossoms of larkspur, she found herself whisked away in a memory, one where she and Babusya spent a lazy summer discovering the world.

Ionna loved that her mother was a biologist and her father a chemist. They brought home exciting stories from work, books about science from the libraries, microscopic slides to analyze with her child-sized scope, and experiments to perform in the kitchen sink that fizzed and changed colors. But what she loved the most about their jobs was it gave her so much time alone with her babusya.

At the young age of eight, Ionna understood *her* Babusya was not the same Babusya who made dinner for the family, went shopping for groceries, and cleaned the house. The family Babusya was stooped, slow to smile, and distant. Her movements were measured and mechanical, sort of like the robots her science class created with motors and metal parts.

But *her* Babusya? Her Babusya smiled widely, teeth showing all the way to the back of her mouth. Her laughter would rush out in a burst of happy noise that filled the room. When she had something important to show Ionna, like a new book, her eyes would dart quickly from right to left and back again, before pulling it out from behind her back, her efforts keeping some unknown spy from learning their secret.

Each day with Babusya was filled with surprises, secrets, treasures, and adventures. Which was why, when Ionna learned her mother would not have her usual time off during the summer months, she was not as unhappy as her mother had wanted her to be.

"Ionna, darling. I know this isn't what you want to hear, but the project at the university I've been working on has hit a snag. They need everyone involved to give it their best efforts, so I won't be able to reduce my hours to part-time this summer as usual."

She had anticipated sobs or at least a mournful expression and frowned as Ionna said, "Woo-hoo! I get a whole summer alone with Babusya!"

Her mother had turned quickly away, and her father had pulled Ionna close, whispering urgently, "You are hurting your mother's feelings. She wanted to be with you this summer. For goodness sakes, please don't be so rude."

Ionna hadn't meant to be rude. She loved her mother dearly, but a whole summer with babusya? Why should she be sad? However, she had dutifully gone to her mother and given her a hug. "I'm sorry, Mama. I didn't mean to make you sad. I will miss you this summer." But deep in her heart, she knew she wasn't telling the entire truth.

But now that summer was here, she didn't dwell on the tiny lie. Instead, she waited anxiously each morning for her parents to leave for work so that family Babusya would magically turn into her Babusya, like Clark Kent ducking into a phone booth and emerging as Superman.

Today, when superman Babusya appeared, she did so with a conspiratorial smile. "Do you know what I planned for today?" she had asked, looking quickly for spies as she did so. "We are going to hide among the sunflowers!"

It was nearing the end of July, and the sunflower fields at the edge of town had grown tall enough to dwarf both Ionna and her diminutive grandmother. "*In* the sunflower fields?"

They had often taken walks next to the fields, watching the sunflowers getting taller as the summer days moved by. Babusya had shown her how the flowers moved with the sun, their blooms bobbing toward the east in the morning sun and nodding to the west as the sun moved toward the horizon in the evening. But never had they gone among the sunflowers.

"Yes! We shall go into the field and lose ourselves

among the sunflowers, just as I did when I was a little girl."

Ionna had trouble imagining Babusya as a little girl with pigtails and suntanned arms being led into the fields by her own babusya. Her crinkled up eyes and hands on her hips caused Babusya to laugh uproarishly. "Yes, my little maslyuk" – buttercup – "I was once a little girl who went on little girl adventures. You may not be able to believe it now, but I was an expert tree climber, could run faster than all my brothers, and could hide among the sunflowers so well that I never once lost a game of hide and seek. Not once!"

She imagined her babusya high up in a tree, her black-shoed and stockinged feet swinging from a branch, and her gray skirt and white apron fluttering in the breeze. Her face cracked open, and she laughed along with her babusya as they made their way to the field.

Babusya had packed a lunch of kanapky, the thick spread of cream cheese holding tight to tiny bits of pickle, boiled egg, and cheese, as well as pampushki, the fried potato balls made so small she could pop a whole one into her mouth. She had even brought along the red-checkered tablecloth. "We will have a picnic right in the middle of the flowers, enjoying their shade and munching on their seeds for dessert."

Ionna was excited but a bit nervous. The sunflower fields were enormous, rolling over the hills until they faded away far in the distance. "What if we get lost, Babusya? What if we can't find our way back out?"

"Do not worry, my love. We will not go in so far that we cannot find our way back out." As they arrived at the edge of the field, Babusya said, "Before we go in, we just need to look where we are. But remember, when we are in the middle of the sunflowers, we won't be able to see much by swinging our heads side to side except a bunch of sunflower stalks. Instead, we'll find our way by looking up." She glanced up as she said this, and then said, "See where the sun is now? How it came up over there?" She pointed her finger toward a grove of birch trees. "If we follow along in the sky, the sun will eventually land over there." She pointed to a small barn with peeling white paint up on a distant hill. "The trees are to the east. The barn is to the west. So, where, Ionna, does that make the road?"

Ionna thought carefully. Her grandma had taught her a secret about directions. She pointed her right hand toward the trees and her left hand toward the barn. Her nose pointed toward the road they were standing on. "North!" shouted Ionna. "The road is to the north and the hills and hills of sunflowers are to our south!"

Babusya smiled warmly, proud that her granddaughter not only learned things quickly but held on to what she learned so tightly. "That's right. So, when we are in the field, all we need to do is remember that the sun will be moving to the west, put our left hand to the west, and follow our nose."

Ionna and Babusya wandered in and out of the rows of tall flowers. Ionna noted immediately that it was cooler among the flowers than it had been standing at the roadside as their long stalks and round, frilly heads cast shadows over them. While they bobbed along, always keeping within sight of the road, Babusya talked of her childhood, how she had played hide and seek among the flowers, how her parents had harvested the seeds, using them for food, oil, and medicine. They also used the beautiful petals to dye their wool and cotton yellow, making beautiful clothes and curtains, and threads for embroidery. They even used the stems, grinding some to make flour and soaking others to make paper.

"The sunflower is the national flower of Ukraine, Ionna. Did you know that?" Ionna nodded. She had learned that in school at the same time she learned the national bird is the white stork and the national tree is the willow.

"But do you know why?" When Ionna shrugged her shoulders, a frown pulling down the corners of her mouth, Babusya gently laid out the checkered cloth, pulled out the picnic and said, "Let me tell you while we eat."

Ionna was amazed at how much her babusya knew about sunflowers. Although there were sunflowers all over Ukraine, Babusya assured her that they were not native here. The seeds were brought to Ukraine by explorers who had been to what is now America. These seeds, along with others brought back from the foreign lands, like squash and blueberries and pecans, grew well here. Not only were they beautiful, and edible, but the people loved how the flowers followed the sun, dropping their gaze toward the ground in the evening. "They said, 'These flowers understand the importance of looking heavenward to find hope and then spending time each day looking down to reflect upon their lives.' Before long, you could find sunflowers everywhere, even in the winter!"

Ionna jerked upright, a pampushki missing her mouth and rolling to the edge of the blanket. As she scrambled to catch the errant ball and stuff it into her mouth, she mumbled around the treat, "Sunflowers in the winter, Babusya? You are teasing me!"

Babusya had smiled. "No, my love, I'm not teasing. Of course, during the deep snows, the flower's seeds lay dormant, waiting for the spring's warmth. But the Ukrainian people didn't want to wait for spring to behold the flowers again. So, they embroidered sunflowers on their clothes and carved sunflowers into their furniture. Store signs. Bed posts. Baby bonnets. Rugs. Sunflowers were everywhere."

Then Babusya grew quiet. "When Ukraine became part of the Soviet Union, that all changed. Ukraine was no longer a country on its own, but part of a greater whole. As comrades, we were no longer Ukrainians. We no longer had a nation, so we didn't have a national flower of our own. Nonetheless, many still held the sunflower in their hearts."

It was as her grandmother related this story that Ionna understood the difference between her Babusya and family Babusya. It was sadness.

Now, as Ionna came to the last block before reaching her home, she shook the memory from her mind, unable to imagine what life would be like without her babusya. No matter how many ways she shifted the pieces of her reality like a puzzle, she simply couldn't create an image that didn't include her grandmother. Every completed puzzle had Babusya smiling, cooking, waiting for her arrival after school just as did every single one of Ionna's memories. No, her babusya was not going to die. Still, that unknown fear ushered her forward.

Chapter 21

2006

Grief stung at her eyes, and a gaping hole stood in the place where her heart had been just days before. The emptiness of that ache was beyond anything she had experienced in her 12 years of life. As she walked toward the gravesite at the front of the procession, she wondered how she would survive the pain.

Despite the calendar declaring spring had sprung, the overcast day was cold and blustery, and the wind whipped around her black stockinged legs. Chilled and shivering, the weather appeared to understand her grief and had provided her with the perfect sensation for a day that would forever be linked to loneliness.

As they came to a stop near the gravesite, Ionna averted her eyes. She couldn't bear to think about the coffin, knowing one she so dearly loved lay inside. Instead, she focused on her mother, who allowed herself to cry freely, creating small puddles on her black trench coat before flowing, unheeded to the ground.

As of yet, Ionna had not wept in public. She was not ashamed of her grief, but it was too private to share with those who had come to the service. Aside from those closest to her, no one could begin to fathom the depths to which her aching fell, and she didn't have the energy to try to explain. Her plan was to hold her sorrow in check until she was home, in her own room, with her own thoughts. Then, she would continue to suffer as she had been doing for the last 48 hours.

Next, she glanced toward her father, standing stoically on her other side, his arm behind her with his hand resting gently on her mother's shoulder. Although he did not cry, she noted the creases on his face had deepened, giving the impression of a man much older than his years.

Finally, she let her gaze rest on the coffin. Babusya. Her beloved grandmother. She wanted to rush over to the horrid wooden box and unlatch the lid, hoping she would step out and yell, "Surprise!" to the startled attendees. This was nothing more than wishful thinking. She understood the permanence of death in theory, if not in practice. But she couldn't help but wonder if Babusya was really gone – forever.

She couldn't remember a single day, before now, in which her grandma hadn't been part of her life. She vaguely remembered the tiny house where she slept on a pallet on the floor of her parent's room and Babusya slept behind a screen in the living room. The night they had a sleepover, however, was very specific. Ionna had put on her best nightgown and taken her stuffed bear and a stack of books into Grandma's "room." Her intent was to sleep there all night, but her grandmother's loud snoring kept her from falling asleep. Her mother loved telling that tale on Babusya, who swore vehemently that she did no such thing.

Despite moving into the bigger house, where they each had their own room, Babusya remained a central figure in Ionna's life. She taught her songs, read her stories, made her snacks, and dressed her for church each Sunday.

When Ionna started school, Babusya was sure to make a special treat for her when she got home. Over cookies or cakes, Babusya would ask her all about her day and then they would begin preparing the meal for when her parents got home from the university, where both were working once again.

Ionna loved her parents with all her heart. But she and Babusya had an extraordinary connection that couldn't be explained in words. It was as if the older woman could read her thoughts and she hers, causing them to lock eyes and smile at one another in unison.

And now? The connection had been severed by this thing called death.

Her parents had tried to prepare her for the inevitable. But Ionna had wanted nothing to do with the conversation, believing in her little girl heart with her little girl faith that her babusya would live forever.

Yet, there she was. Dead. In a coffin. About to be lowered into the ground.

Her deep sadness was accentuated by her fury at God. The priest said, during the funeral, that Grandma was in a better place. Better? Better than being here with her granddaughter and family? He also said God needed Grandma, but He couldn't possibly need her more than her grandchild did, especially given the number of sincere prayers that had left her lips over this specific issue.

In her young, impressionable mind, God was a farce. A fake. At the very least, he was mean and didn't keep his promises. Hatred worked to fill up the empty space left by Grandma's passing, and for reasons she couldn't comprehend, this hatred left her all the more sad and lonely.

She couldn't concentrate on the words or prayers, her mind racing from pleasant memories to living a life without her grandmother and back again so quickly that her breath came in short gasps as if she had been running. Woodenly, she stepped forward to put a single rose on the coffin, as she was instructed, followed closely by her parents and then all those who braved the weather to give their respects.

And then, it was over. The finality of it almost wiped out her resolve to grieve privately as the tears threatened to spill. But Ionna had gotten her grandmother's stubborn streak, and she willed her eyes to contain the tears until they were secluded from sight in the car.

Finally, when no one was within sight, big, wet drops splashed to her lap, and she gladly fell into her mother's outstretched arms.

"It's okay, baby," her mother cooed. "It's all going to be okay."

Ionna wanted to believe her, but the triteness of the comment provoked her to anger. "Okay? How can you say everything is going to be okay and mean it? She is dead, Mother."

At the word 'dead,' Yevt flinched and Danya prepared to discipline his headstrong child, except that Yevt's hand waved him off. Her eyes said, "Let her talk. She needs to get this off her chest."

Ionna continued. "Dead, as in gone forever. Never coming back. And I cannot see a way for *that* to ever be okay."

Yevt's mind flashed back to Katrina who had saved her from herself all those years ago, and her immediate anger at "Everything turns out okay in the end. If it isn't okay, it isn't the end." She understood her daughter's anger and frustration. She was still too young to be able to see past the here and now to find an okay at the end. She also knew better than to share this piece of wisdom, knowing wisdom shared with someone not yet ready to hear it was useless, and could even make the situation worse. Her daughter needed to be heard.

"You are right, Ionna. I am sorry. It isn't going to be okay in the sense that Grandma is coming back. It isn't going to be the same without her at all. I guess, I meant to say, you will be okay. Yes, you will miss her. We will all miss her, but you most of all. Nonetheless, life goes on, and I assure you that you will be okay."

Her words did nothing to soothe Ionna's anguish, who, much like any preteen, pulled out of her mother's arms and lashed out with, "How would you know what I'm feeling? You have no idea. No idea at all."

Yevt sighed. She hadn't told the story of her father to anyone, not even Danya, but it seemed that today was the right day to do so.

Chapter 22

2006

Danya watched emotions flicker across his wife's grief-stricken face as their daughter lashed out about her not understanding. He loved his daughter unconditionally, but at times like these, times when her immaturity, combined with raging hormones, reared their ugly head to assault the two people on earth who would give her anything in the world, he didn't like her much.

Unpinching his lips and leaning slightly forward, Danya prepared to let Ionna know she had no right to talk to her mother that way. But before he could say a word, Yevt held up her hand to him, a signal that she was going to handle it.

He leaned back without relaxing and waited to see what Yevt would say. He was often amazed at her reasoning abilities with their young daughter, wishing he possessed the same skill. Although he was recognized on campus as a level-headed professor who debated issues without raising his voice or getting emotional, dealing with Ionna was a completely different matter. It seemed that within moments, he could feel his blood pressure rising, and, before he knew what was happening, angry words billowed forth from his mouth, Ionna stomped away angrily, and Yevt stared with wide eyes, wondering what had happened to her otherwise calm husband.

"What in the world, Danya? Why do you let her push your buttons like that? She is just a child expressing childish sentiments. Surely, you can see that?"

Yes, of course, he could see it, but only after the fact. Each time he exploded, he vowed to do better the next time. And each next time, he failed miserably. Yevt had begun the habit of stepping between them, both literally and figuratively, trying to keep the peace. Thus, the hand waving him off. Although grateful he had been given permission to let someone else handle the issue and be off the hook so he wouldn't have to, yet again, 'try harder next time,' he bristled a bit at his inability to be the adult in the situation.

He observed Yevt reach out her hand to stroke Ionna's cheek as the young girl flinched away, causing him to suck in a deep breath and Yevt to, once again, hold up her hand to him. Her eyes implored him to let her take the lead.

Forcing himself to sit back against the seat once again, he waited.

"Ionna, darling. I know you don't think I understand your pain. And it is true that I can't know exactly what you are feeling. However, I do know something of grief and loss. Have you ever wondered about Didus? Why Babusya was not married?"

Although Ionna still didn't look at her mother, Danya noted she had stilled and that her posture grew less rigid as she contemplated her mother's words.

"We never spoke of my batko because of the pain it brought to Maty, your babusya."

With that pronouncement, Ionna turned slightly, letting her eyes meet her mother's. Danya, too, watched intently, wondering how much of the story Yevt would tell. He knew little. Just that her father died when she was young, and her mother had to work very hard to keep them from starving. He had probed just once for more information, but the anguish in Yevt's eyes caused him to take back the question. He never brought it up again, and she never offered more information. In fact, she rarely spoke of him.

Her father's death was a turning point in her life, and one that obviously still caused her pain, but it was a pain she didn't share. He often considered the silence on the matter was to protect herself from further pain as much as it was to protect her mother.

Yevt closed her eyes and took a deep breath. "It is time for a story, Ionna – a story with years of pain and grief and sadness and deprivation. It is my story, which makes it your story, too."

Ionna was now fully engrossed, leaning in slightly, breathing in the words coming from her mother's lips.

And Yevt began, "Once upon a time, there was a little family living in Ukraine..."

Now, hours later, long after the sky darkened and Ionna was tucked into bed, he held Yevt whose body wracked with sobs. She was not only grieving the loss of her mother, but after 33 years, she was finally grieving the loss of her father.

She had begun her story with wonderful tales of a happy family who lived a modest life in the Soviet Ukraine. Danya learned many details about the man who was his father-in-law. His appearance, his actions, his laugh, and his capacity to love. He marveled at the breadth of memories from the eyes of a child not much younger than his own daughter. He wondered, if he were to die today, what Ionna might say about him three decades later. The thought made him grimace, given their current relationship. Once again, he vowed to do better.

Then the story took a turn for the worse. A day that started like others, except Batko was not there to say goodbye before she went to school. His work had taken him away early, so Yevt spent the day, happily learning her sums and reading and playing with friends – only to return to a new life – one devoid of a loving father and one that changed her mother forever.

She described, in minute detail, the weeks following her father's death. How her mother either cried or slept but nothing else. How it was young Yetti who received the news that since her father was gone and no longer an employee of the university, they would have to vacate the premises within three days. It was she who packed their belongings. It was she who led their mother out the front door, not knowing where they should go or how they would live.

During this portion of the story, Danya's heart squeezed tightly, and a sob caught at the base of his throat. How could such a young child bear such enormous pressures, all without the support of those she had counted on? He wanted to reach out and hold her, comfort her, but she was so filled with memories that she didn't even notice his hand on hers. He realized she was not in the car with him and their daughter, but far away in a tiny village, a scared, sad, young child with nowhere to turn.

Eventually, her mother regained some semblance of normalcy, but never again was the happy, carefree woman made of sunshine and warmth. She also never let Yevtsye speak of her father. "I tried to talk of him. I wanted to remember him. I loved him. He was my father. But Mama forbade any mention of his name, forbade any memories at all. So, I kept all my love and memories inside...until today."

"But why?" Ionna cried out. "Why did Babusya want you to forget him? Why did she forbid you from talking about him?"

With a sad smile, Yevt said, "Ah, but you are jumping ahead of the story, Ionna," before she continued as though never being interrupted.

Her descriptions of the deprivation were so vivid that Danya felt the gripping cold and his stomach squeezing in pain from lack of food. Despite her lack of similar experiences, he saw Ionna was feeling it, too. Her face had grown concerned and tender toward her mother, taking on a motherly appearance, wanting to protect her from the pain.

Finally, Yevt came to the schooling in the city. Danya had heard this story proudly pronounced many times by his mother-in-law. However, Yevt's story had a secret twist. Yes, she was summoned to take a test, but he had never been told of the interview which followed. Nor had anyone else, because Yevt never revealed it until that very moment.

"After finishing the test, I prepared to find my mother in the waiting area. But, before I could do so, a uniformed man ushered me into the office of the Superintendent of Educational Reform. Each child, I was told, must be 'vetted' to determine if they were truly a quality candidate for further schooling. As you can imagine, I was quite nervous, not understanding how they meant to 'vet' me."

The man behind the desk pulled out a thin, manila folder with her name written in bold, black, uppercase letters on the front. Inside were several sheets of official-looking papers that Yevt could not make out across the yawnng expanse of the desk.

"I see you are a good student, Comrade Rosomakha," he said while looking at one of the pages in her slim folder.

"Yes, comrade," Yevt nodded as she watched him turn the paper over and retrieve another from the file.

"And your mother? She works as a washer woman and cleaning woman?"

Once again, Yevt nodded in agreement, "Yes, comrade." With this pronouncement, the second sheet of paper was put on top of the first, as he held up a third paper for her to see.

"And your father? He is dead?"

Yevt flinched at the words, but said, "Yes, comrade."

Squinting at the paper, pulling it closer as if reading the contents for the first time, he said, "And he died a disgrace to your family?"

At this, Yevt stopped nodding. "No, comrade. He died doing something at work." Although her mother had never told her what had happened, she assumed whatever had taken her father to work early that morning had been the cause of his demise.

The Superintendent slowly straightened the paper and tapped it lightly with his knuckles, seeming to relish the next thing he was to say. "No, Comrade Rosomakha, he died in disgrace at the hand of his lover's husband who set fire to the home where your father made love to another woman."

Yevt stared in horror. Without realizing it, she began shaking her head, saying a silent no.

He spat out the next words, ridding his mouth of the distasteful things held in the file. "His actions left you and your mother homeless and penniless. If it weren't for the good fortune of your intelligence, it is a condition in which you would remain. This is certainly disgraceful, yes?"

Yevt had stared at him blankly, unable to connect the words of this stranger with the memories of her father that she held so dear.

Seeing that Yevt was unable or unwilling to agree, the Superintendent helped her understand what was required of her. "To be part of the program, Comrade Rosomakha, and surely you must want to be part of such a program, I insist you answer my question. You are a bright student, but there is more than aptitude involved in our careful selection. We want students who understand that truth is found within the Party and only within the Party. There can be no hesitation. And it says right here" – he tapped the paper with the official looking seal with his long, pointed finger – "your father was a disgrace. So, once again, Comrade Rosomakha, did your father die a disgrace to the family?"

In the dark recess of her mind where her father lived,

Yevt could not believe what she was hearing, no matter what the official paper said. However, she was old enough to understand the Superintendent's words. Denying the official report would ruin her chances at a better life, and though he had not said so in so many words, it could ultimately mean she and her mother would die, probably in some labor camp. At the young, delicate age of 14, just two years older than her own Ionna was now, Yevt became an adult and swore to Party allegiance. It was the first of many such lies over the years to come. "Yes, comrade, my father died a disgrace to his family."

Yevt continued her story, leaving out no details. Explaining her schooling, her job, meeting Danya, her inner hatred of the Party but her outward acquiescence, the rift with her mother, Ionna's birth, and even her battle with postpartum depression.

Finally, she said, "My father's death was not a good thing, in and of itself. But, in the end, it turned out okay. I got good schooling. By doing so, we were able to make it through some of the worst years of oppression by a communist government. I met your father. I discovered God and helped my mother to do the same. I had you."

With these words, she reached out and took Ionna's hands in her own. "I would do it all again to have you, my darling girl."

Holding her daughter's gaze firmly in her own, she stated, "And now, today, we buried my mother, your dear babusya. I know this looks no better on the outside than when my father died. We have been left alone without someone we love, which brings us pain – and yes, a pain I can understand."

Ionna had the grace to cast her eyes downward,

understanding how wrong her earlier words had been.

Yevt reached out and lifted her daughter's chin. "It will be okay, eventually, Ionna. Not today. Probably not tomorrow or the next day. But eventually, when you can look back, you will find everything has indeed turned out okay."

Part 3

IONNA

Chapter 23

2012

Ionna had permission from her parents to skip school on this day, the sixth anniversary of Babuysa's death. Although the first few months without her grandmother had been brutally difficult and filled with aches and sadness, Ionna's grief had lessened over time, just as her mother said it would.

However, on days like today, the day of her dear grandma's death, the grief had a way of sneaking out of the neat little box she had placed it in and consume her.

She missed her babusya every day, still hoping to find the older woman waiting for her in the kitchen after school, knowing full well that was never going to happen. And she still struggled with her faith in a God who was willing to take such a woman away. However, like the grief, her anger at God had subsided as well, and if nothing else, she was able to show some semblance of belief, praying at mealtime, attending church with her parents, even if the attitude didn't go all the way to her heart.

As she sat by Babusya's grave where she had placed a small bouquet of flowers, she considered what her grandmother would say about the last six years. Ionna had grown two inches in the same year that her grandmother died, but nothing since. Her hair was still chestnut brown, and her brown eyes were still rimmed with a more golden hue. Physically, nothing much had changed. However, Ionna was no longer a little girl and was in her last year of schooling before beginning university.

Hugging her knees to her chest, she began talking to Babusya, as she did every year.

"Hi, Babusya. It's me, Ionna." She mentally scoffed at herself. Of course, it was she, Ionna. Who else would call her Babusya? But she couldn't come up with any other way to start the conversation, so she continued.

"It's me, Ionna. I'm here to visit again today. I wanted to tell you about my year and my plans. I think you'll be happy – for the most part." She added in this bit because she and her grandmother would not see eye-to-eye about God, and she wanted to be truthful with the woman who meant so much to her.

"I'm doing well in school. I'm taking an extra literature course this year to get ready for university in the fall." Ionna had inherited her mother and father's intelligence. She loved school and excelled at whatever she put her mind to. Though she did well in science, even the harder courses like chemistry and physics, she was not drawn to these intellectual endeavors the way her parents were. Instead, she was drawn to books.

She smiled at the thought. She couldn't remember a time when books were not part of her life, and her father confirmed that memory regularly. "You would stand at the bookshelf with one tiny hand on a tiny hip and contemplate which of your many board books you would choose. Of course, the final choice never really mattered because by the end of the day, each book had been read to you at least twice!"

Of course, as she grew older, so did her book selections, and she and her grandma would often pick a book with many chapters and take turns reading to one another each afternoon after school. Once Grandma died, Ionna continued the tradition of reading after school, sometimes reading out loud in hopes that Grandma might be able to hear her from heaven – but only on days when she happened to believe in heaven.

Right before finishing Level II of Middle School, she decided to try her hand at writing and worked hard over summer break so she could get a position on the school newspaper. Becoming part of the staff was highly unusual for a first-year Level III student, but Ionna was not one to let something 'highly unusual' get in her way. And it didn't. Ionna started Grade 9 as a junior reporter.

Although she enjoyed writing for the paper, she quickly determined that journalism was not what she wanted. What she wanted more than anything else was to be a novelist – to create stories that grandmothers and granddaughters could read together after school. This goal pushed her to excel in her studies so she could eventually go on to university.

"The literature class is American Literature, Babusya. We are studying great American authors – in English!"

Although not uncommon to study English in school, taking a class other than English Language in anything other than Ukrainian was. But, given the American Literature was written in English, English was the predominate language of the class.

Prior to the class, Ionna would have said she was quite proficient in the English language. She always did well in her classes and believed she could easily carry on a conversation with someone whose first language was English. Once her literature class began, however, her assessment changed. The class was difficult, and the vocabulary was immense. She spent more time with her Ukrainian to English dictionary than she did with the book she was supposed to study. Even reading small sections of text was laborious and time-consuming.

Nonetheless, she persevered and was now actually thriving. She noted with pride that her English vocabulary had grown considerably.

They were currently reading a book by the author John Steinbeck called the *Grapes of Wrath*, set in the Great Plains of America during the Depression. She pulled the paperback out of her backpack, and said, "Let me read a bit to you, Grandma. 'In the roads where the teams moved, where the wheels milled the ground...'"

She chose to start at the beginning, though what she read didn't matter since Grandma didn't speak more than a handful of words in English. Yet, it was important to her that Grandma hear her read the story. She believed if there was a heaven, and today was a day in which having a heaven was more important than usual, that language wouldn't be an issue. Maybe Grandma had an interpreter or an excellent English to Ukrainian dictionary. Or maybe, her love for Ionna would make anything said comprehensible.

Once she finished Chapter 1, she put the book down, knowing she was putting off the inevitable, but not wanting to mar an otherwise perfect morning with a topic sure to cause contention. But she had always been honest with her babuysa and wasn't going to stop doing so now.

She took a deep breath, and then, before she could lose her nerve, blurted out, "I'm still not so sure about God, Babuysa."

She waited a long while before continuing, hoping her grandmother would intercede in some way, making the conversation easier. But she just sat in silence with thoughts swirling through her head.

"See, it's faith. The whole idea of believing something you cannot know for a fact seems a lot like pretend, doesn't it, Grandma? I mean, Mom and Dad are scientists. They must have proof and facts to do their job. So, I don't understand why we can't have proof and facts for religion. It would make the whole business of faith so much easier, don't you think?"

She had a similar conversation with her mother, who let out a chuckle before answering in the affirmative. "Yes, Ionna, you are absolutely right. Faith would be easier if we had proof and facts, except for one small detail – proof is not faith."

She went on to explain that faith was the ability to take a step forward in the dark believing that God had a plan for you. "If you step forward with facts and proof, you possess knowledge. And knowledge is a great thing, but knowledge isn't what God is seeking from us. He wants us to learn faith. To be able to move forward despite having no proof. Do you understand what I mean?"

Ionna understood the words but couldn't quite grasp the concept or the reason why this was so important. Why would an all-knowing God need someone like Ionna to 'step into the dark' without proof when He could so easily provide what she needed to be certain?

As she explained these words to Babuysa, she wondered how she had come to believe in God. Babuysa, and her parents, for that matter, had grown up in Soviet Ukraine and religion wasn't tolerated. And Mama had explained that Babuysa hadn't always been a believer – Ionna helped change her mind. Though she had no memories of doing so, Babuysa often told her the story.

———————

"After my epiphany in the hospital – that's a fancy way of saying that I understood something I hadn't before – I started questioning my position on God and religion. I wasn't ready to attend church with your mama and papa, but the kinship I experienced with a father-like God who watched over me was comforting.

"I also believed that my parents naming me God's gift was a sign. They didn't do things lightly, so I was confident that the choice was purposeful.

"But believing in God wasn't easy for me. I had all those years of communism that sowed weeds of doubt. And despite knowing that the Party wasn't going to rise again, I was having trouble letting that go.

"Plus, religion nearly tore your mother and I apart. Can you believe that we spent over a year without speaking to one another?"

Ionna had trouble comprehending this. Her mama and

babuysa were so close. "Why, Babuysa? Why would God do that to you?"

"It wasn't God, dear one. It was me. And your mama. But in those early years, I wondered the same thing. In my mind, the church caused my pain, so could such a church be true?"

At this question, Ionna would always say, "Yes, Babuysa! Yes, it can be true!"

Smiling at her earnest young granddaughter, she would continue, "I would sometimes go to services with the family. I said it was to be with you, but I was hoping to learn something. Most of the time, I arrived home more bewildered than when I left. However, I did see others in the congregation who found such contentment.

Then she would go on to explain that one Sunday after she had attended church, her mama wanted to talk.

"I was afraid. Your mama said it was important and made me promise to not allow what she said to hurt our relationship. Then, she asked something so big." Babusya held her arms out to the side, stretching as far as possible while wiggling the ends of her fingers.

"What did she ask? What did she ask?" giggled the excited Ionna despite knowing the story by heart.

"She asked me if she could have a real Ukrainian wedding in a church even though she was already married. Apparently, your papa promised her. Can you believe she asked me that? Even though having a wedding was the very thing that caused us to be angry at one another.

"At first, I wanted to say no. But then I remembered how much I loved your mother. I remembered how much I wanted her happiness. So, I said, 'Yes, my daughter. I can, but it doesn't mean I believe in your God.'"

The next few weeks, according to Babusya, were hectic though the ceremony was small with just family and a few close friends. Despite protests, her mama had worn all the traditional wedding clothing, including the headpiece for single women.

And, as tradition dictated, her babusya demanded more ransom for her daughter. "She is worth more than all the gold and rubies in all Ukraine. This ransom unacceptable." She and Danya haggled until Babusya decided the amount was just right, and then the ceremony continued.

"Your mama had been looking forward to seeing who stepped on the rushnyk first. She intended to be the one who had the final say in their marriage even if she had to cheat to make it happen. Ironically, neither she nor your papa got that honor. Instead, you squirmed out of my arms and ran full tilt toward the canopy. Before anyone could stop you, you stepped on the rushnyk. To this day, you have the final say!"

Although that was the funny part of the story, Babuysa would always become contemplative as she related the rest. "I'm not sure why, Ionna, but seeing you there, with your mama and papa, a pretty white dress and a basket of flowers over one arm...I just knew. I knew God was real. I knew I could find Him in that church. I knew I would believe from that day on. I just knew."

If understanding the truth was as simple as going to a wedding, Ionna wouldn't be struggling. She had been to several weddings and didn't feel anything related to God.

She placed her hand on the gravestone and blew a kiss to Babuysa. Then, Ionna marched home determined to figure out faith and learn how her parents and grandmother had gained an understanding of this elusive concept.

Chapter 24

2012

Although Yevt still worked at the university, budget cuts reduced her hours to two days per week. She continued to be grateful that Danya's hours rarely fluctuated, and his paycheck was rarely late. She had to admit she missed the extra money, but she honestly didn't miss the work.

She was getting older and would be turning 50, half a century, in little more than a year. Although she wasn't ready to haul out the knitting needles and rocking chair, she was ready to slow down a bit and try to enjoy these last years with Ionna, who would shortly become a university student, and likely where her father was not a professor and her mother a researcher.

She had trouble imagining what their house, already oversized for the three of them, would feel like when it housed only Danya and herself. Unlike in times past, they were no longer required to give up their housing as their family situation changed. Their home was truly their home – something they purchased a few years before her mother died.

She laughed at the memory of her mother's eyes when they told her they were buying the house they were currently renting.

"Buy? A house? You mean, you'll own it?" Ivonna had said in utter amazement. She had owned very little in her life and had been able to move into Yevt's home all those years ago with only two boxes of things, so the idea of owning a home was almost beyond comprehension.

Yevt was proud of the home they had created. She spent hours in the garden areas, creating beautiful spots of color and texture. She had seen enough stark, cold, ugliness to last a lifetime and wanted no reminders of a time when beauty was forbidden. Now, as she glanced around her yard, she felt peace and tranquility and hoped this was a feeling she eventually passed on to her young daughter.

The thought of Ionna brought an immediate smile, followed closely by a small grimace. Ionna's teenage years had not been easy. It was true that the moodiness was more controlled, but her incessant questions and demand for answers left Yevt weary – especially those on religion.

Just last week, Ionna had demanded yet another explanation of faith and how to find it. She wanted the details of how her mother and grandmother came to gain faith and expected an answer like, "Well, darling, we went down to the market, went to the Faith store, and purchased a cupful." When she learned that finding faith was a journey which took time and work and required that a person try it out to discover its truthfulness, Ionna looked dubious.

"Why does finding faith have to be so difficult? Why can't I just get faith and move on?"

Yevt had been willing to try to explain, but she realized the questions were far more rhetorical in nature when Ionna flounced out of the room mumbling about the craziness of it all.

What would her days be like when Ionna moved away? Quiet was the first word that came to mind, and then lonely. Without realizing where this questioning would lead, Yevt found herself an observer as she told her own mother she was getting married and felt the pangs of loneliness hit her mother's heart at the pronouncement. Despite her hard exterior during those years, Yevt knew how much her mother loved her, so knowing her daughter would be leaving soon must have hit her hard. And then, came the unbidden thought, "She probably also worried that all husbands were bound to find another's bed."

Tears fell unbidden from her eyes. Ever since she finally released the story of her father's death, thoughts of him quickly turned to sorrow and regret.

She was angry with herself for saying he was a disgrace to their family, though, if the story was true, then he was most certainly a disgrace. But despite the document and the years and her mother's belief that he had betrayed her, Yevt just couldn't bring herself to believe the accusation.

Naiveté was not usually one of her characteristics, but when it came to her father, a child's belief in the goodness of fathers seemed to be the one in charge of the conversation. She had seen the official paper, so what she had been told must be true, right?

"Prove it," the voice echoed in her head. What had she actually seen? A piece of paper that, to a frightened 14-year-old, appeared official. The man had never put the paper in her hands. It could have said anything and been about anybody.

"But why would he do it? What did he have to gain from lying to me?" He needed me to toe the Party line. Maybe he discerned something in me before I recognized it in myself. Maybe this was the first lesson in my indoctrination."

"Prove it," she heard again.

She swiped at the air trying to erase these circular thoughts. This line of questioning was not new to Yevt. At least once a week, she would argue with herself about her father and his death. In the end, each time, she came up with the same problem – no proof either way and no way to find it.

Determined to rid her mind of these thoughts, she began to pull weeds with gusto, willing time to pass by quickly so Ionna would come home. She preferred her daughter's exasperating questions to the ones running rampant in her own mind.

───────────

Danya's last two classes of the day had been canceled due to a fire in one of the other labs. He had no doubt a student had started the blaze hoping to get out of a lecture or test and was disgusted the ruse had worked. However, he didn't fault the administration for their decision. The smoke had been thick, and the acrid odor permeated all six floors of the building. He suspected that even tomorrow, the stench would be almost unbearable.

When he got home, Yevt was pulling weeds at a furious rate, flinging them overhead into a pile on the sidewalk which created a square border around the foundation of the house. He wondered what had gotten her into such a foul mood.

Glancing at his watch, he knew the reason behind the weed flingling couldn't be something Ionna said or did, at least not anything in the past few hours. She had been at school since early morning and wasn't due to arrive for another hour or so. The electricity between the two women in the house was palpable, even to strangers.

He realized, with a start, that time had changed things considerably. Not so long ago, Yevt was the calming influence whenever Ionna pushed his buttons. Now, the tables had turned.

Walking stealthily into the house so as not to disturb the maniacal weeding and the mood that was sure to go along with it, he wondered at the changes between mother and daughter. Oh, they still loved one another fiercely, but small, inconsequential statements by either mother or daughter could turn into something closer to a mountain than a molehill.

Yet, with him, she was all sweet sugar and smooth honey. She would talk with him for hours about his lectures and her studies at school. She sought his opinions about universities and majors. She had even gone back to holding his hand when they took their Sunday walks after church. The closer the two of them got, the more estranged the girls became.

He doubted the reason was jealousy on Yevt's part. He and Ionna, minus those few short preteen years, had always been closely connected. Perhaps they were just too much alike. Not physically. Ionna's appearance came most definitively from his side of the family. But in thoughts and emotions? She was her mother's twin. "It is really no wonder they constantly challenge one another, quibbling over the smallest issues," he mused.

Of course, there was an added dimension to the problem – his daughter had yet to learn socially appropriate tact. He cringed at the thought of a recent conflict between the two. While eating dinner, Ionna made a declarative statement. "When I grow up, I don't think I'm going to marry."

He had smiled to himself, knowing this sentiment was not unusual for a child of her age. Without real interest, and more to say 'mmhmmm' than anything else, Yevt asked, "Oh? Why is that, dear?" Danya wasn't even sure his wife's mind was on the conversation. But her inattentiveness didn't last long. Ionna's next statement hit the kitchen like a nuclear blast.

"I don't want to end up like Babuysa who had a cheat for a husband and left her stranded to make it on her own."

Yevt's head jerked upright, and daggers appeared where her eyes had been just moments before. With quiet precision, each word emphasized, each becoming its own sentence, she responded, "Do. Not. Ever. Say. That. Again."

Danya's eyes flew to his daughter's bewildered face. Could she really be so naïve? "Why? Isn't adultery a good reason to stay single?" she said as she shoveled in another mouthful of supper while waiting for a discussion on the merits of marriage.

A bit louder, but with the same staccato of words, Yevt said, "My. Father. Was. Not. A. Cheat. Not." And with that, she stormed from the room.

Knowing he needed to go comfort his wife, Danya still took at moment to ask, "Why in the world would you say that to your mother?" to which Ionna replied, "It's true, isn't it? Mama told me so on the day Babusya was buried. What's the big deal?"

"The big deal is that your mother loves her father, despite any of his faults, and it is insensitive to bring up those faults to your mother or about a man who is not here to defend himself. I thought I had taught you better than to be so unkind and so rude. Please excuse yourself from the table and go to your room. I'll join you there later for further discussion." And with that, he had gone to his wife.

To say she was inconsolable was an understatement. It wasn't so much the idea that her father had cheated on her mother. It was that she had bared her soul to help her daughter through a difficult time, only to have this difficult part of her life thrown back in her face. Had it been up to her, this 'insolent and impertinent daughter' would have been grounded for the rest of her life, leaving her thoughts on marriage inconsequential.

She was right. Their daughter had been more than a little impolite, but he didn't think she fully comprehended the impact of her words. When he tried to say so, Yevt exploded.

"Not understand? Did you see the brazen look on her face as she oh-so-casually threw that remark at me?"

Danya hadn't been looking at their daughter as she spoke but had seen the bewilderment cross her face at the response. If she had tried to provoke her mother, surely, she would have looked satisfied rather than surprised.

"Look at you!" Yevt had snarled. "Taking her side again. Your precious daughter who can do no wrong. Well, mister, this was wrong. And you are wrong." She turned to face the wall, refusing to continue the conversation.

After sitting there, silently, long enough to let Yevt know he was not leaving in an angry huff, he said gently, "I'm sorry she hurt you. She was insensitive and rude. I will go speak to her now."

The conversation with his daughter was long and arduous. She couldn't grasp why stating the truth was so bad. Finally, he said, "Before opening your mouth, you should analyze what you want to say against these three statements. Is it true?"

Before he could go on, she said emphatically, "But I did speak the truth!"

"Let me finish," he said calmly but firmly. "Is it true? Is it kind? Is it necessary?" He stopped and let all three conditions sink in.

"So, in terms of this conversation with your mother about marriage, what you said meets the first criteria, at least as far as we understand the circumstances. But was it kind?"

"Well, I guess since Mom still loves her dad, what I said could be seen as unkind...but it isn't how I meant it," she said, not sounding quite as sure of herself.

"And let's not forget the last criteria. Is it necessary?" He looked at her again. "Do you think bringing up your grandfather's indiscretions to get your point across was necessary, or could you have done so in a less hurtful way?"

Ionna let her face droop between her shoulders, the

tears slipping down her cheeks. "I wasn't trying to hurt Mama. I had just been thinking that marriage was hard and doesn't always turn out well. Since I had also been thinking about how much I missed Babuysa, I thought of her marriage."

Danya put his arm around his daughter, "In which case, when your mama asked you why you didn't want to marry, you could have left it at 'marriage seems to be hard and doesn't always turn out well.' There was no need to bring in something so personal. Do you see?"

"Yes, Papa. I do see. I'm sorry. I'll go tell her I'm sorry."

Danya quickly put out his hand. "It's not a good idea right now. Your mama has been hurt, so she probably won't be able to accept an apology yet. But I have an idea. You want to be a writer, so why don't you write your apology? Give it to me before you let your mother see the letter. I'll help you stay on the right track without saying something that could be taken as unkind or unnecessary."

Ionna sniffled. "Thank you, Papa. I'll go write the letter immediately."

She spent the better part of the evening crafting an apology letter that Danya found no reason to alter. She had clearly understood his words, and he hoped such an event never happened again.

Although Yevt had accepted the apology and life moved on, Danya still noted a coolness between the two. Which was why he hoped her weed pulling was unrelated to his daughter, her actions, or her words. The longer the two went without a blowout, the more likely it was that his wife would be able to truly let the incident go.

Yevt walked into the kitchen, breaking his reverie. "Hi, sweetheart! I didn't know you were home." As he told her the circumstances of his early arrival, he studied his wife for the telltale signs that she was upset, but he didn't find any. She kissed him lightly on the top of his head, saying, "Well, let me get dinner started. Did you want potatoes, potatoes, or potatoes?"

And then laughed a tinkling laugh when he said, "Um, I think I'll go with potatoes."

Chapter 25

2012

Lyaksandro walked briskly home from the lecture series he was attending on the psychology of happiness. He had always loved learning as a child and as a young man and had rediscovered his desire to expand his mind with new thoughts and concepts once he had finally found space in his psyche for the death of his wife and daughter and his direct hand in it.

Over the past 20 years, he had taken free courses, listened to lectures, watched documentaries, and had begun listening to podcasts, though he preferred the interaction from in-person encounters. His interests were broad and included literature, sociology, anthropology, history, physics, and, as of late, psychology.

For years, he had avoided psychology, concerned that something he learned would shake loose the tenuous peace he had created within his mind. And there was always the fear of discovery. He imagined sitting in a lecture hall, the professor armed with a doctorate, theories, and insights, explaining something about the nature of people. A brightly lit arrow would pop up directly over his seat, pointing in his direction. Staring, the professor would say, "You, in the dark suit," and aim a slim finger at a spot between his eyes. He would slide down in his seat, lowering his head into his shoulders like a turtle trying to escape danger, but she would continue to point. "Yes, you. The incredibly shrinking man." Everyone in the class would begin to laugh and strain in their seats to get a better view of the spectacle. "You, my dear sir, are a coward. Aren't you?" And then with more fierceness, more intensity, more derision, her finger stabbing with each word, "Aren't you?"

He began the pursuit of psychology quite accidentally and in the privacy of his home. He had discovered a documentary exploring the ways grief was expressed in different cultures of the world. The focus had been on grief following the death of a loved one, but also touched on the burial practices and the emotional significance of grieving. The three-part, six-hour series had explored the merits of keening and wailing, the differences between somber burials and jubilant parties ushering the dead on to the next life, the wearing of specific apparel to signify a mourner's loss, the tearing of clothes, the smoking of pipes, the covering of mirrors. It had been fascinating. And frightening.

The documentary had pulled at tiny threads in his mind, each attached to how he had dealt with his own losses. He identified with the keening, remembering the discordant sounds escaping his lips in that room so long ago. He was in awe at those who sent loved ones on with dancing and music and feasting. It had been years before he felt anything akin to happiness, and to this day, he wondered if he would ever again experience true joy. He had considered his own mourner's apparel – filthy clothes, matted hair, crazed eyes – and wondered at the ease of black clothing.

Those six hours began a quest, though painful with memories, had helped him get to a place of rest, if not actual peace.

During this process of discovery, he had come to hate the term 'moved on' when discussing the healing process after the death of a loved one. He found these words to be trite and patently false.

'Moving on' suggested some unnatural ability to put those he had negligently killed in some box he kept in the back of the guest closet, forget they ever existed, and start afresh. Lyaksandro had no such ability, nor did he feel he deserved the reprieve it might bring him. Instead of 'moving on,' he saw it as a moving through, like an expert swimmer caught in a riptide who understood when to swim and when to just let the current take him away.

And now, ironically, he had progressed to the psychology of happiness. Today was the first day, and the professor spent a long time on the history of this field of study and the many different constructs. But the most important thing Lyaksandro had learned was that happiness was more than experiencing a positive mood. Happiness had to do with how people evaluated their lives.

This tiny tidbit of information had almost been an afterthought, a mere parenthesis in the scheme of the lecture, but it held the truth Lyaksandro had known instinctively. The truth he had lived every day for the last 29 years.

For those first several months after learning the KDB had taken Ivanna and Yevtsye, likely minutes after he snuck out of his home for the last time, Lyaksandro swam against the violent currents of his grief, exhausting himself and getting nowhere. He fought against the waves, sucked in great gulps of water that burned his lungs, begged to drown. He rarely let his mind go back to those months, but when he did, he could only retrieve small packets of memories, as if the days, months, weeks had shattered into tiny fragments, and when finally glued back together, the empty spaces held more significance than the memories.

His handlers had not left him completely alone, though they could have stood by to watch the implosion without any worry of repercussion. No one knew him or that he was in the country. That they stood by him showed something of the character of the organization in which he had ensconced himself, though nothing of his own character. They had done what they could for his family, and then they did the same for him. For this nicety, he experienced both thankfulness and hatred.

Had they not brought food or insisted on at least some modicum of self-care, he would have died. Of course, that was what he wanted. He still harbored a fantasy which used to haunt him daily, even hourly, of his last night in Ukraine, but now only surfaced when he recognized an important date – a birthday, an anniversary, the date of their deaths – or when he considered a milestone Yevt would be achieving if she had lived – graduation, marriage, the birth of a child.

The fantasy was one in which he would valiantly say, "I will never leave my wife and daughter. If they are not leaving, I am not leaving." Then he would have closed his eyes, the barrel pressed ever more slightly against his skull as the man's finger squeezed the trigger, heard a rush of air, and before the sound of the explosion could even reach his ears, nothing.

But Lyaksandro, as he learned, was a coward and did exactly what a coward would do. He ran. He protected himself while leaving those he loved to fend for themselves. Never mind that they were likely dead or worse, being tortured until they died, when he made the decision. The truth of their situation didn't matter because he had chosen to save his life with the naiveté of a fool believing the Soviet machine would say, "Ah, Comrade Rosomakha has made a grave error in judgment, spying for the rebels. But surely, he said nothing to his wife and child. Surely, he kept all this to himself. In this one case, just this one, we shall let them live."

But he was more than a mere fool. His simpleminded belief that his silence, his lies of omission, would be enough to keep his family safe, was rash and reckless. He had killed his wife and child as surely as if he had encircled their soft, white throats and squeezed.

And now, Lyaksandro lived each day completely aware of who he was and what he had done. It didn't matter that he had a new name. It didn't matter that he had a new biography which didn't include spying, a wife, a child, or an escape from the country he loved. It didn't matter that those who knew him now would pronounce upon him adjectives such as kind, charming, intelligent. It didn't matter that he went to lectures and learned about happiness. He, Lyaksandro Hadeon Rosomakha, would always know the truth and swim with the weight of that truth into precarious currents that tortured but never drowned him.

Chapter 26

2013

Yevt moved about the kitchen listening to the heated conversation between father and daughter. She was delighted to have Ionna home from school. Although she had hoped Ionna would stay close by, her daughter chose a school, H.S. Skovoroda Kharkiv National Pedagogical University, nearly seven hours from their home.

The school was renowned for their courses in the arts and literature and was a perfect fit for a young lady who wished to pursue a writing career. Of course, learning that one of her favorite contemporary authors, Serhiy Zhadan, not only graduated from there but was often a guest lecturer did much to sway her decision.

This did not go over well with her father, who did not think highly of a man willing to write about the disillusionment brought on by the collapse of the Soviet

216

Union. "What is he trying to prove?" he had asked his daughter. "Rather than write about how people are unhappy with how things are turning out, why not DO something about it?"

Ionna had responded with, "Writing is doing something, Papa. He is showing that breaking away from the USSR wasn't all happiness and roses. That Ukraine isn't perfect. That our country still needs to evolve."

Danya had snorted. "Of course, the transition hasn't been all roses and happiness. It doesn't take a writer to help people understand. Hell, I lived it. And he seems to be just a bit too cozy with Russians if you ask me, as if he might want to create a bigger bed with them. Why else would his works be so popular they'd make Russia's National bestseller list?"

Danya had never given up his hatred of Russians, so anything or anyone who appeared to glorify the nation or the people in any way caused him to explode in anger. In the end, Danya gave in, realizing the school was a perfect fit for her desired occupation and determining that Zhadan's influence would be limited given he hadn't taught there in a decade.

As she listened to them argue, she wondered if Danya had simply not considered how close the school was to the Russian border when he agreed, or if he didn't assume the proximity would matter since the school was in Ukraine. Either way, his lack of foresight caused loud outbursts each time their daughter came home from school.

"Papa," she exclaimed in exasperation. "You are so old-fashioned. There is nothing wrong with being a Russian. I have lots of Russian friends. I have even dated a few Russian boys."

Yevt poked her head in the room before Danya died from apoplexy. "It's time to eat, you two. No political talk at the table." Then, she caught her daughter's eye and mouthed the words, "True. Kind. Necessary." She and Danya had eventually discussed their daughter's rude comments about her grandfather, as well as Danya's lecture. At the time, Yevt believed she had gotten off lightly, but she readily admitted this three-pronged analysis had helped her daughter stay more within bounds.

This time, however, based on the broad smile and twinkle in her eyes, Yevt understood the last comment about the friends and the boys was calculated – not a faux pas. She swatted her daughter as she passed and wondered if they would make it through the Spring Break without irreparable damage.

Despite her insistence that politics not be brought to the dinner table, Danya simply couldn't let the conversation drop. It seemed his daughter was being indoctrinated, and he wasn't going to let that happen without a fight.

"I will concede," Danya said, with some consternation, "that not all Russians are bad. Our friend Katrina, for instance, is of Russian heritage." He had learned this fact during one of Katrina's visits when Ionna was still a young child. He had been angry at some recent Ukrainian-Russian agreement, and without considering his guest's political stance, ranted and raved, much to his later chagrin, about the lunacies of partnering with the Russians on anything – anything at all.

"Why would Ukraine submit themselves once again to the likes of the Russians? We know what they did in the past. We know what they will do in the future. People don't change, not really. There simply isn't one Russian I would ever befriend. Not one. They aren't to be trusted."

Yevt had been irritated with the tirade since they had a guest but would caution Danya about airing his views in front of guests once they were alone. However, she never got the chance. Instead, Katrina stood, quietly, and gathered her hat and coat. Then in a soft voice without any recrimination, she said, "I'll be on my way home, Danya. I wouldn't want to be the reason someone called you a hypocrite."

Bewildered, he tried to understand how Katrina's presence in his home could be seen as hypocritical by anyone. Then, a thought shot into his head like a bolt of lightning and thundered in his ears. "Katrina is a Russian."

Danya had the good graces to apologize and mean it. Katrina had the good graces to accept his apology, remove her jacket, and resume her visit as though he had never uttered those words. For weeks after that visit, Danya didn't mention Russians at all. Eventually, he made peace with his ideals, believing some Russian people were decent human beings, but not as a nation. However, he rarely mentioned this to anyone other than his family.

Like today, as he argued with his daughter. "However, as a whole, as a nation, they are bad for Ukraine." Then he went into a lengthy explanation, trying to help his daughter to understand why foreign relations with Russia was like sleeping with the devil.

"Russia hasn't wanted Ukrainian sovereignty from the very beginning. They've been contesting our freedom since we claimed independence before you were born. The only reason, and I mean the ONLY reason Yeltsin agreed to our independence was doing so was the only way for him to defeat Gorbachev. Unless the 1922 Union Treaty was dissolved, Gorbachev would remain in power. Ukrainian President Kravchuk insisted the new treaty gave every state veto power rather than creating some kind of confederation. Yeltsin gave in, but he wasn't happy."

Ionna sighed. "Papa, that was years ago. Years. What difference does it make now, a quarter of a century later that Yeltsin didn't want Ukrainian independence? We enjoy our freedom, don't we?"

Yevt watched with some amusement as her husband's face tightened and grew a few shades more red. "This," he said, jabbing his finger on the table, "is why youth should not vote. They have no idea about how the history of this country affects current foreign relations which affects such things as what is available for dinner."

Ionna rolled her eyes, stabbing the boiled cabbage roll and popping the bit of holubtsi into her mouth. "I've taken plenty of history, Papa. And I read the news. I know what is happening."

"No, no you do not." He put down his fork and continued to explain the relations between Russia and Ukraine since 1991.

"From the beginning, Russia wanted us to concede our military, our nuclear weapons, and our monetary policy to the CIS. But we weren't so stupid. We knew the CIS would give too much power to Russia and leave us with nothing. A nation cannot be sovereign without a military and without money."

Yevt had the same opinions held by her husband, though not with the same passion. She remembered the years of the USSR and believed that granting such powers to the Russians through the CIS would be doing nothing more than creating another USSR-type government that would do nothing for her country. Yet, she also knew that their insistence of having their own currency led to the hyperinflation that left a majority of Ukraine starving about the time Ionna was born. She would never forget taking sacks of money to the store in hopes of buying a loaf a bread.

"And don't get me started on Crimea," Danya was saying. This was another of his favorite topics when proving to others that Russia was nothing more than a power-hungry nation. "I'll never forget the insolence of Yeltsin, stating, 'The Black Sea Fleet was, is and will be Russia's. No one, not even Kravchuk will take it away from Russia.' The balls of that man, thinking he could come in and take Crimea from Ukraine by passing resolutions and trying to starve us of gas to get what they wanted." Yevt was surprised he didn't turn his face to the side and spit for emphasis. "To this very day, Russians still say Sevastopol is a Russian city, despite signing treaties stating otherwise."

Ionna could not sit and listen without interjecting. "But Papa, who cares that some Russians think the Crimea belongs to them? It doesn't. Ukraine has the region, don't we?"

Danya, working hard to control his temper and treat this discussion like a college lecture, lowered his voice a decibel and took on the tone of a professor. "Tension about our independence has existed every day from our declaration to the present because, fundamentally, Russia believes its role is one of protector over everyone else, and this protection comes at the expense of everyone else's freedom. You can see this in how they have dealt with NATO over the years and with the EU."

Ionna couldn't take any more debate. She was on break and hadn't really wanted to fight with her father about Russia. She wasn't pro-Russian. She just wasn't anti-Russian. "You win, Papa. Russians want to take over Ukraine and always have. There, I said it. Does that make you happy?"

"It would...if you actually believed what you said," he stated.

———

The rest of Ionna's break was pleasant. They discussed a myriad of topics from Western literature to the role of the written word in civilization to the latest styles to boys. Based on Ionna's detailed descriptions of the latter, Yevt assumed her desire to remain single the rest of her life had been a passing whim and not a permanent stance.

For the most part, politics didn't enter the conversation, and when it did, the subject was short-lived. Yevt did wonder if Ionna was becoming a bit too comfortable with Russian ways and people. Living so close to the border, she met many more Russian-Ukrainians who still spoke Russian around the dinner table and felt Ukraine was making a mistake by its consideration to join the EU. On the other hand, Yevt had always believed one couldn't hold a nation's policies against any individual living in that nation, or in this case, against someone with that heritage. However, she would be glad when Ionna's Russian Civ and Literature combination class ended, thinking the influence of such a class might be too strong.

Despite her uneasiness about Ionna's ready acceptance of Russian culture, she was quite delighted by Ionna's love of all-things-Western and her ability to speak English so fluently. Yevt had been trying to learn English for many years since English was the predominate language for scientists, but language was not something she excelled at. She had several phrases and knew the English words related to her scientific research, but would never be able to hold a conversation beyond, "What is your name?" or "Where is the bathroom?"

Ionna had a love for languages and words. She now spoke Ukrainian, Russian (much to her father's annoyance), English, and French. Her intent was to learn Spanish before graduating.

"Have you changed your mind about writing? Perhaps a linguist?" Danya had asked as Ionna expounded on her desire to learn yet another language.

"Oh, no, Papa. I love writing and reading and cultures and....it is just so much better to read works in the original language rather one that has been translated. Plus, I want to travel the world and see things I cannot see here."

She noted her father's concern and quickly added, "I will always be Ukrainian, Papa. I love my country. I just want to experience other places, too. Maybe I can find a way to bring the best of what I find home through my writing."

Yevt was excited for her daughter. As a young girl, she didn't have the possibility to travel. She couldn't even move from one part of Ukraine to the next. And now, though permitted, they simply didn't have the time or the money. Nor, in reality, did Ionna.

"I hope you do have the opportunity to see the world,

Ionna, but you are going to have to marry somebody rich to make that happen," she said with a laugh.

Ionna laughed, too, but then grew a bit more earnest. "Actually, there is a program I'm considering." She let the words sit alone in the room for a moment until she was sure she had the attention of both of her parents. "I can't do it this year. The applications are already in. I didn't find out about the program soon enough. But I'm already working on my application for next year. I'd be going to America to work for the summer. I'd be given a work Visa and then have about a month to do a little exploring on my own through an organization called CCUSA."

"CCUSA?" Danya asked, inquisitively.

"It's Camp Counselors USA, Papa. I'd be working at a summer camp. CCUSA helps students like me find a camp counselor placement in the United States."

Danya snorted. "A summer camp? With tents and bugs? Ionna, you hardly go outdoors here in Ukraine! And you were never interested in anything like Girl Guides. Why would you choose to spend a summer camping?"

Looking a bit hurt by his lack of enthusiasm for her idea, she retorted, "I do like the outdoors. And not all camps in the United States are in tents. I could just as easily end up in one with air-conditioned cabins. And even if I do end up in a tent" – her eyes became glassy and distant – "just imagine how much English I would learn!"

Hopeful puppy dog eyes watched her parents. "May I fill out an application? Going to America through CCUSA won't cost us anything. I'll actually receive a small stipend for working. And be able to see the US and learn more English. Think of it as an advanced English class – far better than anything you are paying for at university."

Although Yevt was willing to agree immediately, caught up in Ionna's enthusiasm, Danya said, "It sounds like an interesting opportunity. Get your mother and me the information so we can look it over. Once we have, we'll let you know our decision."

Ionna's face fell slightly, but Yevt saw the wisdom in it. Who was in charge of the organization? What would happen if Ionna fell ill or was injured? Although the opportunity was 'free,' what would be required in terms of clothing, supplies, and international travel? And, whether she wanted to admit it was part of the decision or not, would they be able to live without her for a whole summer when they had assumed she would be coming home yearly until graduation?

This was a bigger consideration than she would have realized before these months since Ionna left for school. Yevt was not unaware of the concept of "empty-nest syndrome," but she had always assumed the stories were a bit overblown – that was, until Ionna left their nest so empty.

The house was too quiet. Meals were too quiet. Everything was just too quiet.

Of course, Yevt wanted Ionna to grow up and be independent. Everything she taught her since she was an infant was aimed at helping her be an adult and on her own. But with her gone? She had been surprised at the depths of her sadness and loneliness. At times, the grief resembled that of when her mother had died, though Ionna was merely living seven hours away rather than at home.

She was also surprised at her feelings that there was nothing left to accomplish. She had been a researcher, but that era of her life was quickly coming to a close, as was her motherhood. Now what? She had thrown herself into learning English and creating a beautiful yard, but both seemed to be Band-Aids on a gaping wound.

Although she broached the subject with Danya, he didn't seem to be as bothered by her absence. Sure, he missed her, and yes, the house was quiet with her gone. "But quiet is wonderful. We haven't had quiet in 18 years!" Which was exactly what she was saying but without the enthusiasm. She found it amazing that the thought of raising Ionna had been almost too much to bear when she was born, and now, the thought of letting her go felt equally as difficult.

So, a summer in America, though a fantastic idea on paper, was not going to be easy on her in reality.

In the end, she and Danya agreed Ionna should apply. Yevt only felt slightly guilty to be happy to discover there was only a 30% acceptance rate.

Chapter 27

May 2014

Ionna hadn't yet learned that things didn't always go her way. Except for her grandmother's death, which was something that never diminished in size, navigating her life was easy. When she wanted something normally difficult to find on store shelves, her father found a way to bring it home to her. When she wanted to join the school paper a full year before most students got the chance, she was given a junior reporter position. When she applied to university, she got her first choice with an academic scholarship to boot. And now, when she desperately wanted to go to America, she got one of the limited slots.

School had let out for the summer barely a week ago, and she had eight days left before embarking on her summer adventure. She sat in her room watching her mother flit to and fro like the long-tail blue butterflies in

the garden, fretting over clothing and lists, not understanding what all the fuss was about.

"Mama. Stop! Please! It's fine. We've been over the list
a dozen times since this morning. I have everything I need
except a second pair of sneakers, and we decided I will buy
them when I arrive. My letter from Camp Shenna says the
nearby town has a large store with everything I'll need.
The camp director will take me and the other foreign
counselors once we arrive."

Yevt stopped refolding Ionna's shirts. "I know. Really,
I know. It's just that...I mean...you're going to be gone for
three months in a foreign country. What if you don't have
what you need? What if you get sick? Or hurt? Or...
or...homesick?"

Ionna laughed. "If I'm sick or injured, they have
hospitals and doctors. And I won't get homesick. I've been
away at school for two years now and have been away
from home for almost three months on several occasions."

Yevt stated matter-of-factly but with a trace of
smugness, "You've been in Ukraine. That's home. America
is...NOT Ukraine. Everything will be different. The people.
The food. The language. The weather. Everything."

With an equally haughty expression, Ionna stated, "I
know! Isn't it fabulous? What's the point of an adventure
if it is no different than being home?"

Yevt wasn't sure she would use the word fabulous. Or
even nice. It was terrifying. Her little girl was flying over
8,000 kilometers to land in some Godforsaken place called
North Carolina to spend the summer in a tent.

That part did make her smile a bit. Although Ionna
hadn't said anything about the accommodations, Yevt was
sure she wished she had an air-conditioned cabin rather

than a tent. But her daughter would never complain at this point, not when her father had said she couldn't manage a summer in the heat.

"Are you sure you want to do this?" he had asked. "The temperatures in North Carolina often reach well above 32C, sometimes reaching 38C and 39C. And the humidity is so high, you will feel like you are swimming in sweat. And to my knowledge, Ukrainians haven't perfected the growth of fish gills. You can still rethink this and stay home, you know."

Yevt wasn't sure if it was Danya's intent to make sure his daughter went to America despite the heat and the tents or not, but the resolve on her daughter's face said it all. "I am going and going to have fun. I can't wait!" She had flounced back to her room, and that was the end of the discussion. That had been Christmas, and now, here it was, almost time to go. If Ionna was merely acting excited to 'show' her father, she deserved to win best actress in the Academy Awards.

"I'm glad you are excited, but honestly, Ionna, I can't help but worry. It is far away. We will be far away. Anyone who knows you and loves you will be far away. Aren't you the least bit worried about getting homesick?"

"Oh, Mama! I'll be fine. Plus, we can Skype once a week. I'm told the Internet at camp is pretty lousy, but we get time each week to explore. I can Skype. We can talk. It will be fine."

Ever since Christmas break, Ionna had been Skyping with her parents on a weekly basis so they could get the hang of the technology. Not that they were technophobes. They both used computers at work, but they had not kept up with all the communication platforms available – or social media. She and Danya each had a Facebook account as well and learned how to use the instant messenger, send and receive photos, and even send documents – not that Yevt assumed that would be necessary.

She took the list from Ionna, who groaned as Yevt said, "Let's look this over one more time."

––––––––––––––

Although a boy at school sparked a bit of interest, Ionna didn't consider herself 'taken.' So, she didn't have any lengthy goodbye or promises to send in the mail. She had already said goodbye to her closest friends at school, but that would have been true with or without a trip to America.

In terms of local friends, she realized few were left. Most of the girls her age had either gone off to another school and drifted apart, or they had gotten married and started families. Though Ionna loved children, she wasn't in a hurry to have her own, and she had little in common with those who had.

The only real goodbyes she needed to attend to were that of her grandmother and her parents. She set off for the cemetery with an interesting book and some flowers, intending to tell her babyusa everything going on in her life.

"Hi Babuysa! It's me, Ionna." She still started every conversation the same way she had done since she was just a child of 12. "I told you at Christmas and again at Easter about my big trip. My adventure is almost here. I leave in two days. I'm really excited."

She babbled on and on about everything she would see and do and learn, completely forgetting about the book she had planned to read.

"I've been studying all about America, Babusya." In truth, most of her 'studying' had been accomplished by watching the American films that were so popular on campus. She was under the impression that nearly everyone lived in a city like New York City, on a ranch with horses and cows, or in California on the coast. She couldn't wait to learn to surf, shoot a gun, meet Mickey Mouse, and get the signatures of all her movie-star crushes, and hoped she could do quite accomplish a majority of these must-do items during her free time on weekends.

"By the time I return, I will have such a great command of the English language that I should be able to teach classes. I'm already fluent, so I figure these next three months will give me just the boost I need to teach a few classes. I'll use the money I earn to help Mama and Papa with the cost of tuition."

She was sure her babusya would be proud of her for her entrepreneurial spirit and magnanimous gesture.

"But going to America is more than just learning English, Babusya. It's about gaining experiences. You know, you can't actually be a writer if you haven't done anything or seen anything or been anywhere. I've only lived in two houses my whole life, and both have been within a mile of one another. My life has been so boring. So normal. So predictable."

Ionna loved her parents and was grateful for all they had given her. But she knew every night what would be for dinner. She knew what each day would bring. Her parents were old, settled, content.

Ionna wanted so much more. She wanted each day to be new, never knowing what might happen, always having to be ready to make a swift decision and act before the day left without her. She didn't want a job that started at 8 o'clock each morning and ended at 5 o'clock each evening. She didn't want to teach the same lectures one year after the next to students who didn't care about the subject but only took the class to get the credits needed to graduate. She didn't want to spend her life looking at microscopic organisms wriggling around on slides with nothing of note to show for the effort.

Ionna firmly believed she was different. She couldn't imagine her parents had ever been anything other than dull, methodical people who hadn't lived unique lives, but had simply lived the same day over and over until the years had passed. She would never settle. It's why she insisted on going to school so far away. It's why she hadn't followed the traditional 'go to school to find a husband' path and stubbornly refused to let some boy derail her plans. It's why she argued with her father about Russians and politics. It's why she was going to America.

When she was finally out of words, she said solemnly, "I will miss you, Babusya. I always miss you. I sure wish God had a Skype to heaven. I'd use it every single day. I'll see you in a few months."

With that, she kissed the gravestone and wandered home. Her goodbye to her parents would be far more difficult.

The night before her flight, they took her out to a fancy restaurant to celebrate. This was a rare treat because of the expense, but her father said his daughter, the world traveler, was worth the expense. He made a bit of a scene, letting everyone know about her trip and how proud he was of her. The entire restaurant applauded and held up glasses for a toast to the young lady on her way to America. Ionna thought the whole thing felt more like a poorly written movie script than a going away dinner for a teenager, but she let her parents show off their pride without too much of an eye roll.

The next morning, before the sun was above the horizon, Ionna and her parents were in taxi on the way to the airport. Despite a better economy, her parents didn't own a car. Even if they did, the car would sit unmoving in the driveway. Neither knew how to drive. There had never been a need.

The airport loomed into sight, her father paid the driver, and a porter took her bags to the ticket counter. She checked in, found her gate, and confirmed she had her passport, one last time. As always, it was in the pouch around her neck that her mother had purchased.

It was time for her to depart for her gate, but her feet seemed to be stuck in concrete. She didn't move. Her parents didn't move. They all just stood awkwardly, silently looking at each other, until finally, her mother let out a sob and grabbed her around the waist. "I will miss you, Ionna. Enjoy yourself. Be good. Remember who you are."

Her father joined in the hug, saying little, while trying in vain to hold back his sobs. Finally, he choked out, "I love you, my girl. Show them what it's like dealing with a Ukrainian!"

His joke eased the tension somewhat, as Ionna gave each one a kiss. "I promise to enjoy myself and be good and remember who I am and show them a real Ukrainian. I'll miss you, too." And with that, she got on a plane and journeyed West.

Chapter 28

May 2014

And just like that, Ionna was gone. A quick kiss, a hug, the perfunctory tears, and Yevt was left with an empty nest and markedly emptier space in her heart where her child had been only days earlier.

Yevt was doing her best to shake off the feelings of gloom, using all her analytical thinking and reasoning skills no longer needed for her job. This 'empty-nest' wasn't a permanent state of being – not yet, anyway. Ionna would be home at the end of the summer, albeit briefly. Of course, she would be home again between semesters and at the end of the summer. There was no reason for Yevt to have a full-blown crisis over a temporary condition.

Plus, there was the fact that Ionna was doing something marvelous. What parent didn't want their child to have the opportunity to travel and gather new experiences? It wasn't like she had decided to quit school and work in some seedy bar.

Finally, Yevt reminded herself that she raised her daughter to be independent. Independence did not mean firmly fettered within the circle of her mother's arms. She had known, hadn't she, that Yevt would become her own person and want to live her own life on her own terms. Of course, she had. She wasn't daft – though she now realized she had hoped 'independence' would be far closer to home.

She had managed to keep her tears at the airport to a minimum, reminding herself she was happy for her daughter. However, as soon as Ionna had disappeared down the tunnel leading to the plane, her dark hair no longer visible even to the straining eyes of a mother, she let the tears come.

Danya had held her close, rocking her gently to and fro, murmuring, "It's okay. She's going to have so much fun. Before we know it, we'll be here to pick her up. Shhh. Shhh." Despite his later insistence he was unbothered by her departure, Yevt supposed those murmured words were as much for his sake as they had been for hers. The difference was that, a week later, Danya was fine and Yevt still struggled.

It made no sense, really. Ionna had been gone for weeks during the school year and Yevt had no problems filling her days. She gardened. She read books. She chatted with the neighbors. She cooked. She talked late into the night with Danya. But now? For inexplicable reasons, each day crept by with hours which felt like days and days which felt like weeks. She never had enough to do to keep her mind occupied and away from the topic of Ionna in America.

As she had done before Ionna left, Yevt tried talking to her husband about her problem. But although he was typically an astute listener and gave wise counsel, he seemed completely unable to grasp the problem.

Just this morning he had said, "She's been gone a week, Yevt. She was gone longer than that the last four semesters of college, during which time I rarely heard you complain about missing her and never heard you say you had nothing to do. But for the last week, it's all I hear."

His words – and his placating tone – infuriated her. She did not complain all day, every day. She spoke to him about many things beyond her current misery. And hadn't she told him before Ionna left that she was bored? Yes, she was certain she had, mentioning that English and gardening didn't seem to be enough.

Danya still had his work. He left the house each morning and returned each evening, with the hours in the middle filled with lectures, students, colleagues, and ideas. She, on the other hand, spent a majority of her day at home, either creating beauty in the garden or keeping the house clean and trying to come up with something new to eat given they had the same tired ingredients. She said as much, and he stared at her, one eyebrow raised slightly higher than the other.

"Didn't you say you were glad they cut back your hours? I thought you said you wanted to retire."

"Honestly, Danya. I may as well be trying to explain myself to the cinder block fence. You simply aren't listening to me. Either that, or you are pretending to be dense." With that, she walked from the room, with a bit more speed and significantly more noise than was usual.

She had talked with her neighbor, Olena, while pulling

weeds at the fence line. Olena was of similar age to Yevt but had children earlier and was well into the babusya phase of life. As Yevt talked about missing Ionna and not knowing what to do with herself, Olena gave a slow nod.

"Oh dear, you are bringing back some miserable memories," she said, her broad smile belying her words. I was a mess when my Ruslana left home. Even though I still had three other girls in the house, her absence was a hole I couldn't fill. My Dmytro didn't understand anymore than your Danya does," she laughed.

Yevt worked hard to keep the irritation – a regular occurance these days – from showing on her face. There was nothing funny about what she was feeling. On the other hand, if Olena had been through it, then maybe she had some suggestions, even if she now found the whole thing too humorous to recount without levity.

Mechanically, hoping her voice didn't sound as piqued as her mood, she asked, "So, how did you handle the absence? How did you help Dmytro understand?"

Now, Olena's laughter burst out, and she put one hand over her mouth as if to keep more from escaping. "Dmytro never did understand. He doesn't understand to this day!"

Yevt no longer tried to hide her displeasure. "I don't see how a husband who can't understand a real problem his wife is experiencing is funny. Nor am I enjoying your mirth while my heart breaks in two." Then, much to her horror and shame, she began to cry, heaving sobs she hadn't realized were just waiting for the right moment to escape.

Olena walked quickly around the fence, into Yevt's yard, and opened her arms, an invitation for Yevt to step within their warmth and comfort. Despite her anger, she fell into them eagerly. "Divchynka. Divchynka. Baby girl, baby girl. Shhh, now. It will get better. I promise. Shhh."

When she was devoid of the energy needed to cry and only a few stray hiccups remained as proof of her breakdown, Olena said gently, "I'm so sorry, my friend. I was not laughing at you but at women. We can't wait to start a family. Then, we can't wait for the children to leave. Then, when they do leave, we want them back again. And as for our husbands? We expect them to think the way we think but would be mortified if they did so. Can you imagine your husband coming home from work today, explaining that a colleague had laughed at an inappropriate moment, and then beginning to blubber?"

A mental image of Danya sobbing and hiccupping filled her mind, and she began to laugh. Olena joined her until they were wiping their eyes, but this time, it was to get rid of the joviality rather than the sadness.

Yevt invited Olena in for a cup of tea, and while the water heated, Olena sat at the table, her chin in her palm. "The only real way through these feelings of yours, the ones society has trivialized by gathering it all up under a ridiculous phrase about empty nests, is to get through it."

Yevt, now pouring the tea into mugs looked at her quizzically.

"Do you remember when Ionna was a newborn?" she asked.

Yevt nodded.

"Do you remember how tired you were? How everything seemed to be hard, or completely impossible? The times she wouldn't eat or wouldn't sleep? The bouts of crying that had no sensible solution?"

Yevt nodded again. Those had been difficult months,

especially as she worked hard to put the depression behind her.

"Do you remember other women, perhaps your mother, perhaps a neighbor, maybe even a magazine article, that told you 'the one thing' you needed to do that would make it better?"

Yevt, now nodding enthusiastically and smiling, felt she knew where this line of questioning was leading.

"And do you remember how well those tips worked?"

Yevt, smiled broadly. "Not one bit. In fact, the more they talked, the worse I felt."

"Exactly," stated Olena, letting that sink in for a moment. "I could tell you what I did and what worked for me, but the truth is, the same thing that worked for finding myself with no birds in my nest is the same thing that worked for raising babies – time."

With 'I've been there. I know. You can trust me.' In her eyes, Olena said. "Give yourself a bit of love. Wallow a bit in your sadness if you need to. Then, find things to do. And before you know it, you'll be able to look back and laugh."

She was thankful for Olena's words and understood they held a lot of truth. However, this was one substantial difference between the two women. When Ruslana left the nest, there were still three girls at home. By the time her last daughter moved out, Olena had grandchildren to take their places.

Yevt hadn't been that lucky.

Yevt began to long for another child. She had not been young when she married and several years stood between that date and her first child. Now, with Yevt's 32nd birthday come and gone, most of her peers had teenage children, and those from the village she grew up in would soon be grandmothers.

She wasn't displeased she had waited to have Ionna. She had gotten established in her career, met a man that, though not perfect, was perfect for her, and had been blessed with a beautiful daughter. But she realized if they were going to have another child, it needed to be sooner rather than later.

She and Danya had discussed family size, and he was content with one child but would be "More than happy," – said with the sly grin that only a man could pull off – "to try for more." She had swatted his arm as her mother tsked from behind her screen.

"Seriously, though, Yetti. I'm not against having another child, but where would we put him?" Despite producing a girl the first time, Danya could not fathom having anything other than a boy on the next go around.

Within weeks of having that conversation, Danya came home with news about a house. "It's for rent. It has three bedrooms, Yetti! Three. And a study! I could be home more often because I'd have space to do my paperwork." The house was a short distance away and belonged to a literature professor at the university. He was retiring, and they were going to go live near their eldest son.

He had told Danya, "I'm not ready to sell the house. I may not like living near my son, so close to the Russian border." He and Danya both pretended to spit. "But I'm willing to give it a try. My wife longs to be near the babies, and who am I to deny her that simple pleasure?"

One tour of the house, and they were sold. "Look at the bookcases," Danya had breathed. "Floor to ceiling," Yevt had agreed. By month's end, they had moved and the topic of growing their family began in earnest.

———————

Despite several months of herbs and supplements supplied by Katrina after Yevt confided that she wasn't getting pregnant again, there was still no baby. However, both she and Danya remained optimistic. As Katrina had said, "You have one healthy child. You'll have another!"

Both were certain their second child would be a son, and Yevt desperately wished to name him after both her husband and father. However, each time she brought up the idea to her mom, she would go rigid with fury and refuse to talk.

Yevt understood her father's passing had left deep scars, but it was so long ago. And it wasn't like she wanted to name him Lyaksandro. Instead, she wanted to give him her husband's middle name paired with her father's middle name – Faddei Hadeon – Valiant, brave warrior. It was a strong name for a son and honored the men in his life. Certainly, her mother could see that and understand? Wasn't it time to let go of the hurt and move on with her life?

But Ivanna didn't see it that way at all. "Just slap me across the face. Go ahead. Do it." She lifted her cheek toward Yevt. When her daughter didn't move, she said, "Slapping me would be far less hurtful than giving your innocent child that man's name. If you cannot slap me, then how can you consider giving your baby a name that I could never bear to say?"

In the end, they determined that if they had a son, they would name him Faddei Marko Hadeon on official church records at baptism, but on the governmental records, he'd simply be Faddei Marko. It was a compromise Yevt planned to live with and one to which her mother would not be privy. If they had a daughter, they still had their list from Ionna's birth.

Unfortunately, naming their son did not hasten his arrival. In fact, nothing Yevt attempted was successful. She even stooped to taking advice from the older women from the nearby villages who believed in nonsensical ideas like eating honey and cinnamon daily to aid in conception or timing your lovemaking based on the phase of the moon. But month after month, she remained barren.

At first, she and Danya discussed their infertility issues regularly, sure that, with time, they would conceive. By Yevt's 40th birthday, having a son was a taboo topic that caused too much sorrow. Even Ivanna had quit asking about more grandchildren. The flicker of pain each time she pointed out a baby in Yevt's presence was too much to bear.

In time, she resigned herself to the fact that Ionna would never have siblilngs, that she would never be a mother to a son. Although regret flitted around the edges of her mind, and an ache for something she had never known could rise from her toes and squeeze a deep sigh from her chest, she focused on Ionna. Instead of lavishing love on a large family, Yevt had poured all her love, all her needs, all her mothering into the child she had been given.

Now, Ionna, her only child, her sole reason for existence for the last eighteen years, was on the verge of creating a life that would only include her mother on the periphery.

Chapter 29

June 2014

Weekend! That was Ionna's first thought as the first week's worth of campers left for home. She was free to do what she wanted until Sunday at noon. It was now Friday, shortly after two in the afternoon, and the only thing she really wanted to do was sleep. She could not recall a time when she had been this exhausted.

Of course, she had been beyond tired since leaving Ukraine. The flight to North Carolina was uneventful but long. By the time she arrived, she had been flying or waiting for 20 hours with very little in the way of sleep. After going through customs, she walked briskly toward the lobby of the airport in a town with an unpronounceable name. R A L E I G H. Rah–LEE-I-Ghah. She wasn't sure where to put the emphasis and decided it was on the Lee. Quite different from places in Ukraine like Kyiv,

Donetsk, and Mykolaiv.

She emerged from the long hallway, past the "no one but passengers beyond this point" sign into a crowd of waiting people. She smiled broadly despite a bit of anxiety and patiently stood with her bags. No one came up to her, so she assumed her contact must not be able to spot her through the throng. She dragged her two suitcases to the right to separate herself a bit and replaced the broad smile. Nothing.

In fact, 15 minutes later, when the crowd had dissipated and a new crowd was forming for a different flight, Ionna's smile had not only faded but disappeared. She felt icy fingers grip her heart as she began to panic. Prior to this experience, she had never flown and never been in an airport. She had never been outside of Ukraine. She had no idea what step to take next and wanted to sit down against the wall and cry.

She gave herself a mental shake and spoke to herself as if she were speaking to a child. "Calm down. I can't have an adventure without a few tiny hiccups. It's fine. I speak English. I have the name and phone number of the person who was to pick me up. I'll simply find someone who can help me." Taking a deep breath to steady the last jumble of nerves, she searched for someone who with a kind, helpful face and a phone.

At a counter with 'American Airlines' hung in illuminated red and blue letters on the wall, stood a smiling woman not much older than Ionna. Her queue was empty, so Ionna rolled her bags toward the woman and said in her best English, "My benefactor not come to vestibule. Yearn for phone."

The woman, with an unusual name, Julia, continued to

smile while cocking her head to one side. "I'm sorry? Can you repeat that, please?"

Ionna wondered if she was hard of hearing, so she spoke a bit louder and separated each word a bit more. "My - benefactor - not come to - vestibule. Yearn for - phone."

Julia's smile drooped a fraction of an inch, and her eyes held some confusion. "Can you wait a moment, please?" Ionna understood the woman, though her accent was different from that of her teachers. Please, which was a word she had learned in first year English, had two syllables instead of one and was said at a slower pace. While she waited, she mimicked the word in her mind. "Puh-leez, puh-leez."

Julia came back with an older gentleman, who asked, "May I help you?"

Ionna, unsure why she needed to repeat her request, tried one more time. "My benefactor not come to vestibule. Yearn for phone." Then she added, as sweetly as possible, "Puh Leez."

Julia regarded the man, whose name tag said Donald, and shrugged her shoulders with a 'See, I told you so' look. Donald stared directly at Ionna and said, "Are you lost? Do you have someone here waiting for you?"

Ionna was exasperated. She had clearly let them know no one had arrived, and she needed to use a phone. Were Americans unintelligent or were they merely prone to terrible customer service?

She tried one more time, this time using hand motions. "I fly from Ukraine," she said slowly while flapping her arms up and down. "I stay vestibule" was said while pointing to her watch and "Benefactor no" while shrugging her shoulders. Finally, with a sweet smile, she said, "Phone, puh leez" while holding her hand up to her mouth and ear, pretending to speak on a phone.

Donald's eyes lit up, and he smiled. "You need to use a phone. Okay. Is that the number you need to call?" He gestured at the paper in her hand which had her own name, Sephi's name and phone number, and the address of the camp. Ionna handed him her paper even though she wasn't entirely sure what he said.

"I'll call this number for you and speak to Sephi. Try to find out why she isn't here to pick you up. Sound like a plan?"

'Sound like a plan?' She searched through the English vocabulary bank in her mind and couldn't fathom what thing called a 'plan' would make any type of noise or what this had to doing with calling Sephi at camp.

However, she didn't want Donald to put down the phone, so she smiled and once again said, "Puh Leez."

As he dialed the phone, he said, "Are you new at speaking English? You didn't do too badly for a beginner." It was then Ionna realized despite her years of taking English, she was not nearly as proficient as she had thought.

Her face flushed as she considered the number of times she'd spoken English since boarding the plane to America and wondered how many others took her for a beginner. She also wondered for the second time in less than an hour if she had made a huge mistake coming here and if it was too late to back out and go home.

It turned out that Sephi, the camp director, had gotten busy and forgotten she was coming into the airport that day. It had taken her two hours to arrive, during which time, Ionna catnapped in an uncomfortable chair with constant reminders over the intercom to keep her bags with her at all times and report anyone who looked suspicious.

Based on body language and tonal inflections, Ionna felt certain Sephi was apologizing when she finally arrived, though, quite honestly, she couldn't understand one word of what she was saying. Nonetheless, she smiled, and hauled her cases into the back of the 12-passenger, white van with Camp Shenna emblazoned on the side.

As they got into the car, Sephi began talking again, so Ionna tried to listen as carefully as she could. However, as with the people at the airport, she wasn't sure Sephi was speaking English. Ionna finally put up her hand. "I sorry. No understand? Slow, puh-leez."

Sephi laughed. "Oh, sorry. Your form said you spoke English fluently, so I thought...well, never mind what I thought." She slowed down her speech and picked her words carefully. "Do you have everything from the list? Do you need to go to the store?"

Ionna breathed a sigh of relief. Though still not like school, she understood the question. "I have list. Sneakers. Bedding. Towels." She glanced at Sephi to determine if she was understood and was happy to find her nodding.

"Perfect," Sephi said. "We'll pass a Walmart on the way to camp. We will stop there."

"Walmart?" asked Ionna with a thick accent. "I know not a Walmart."

Sephi laughed again. "You aren't the first and won't be the last international who hasn't heard of a Walmart. Big store. It's a big store."

Ionna grinned and added another word to her vocabulary.

However, when Sephi stopped at the 'big' store, Ionna couldn't believe what she saw. It was not just big. Her English teacher had explained there were many English words for something large. The largest of things could be enormous or gigantic. Ionna turned to Sephi holding out her hands in an expansive arc, "Walmart is not big. Walmart is enormous and gigantic both."

She couldn't imagine a store so immense for bedding or towels or shoes. "They must sell every color and every material ever created," she thought. "How large would the other stores be? Was everything this big in America?"

If the size of the building surprised Ionna, it was nothing in comparison to finding out a Walmart store wasn't just for bedding or towels or shoes. It was for bedding AND towels AND shoes and pots and car tires and toothpaste and baby dolls and swimsuits and lettuce – all under one roof.

"I no see store with so many things." She shook her head, trying to clear away the confusion to make room for this new concept. "All America cities have gigantic Walmart with so many things?" Sephi nodded in the affirmative and led her to the bedding, then the towels, then the shoes. "Do you have everything you need for personal hygiene?"

Ionna's blank expression gave the answer.

"You know. Toothpaste? Shampoo?"

"Ah, hihiyena," Ionna thought to herself, adding a second word for the day. Then out loud stated, "I do have all personal cleaning things."

Sephi didn't try to hide the fact that she found Ionna's

English or her accent hysterical. With a burst of laughter at 'all personal cleaning things,' she said, "Good. Now, let's buy you some snacks. You know snacks? Junk food? Desserts? Chips?"

This one, Ionna knew. "Munchies," she said with a grin.

The next two weeks were packed with trainings. How to handle the campers. How to canoe and kayak. How to stop someone from choking. How to build a fire. Ionna had never done any of these things before and learning about them in English wasn't easy. However, she was a fast learner and discovered most things could be understood simply by mimicking the actions she saw others performing.

The hardest lesson, though, was unrelated to campers. It was worse than not understanding the English or discovering all her 'weekend' plans were ridiculous given where North Carolina was in relation to California and New York, and just how expansive the United States was. It was worse than homesickness. It was almost as bad as losing her babusya because it made her wonder if she were good enough and could ever fit in. For the first time in her life, she didn't belong, and she had no idea how to handle it.

She was given a tent assignment for the training weeks and put with three other camp counselors – all from America. On her first full day at camp, she learned there were six international counselors at Camp Shenna that summer. Three of the girls were from Australia, and the two boys were from Scotland and England. Ionna was the only one from the Urkaine, and it meant she was the only one who had difficulty speaking the language.

Although she had always been at the top of her English class and understood all the assignments, she couldn't follow the counselors' conversations. They all sounded different from her teachers in Ukraine, and they sounded different from each other. One would say 'Puh Leez,' another would say 'Pleez uh' and still another would say 'Pleez.'

But worse than the accents were these phrases she had never heard of before and that made no sense at all. She'd been asked to 'cut out the lights,' and when she stood there trying to figure out what they wanted her to do, another counselor had said 'Bless her heart.'

By the time darkness came that first full day, Ionna had slumped into her tent, sat heavily on the cot, and fallen quickly into a deep sleep with dreams with policemen urging her to do things she couldn't understand and being hauled off to prison for not obeying.

When she rode into town with Sephi on her second day and spoke to her mother, she tried to appear lighthearted despite feeling despondent.

"How's America?" her mother asked brightly. Hearing her mother speak in Ukrainian was just too much, and Ionna began to cry. She tried to talk, but the homesickness caught in her throat making what few words escaped sound squeaky and childish.

"What's the matter, Ionna? Are you okay? Are you sick?"

Ionna struggled to regain her composure. "No, Mama.

I'm okay. Really." She sniffed and swiped at her eyes with the back of her hand. "I guess I'm just missing home more than I thought I would. I'm...I'm not as good at English as I thought I was."

She hung her head, sure her mother's eyes would express an "I told you so," but when she finally glanced back up, her mother's emotions mirrored her own. "Oh, Ionna. Don't be sad. Your English may not be as good as you had believed, but I'm sure it is better than their Ukrainian!"

They both laughed, and Ionna felt immensely better having simply admitted to feeling down. "Except for the English, I'm doing okay. And I understand quite a majority of most conversations as long as whoever is speaking slows down a bit. I'm sure that by the end of the summer I'll be the best English speaker at university! And Mama, let me tell you about Walmart."

Despite a bit of peace after talking with her mama, becoming acclimated to the English language, to Camp Shenna, and to the people she met was not an easy task. Once she had been in America for three days, she was over her jetlag and was beginning to feel more confident. However, none of her tent mates spent much time getting to know her. In fact, except at bedtime, if she entered the tent, they all left within moments. She assumed it was due to the language barrier and tried to assure them that she understood quite a bit of what they said.

"Puh leez. You no have to leave. I talk to you. I tell me America stories? My English is not so good, but I try hard." She smiled broadly, hoping to make some friends. But all three girls scurried out, one muttering under her breath. Later at lunch, as she approached a table full of happy, chatting counselors, everyone spread out in such a way as to keep her from having space to sit, and she found herself eating alone. It happened again at supper.

That evening, while learning CPR, the counselors were put into pairs, one to do the breathing, the other to do the chest compressions. Her partner, a nice-looking boy who reminded Ionna of those she saw in the American movies, moved his chair further away and leaned uncomfortably to one side. The girls at the next table giggled, and her partner made a bigger show of leaning until he almost fell on the floor, arms dragging the carpet and his tongue hanging out to one side.

He didn't speak one word to her that wasn't necessary and moved to another group as soon as their assignment was complete. As the class ended, the counselors moved away, looking at her while whispering behind their hands. She didn't understand why, but she did understand what – Ionna was not liked among her peers.

She walked in the dark toward her tent, alone and lonely. She was not surprised when her tentmates stopped talking as she stepped beneath the tent flaps, nor was she surprised when they quickly filed out. Still, these actions hurt.

As she climbed into bed, she began an internal argument with herself, like a good angel and bad angel sat on her shoulder.

"See? You should have never come to America. This was a terrible idea. You don't fit in. You won't fit in. You should just go home."

Then, from the other side, "I'm on an adventure. Of course, it is going to be difficult to adjust. I've never been in a foreign country before. If I work harder, I'll get the hang of it."

Before the girls came back to the tent, Ionna had shushed the bad angel and was determined to try harder the following day. "I'll make friends. You'll see," she whispered. "You just wait and see."

However, her fourth day at camp was no better than any of the previous days. Her tentmates ignored her. She ate breakfast, lunch, and supper alone. The only people who spoke to her were those forced to pair with her during training assignments. By nightfall, Ionna knew what she had to do.

CCUSA would not send Ionna home because she was homesick. Nor would they send her home because she had, in her own words, 'made a dreadful mistake.' She knew her parents would bear the burden of her return trip plane ticket, but she had no choice. She would go to the airport, send her parents an email asking them to purchase a ticket home, and be back in Ukraine before the week was out.

Once back home, she would find a summer job to repay her parents and CCUSA for her flights. If she couldn't pay for it in one summer, she would work while in school, or even take a semester off. She understood the failure was hers and, as such, the burden was hers as well. She would do whatever it took.

Asking Sephi for a ride to the airport was not something Ionna was willing to do. Sephi had too many responsibilities to take another four hours out of her day. Plus, Ionna was certain Sephi would try to talk her out of going home assuming this was a simple case of homesickness.

Instead, she would walk into town where she would use what little money she had to buy a bus ticket to the airport. She hoped what she had would be sufficient and the person working the counter would be able to understand her request. She no longer trusted her English skills.

That night, when everyone had finally fallen asleep, Ionna slipped out of the tent with her largest suitcase. She left her bedding and the smaller suitcase. So many things were purchased for a hot North Carolina summer, and her heart squeezed at the thought of never using them as she had imagined.

The first half-mile would be the hardest. She had to wind her way on a gravel path through different camp sites full of sleeping counselors. The wheels on her suitcase scraped and twisted on the rocks until Ionna grabbed it by the handles and pulled it firmly toward her chest.

By the time she made it to the road that led into town, her arms were trembling from the strain. She put the suitcase down, sitting on it to catch her breath. It was midnight, and she had until daylight to walk the 10 miles. She had no idea how often the bus ran but hoped she would be able to find a seat on the first one. Now that she had made up her mind, there was no reason to tarry. The sooner she got to the airport, the sooner she would be home. Despite her resolve, she couldn't seem to remove the word 'loser' from her mind.

The walk to town was uneventful. No one drove past until she was nearly to her destination, and they paid no attention to her as they sped by. Greeley was small with just two primary roads and half a dozen cross streets. The bus station was easy to find, situated across from the bank and next to the laundry mat.

Despite the sun barely peeping over the horizon, there were several passengers milling around the station. Ionna went to the ticket counter and spoke the lines she had been rehearsing in her mind during the long walk. "I need ticket to airport, puh – leeze. What time does bus leave?"

The woman at the counter smiled kindly. "You aren't from here, are ya?" When Ionna shook her head, she continued, "I love your accent. It's so different than anything I ever get to hear around here." While she spoke, she printed up a ticket. "That will be twenty-five dollars."

Ionna reached into her bag with a sigh of relief. Her mother had given her $100 to buy the necessities, but Ionna hadn't needed even half of that when she went to Walmart. She handed the girl two twenties and waited for her change.

"Here ya go. The bus leaves in 45 minutes. You've got enough time for some breakfast at the café." She pointed to the busy building next to the bank. "Or you can buy some coffee and snacks at the vending area." She pointed behind Ionna. "I hope you enjoyed your visit to North Carolina." And with that, she was helping the next person.

Enjoyed her visit to North Carolina? If it wasn't so sad, the comment would be funny. She had never enjoyed anything less.

Ionna chose coffee and snacks from the vending machines, sat herself down on the hard wooden bench, and waited for the bus to depart.

———————

The bus ride had taken much longer than the trip with Sephi. The traffic was heavy, and the bus made several stops, picking up people on their way to the airport. By the time they pulled under the airport portico, the bus was completely full.

Ionna glanced at her watch. It was now 10:15. It would be just after five at home. Her father should be on his way home from work. She needed to talk with her parents as quickly as possible. With it so late, she worried whether her parents would be able to find a ticket or if she'd have to wait until morning. Without a doubt, $14.72, what she had left after her meager breakfast, would not be enough to buy a ticket home.

Ionna found a seat in the crowded Internet café, once again, having an internal debate. She wanted to email her parents so she would have more time before she had to face them. Her stomach squeezed as she imagined their disappointment in her. On the other hand, she knew an email could go unseen for hours. Finally, fear of being stuck in the airport outweighed the fear of her parent's disappointment.

However, just before she connected the call, she heard Sephi's voice shouting her name.

"Ionna! There you are! You gave me such a fright! I've been trying to catch you since early this morning. Thank goodness you are alright!" Then Sephi's arms tightened around her shoulders, pulling her backward in her chair until the back of Ionna's head was against Sephi's stomach.

The love and concern were enough to start Ionna on a crying jag, one that had been a long time in the making.

"Oh, Ionna, honey. I'm so sorry that you've been so unhappy. I wish you had talked to me. We could have worked something out. I can't believe you snuck away in the night, caught a bus, and almost got on a plane before I could catch you." She rocked Ionna side to side, lowering her face to rest on Ionna's soft hair. "Please don't go, Ionna. I need you at camp."

Ionna heaved away from Sephi's embrace. "No. You not need me. I not speak English very well. I not have any friends. I not do well at camp. I am big failure." She pulled her hands to her face as the sobs became loud enough to attract the attention of other patrons.

Sephi murmured, "No, Ionna. You are wrong. You are not a failure. Just look at what you've accomplished. You don't know the language, but you've managed to come over 100 miles on your own, purchasing tickets, getting Internet access. I can't imagine any of my American counselors able to do anything like that. Not even close."

Sephi reached out and touched Ionna's arm. "Honey, let's go talk. I learned a few things that didn't make me too happy this morning." At the expression on Ionna's face, she said, "No, not about you. About the other counselors and how they've been treating you." Ionna lowered her gaze, hot embarrassment flushing her cheeks.

"I'm appalled at their behavior. Utterly appalled. And they are now well aware what they did was wrong. I have half a mind to send them all home and replace them. I shudder to think if they treated the campers the way they've treated you!"

Ionna shook her head. "It not matter. I think coming to America was mistake. My English not as good as I thought. I never slept in a tent before. I never work with children before. Learning about boats and first aid is not easy when English isn't good. I was wrong. I want to go home to Ukraine."

"Ionna, please. Let me try to explain what is happening

and why I think it is important for you to stay. Let me help you find a solution. If, after our chat you haven't changed your mind, I'll call CCUSA and tell them that this placement isn't working out. At least that way, you won't have to pay for your ticket home. But Ionna?"

Ionna turned back to Sephi. "I'll be telling CCUSA that you didn't work out to help you make it back home, not because I believe it."

Sephi had come to breakfast that morning to find out Ionna was missing, and no one knew where she had gone or why. "She wasn't in the tent this morning, and her suitcase is missing," said one of her tentmates. "She was there last night when we went to bed," another had assured Sephi.

But when Sephi had asked why, everyone stared nervously at the floor before saying, "We don't know."

"I think you do. I think every one of you knows why, and I want someone here to tell me," she demanded.

"She's weird," one of the girls blurted out. "She can't speak English. She tries to say words with a southern drawl. It's ridiculous."

"And she staaanks," said another, feeling emboldened by the candor of the first girl to speak. "Her body odor is so bad – even after she showers. We've had to leave the tent every time she comes in. And lordy, we don't want to eat with her. The stench will ruin our appetite. It's probably good that she left."

The dining hall filled with a buzz of agreement until Sephi said quietly, "Are you telling me that you ostracized one of our international counselors because she was different?" She eyed each counselor in turn, waiting until their gaze dropped in shame, then went on, stiffly, "That because she had trouble with the language and smelled differently than you, that you knowingly made her feel bad enough to leave camp in the middle of the night?... and that you don't find anything wrong with your actions?"

The only sound in the dining hall was the occasional chatter from the cooks in the kitchen. "As the camp director, I can only assume your behavior reflects how you will act when the campers arrive. I can only assume if a camper stutters or wets the bed or gets homesick or talks incessantly about Legos or baseball stats or can't swim or cries during storms that you will what? Walk away? Laugh at them? Is that what I can expect?"

Several of the girls were now crying, murmuring that they were sorry. "Don't apologize to me. I'm not the one you hurt." With that, she left to find Ionna.

She started at the bus station, and the girl at the counter remembered Ionna. "Oh yes, she had a lovely accent. She bought a ticket to the airport. The bus left about 25 minutes ago."

Sephi had driven to the airport, taking the backroads to avoid the heaviest commuter traffic. She fretted that she would be too late. When she got to the airport, she ran straight to the flight display, quickly scanning for flights to Ukraine. One had left that morning at 6:30, long before Ionna could have made it to the airport. The others, thankfully, didn't leave until the evening.

She ran first to the American Airlines counter and then United, Delta, and Turkish Air, enquiring after Ionna. No one had seen her. Sephi had begun to panic until she realized Ionna didn't have the money to purchase a ticket without first talking with her parents. She moved swiftly to the Internet café, and to her relief, saw her sitting in one of the cubicles.

———————

The personal hygiene lesson, which took place in a restaurant booth, was both enlightening and embarrassing. Ionna could hardly resist the urge to sniff underneath her arms to see what Sephi was talking about. She had never noticed an odor there before and couldn't detect one now.

"You see, Ionna, in the United States, most people use deodorant under their arms to keep from having body odor. Your country doesn't use it, so you are used to the natural odor of the body. The girls from the US are not. To you, it is fine. To them, it is not."

This time, Ionna didn't resist the urge. She raised her arm and took in a big noseful. "I not smell anything."

Sephi smiled. "I know. It is what you are used to. But my underarms smell differently because I use deodorant."

When Ionna moved as if she might try to sniff her pits, Sephi held up her hands, "No. You are going to have to trust me. So, we use deodorant. It is like a...cream...that you put under your arms. I have some back at camp that I will give you if you choose to come back."

Sephi smiled at her with encouragement before adding, "There's one other thing. It isn't required but it may help. Most American women shave the hair under their arms. Clean. Like this." She held up her arm so Ionna could see beneath. "We shave our legs, too." Ionna looked down and noted her smooth leg, unconsciously trying to hide her own.

"Shaving is optional, Ionna, but if you want to try it, I

have extra razors, too."

Once the hygiene lesson was concluded, Sephi did what she could to help Ionna gain back her self-confidence. "The counselors have been rude, Ionna. Most of them haven't ever been beyond their backdoors. They don't know how to deal with people who look different or sound different."

"Or smell different," Ionna interjected.

"Yes, or smell differently. Honestly, if I were going to send anyone home, I'd want it to be those who decided that being different was equated with being wrong. Do you understand what I'm saying?"

"I think, yes? You are trying to say that I smell different but that is not bad as rude?"

Sephi laughed, "Exactly. Ionna, don't go home because some girls couldn't find a way to be kind or wouldn't come to you to help you fit in. We need counselors like you who understand how to help everyone fit in. We'll have kids this summer who stand at the edge of the group, afraid to participate, sure they won't belong, hoping we'll call their parents so they can go home. If you go, who will these kids look up to? Who will understand them?"

Ionna considered this. She tried to imagine a small child, afraid and alone, with no one to help. She tried to imagine those counselors who had made her feel bad enough to want to go back to Ukraine as the ones helping that sad child.

"Thank you, Sephi, for finding me. Thank you for helping me know why people no like me so much. I will use deodorant. I will try to shave the pits. I stay for help these small children who feel bad to come to camp. I help them feel good like you do to me."

When they arrived back at camp, Sephi took Ionna straight to her office. "You've had a long day. I want you to rest here until bedtime. You can begin your training again in the morning. Do you like pizza? I can order some for dinner tonight?"

Ionna was grateful to Sephi. She nodded enthusiastically about the pizza. Though she had never eaten it before, she had seen it in the movies, and the thought of pizza tingled her tastebuds.

That night, when the girls from her tent were ready to go to bed, Ionna strolled in and announced, "I use deodorant. I shave arms and legs. My pits no stink anymore. I learn the American ways. It is time for you to learn to be kind and not rude." Then she climbed into bed, careful not to knock off the three Band-aids from her shins.

Chapter 30

August 2014

Except for the heat, Ionna was enjoying her time at camp. Her English was improving, though she still had trouble understanding all that was said to her and found that others had trouble with her pronunciations.

She loved working with the campers. She noticed she gravitated toward the kids that had trouble fitting in, exactly as Sephi had predicted. Everyone was much kinder to her than they were in the beginning due to the lesson in hygiene, and a stern lecture from Sephi, but her inability to speak the language fluently meant she didn't catch the jokes, had trouble watching the movies, and spent most of a conversation trying to keep up rather than contributing. She wasn't quite ostracized, but she was often excluded.

However, she had made a few good friends that seemed willing to put up with her slow English. Her very best friend was Capuchi. Of course, that wasn't her real name, but all the counselors and staff had a camp name. Some people chose animal names, like Sunfish and Capuchi. Some chose superhero names like Batman and Robin. Others chose names from nature like Rain and Storm. Ionna had chosen Rabbit because the English word was somewhat similar to the Ukranian one – раббит.

Capuchi, Elizabeth to anyone not from camp, lived in North Carolina and took Ionna home one weekend to meet her parents. Everyone was so nice to her and promised to keep in touch once she went back to Ukraine in the fall. They even helped her plan her tour of the US after camp was over. She had already seen much of North Carolina including the coast and mountains, so in mid-August, she would explore some of the places on her adventure list.

Hannah, Capuchi's mom, was a travel agent that hooked her up with a tour in New York, stating she shouldn't try to go there alone. She would do Disney and the Grand Canyon with nothing but her Ukrainian to English dictionary and some brochures, and then Hannah booked another tour group for California that included such stops as San Francisco, Hollywood, and the giant redwood trees. There was simply no way to see all America in one month, she learned, but she would enjoy what she could.

Now, the weekend before her last group of campers, Ionna called her parents for their weekly phone conversation. It was August 16th, a full three months since she had last seen them, and it would be another five weeks before she made the journey home. She gave herself less than a week to recoup before leaving, once again, for school, but she didn't want to waste this opportunity, not knowing when she might be able to come again. She had talked with Sephi about applying for the following summer but hadn't yet broached it with her parents. She wasn't sure what they might think and figured it was best brought up once they had her home again.

She hooked up the camp laptop at the local coffee shop and signed into the internet, opened Skype and began the call. Almost immediately, her parents popped into view.

"Hi Mama. Hi Papa," she said in Ukrainian, waving at them like a little child. "It's me, Ionna." And then she laughed. She told them all about her week and the child who had nearly capsized their boat and the s'mores, which had no Ukrainian translation and needed a lot of explaining, and her upcoming adventures across America. Although they were obviously happy that she called, her father looked distant, and her mother looked anxious.

Finally, when their mood didn't seem to lighten up at all, she said, "Is everything okay? Are you well?"

Her mama piped up quickly, "Oh, yes, Ionna. We are fine. Healthy. There isn't anything wrong." But her father mumbled something she couldn't make out.

"What, Papa? What has you so uptight?" she asked, experiencing a small nibble of fear that whatever was bothering him was so weighty he didn't care to hide it for a 30-minute Skype call.

"It's the Russians," he said.

Ionna tried not to roll her eyes and couldn't believe they were going to talk politics now. But before she could say anything, her mama interjected, "It's nothing. Really."

What was meant to be a calming statement sent bolts of electricity through her chest that radiated out to her fingertips and toes. It must be more than politics if her mama was trying to play it down. "What's nothing, Papa?" she asked.

"There's just been a lot of military movement around here. Everyone is up in arms about Crimea again. Everyone is talking of war."

Ionna's alarm caused her mother to push her father out of the camera and say, "Honestly, darling, the whole thing is nothing. You know men and their talk of war and guns and anything big and loud and manly. It's simply talk. Russia has had their eyes on Crimea for years, and it's always just talk. Don't let you father ruin your last week of camp or your upcoming adventure." Then, to change the subject, she said, "So, tell me. What will you see in New York City?"

Even though nothing more was said of Russians or war, and the conversation stayed firmly on the Statue of Liberty and Mickey Mouse, Ionna felt unsettled. As she said goodbye, without completely understanding why, she added, "Be careful."

———————

One week and a day later, her father's fear came true. Russia invaded Ukraine, taking over the Crimea. On that day, Ionna was happily enjoying the first day of her four-day tour of New York and didn't learn of the fighting along the border until the following evening, when she quickly Skyped home.

"Mama!" she cried when her mother's face flashed on the screen. "Oh, Mama! It's all over the news. War and guns and bombing."

Her mother's appearance was haggard, but she quickly put on a smile. "It's fine, Ionna. They made a big production of it, but it isn't war. Merely a lot of noise and bluster. The president says Crimea will be in our possession again by week's end. It is just a Russian show trying to prove they are big and mighty and powerful. Don't worry, darling. We are fine."

Ionna wanted to believe her, but the news didn't make it look fine, and her mother's eyes were not convincing either. "Where's Papa? I want to hear what he has to say."

Her mother waved a hand toward the door. "He's gone out to the pub to see what news he can glean. As you can imagine, our news only tells one side, and your papa wants to get all the dirt. You know him," she said, forcing a laugh which sounded more like a cough.

"Honestly, Ionna. I don't think it will end up being much of anything. They are showing off and displaying their strength the way a peacock shows off its tail feathers. The sight is impressive but doesn't mean much. Our president will work with them, and they will leave. By the time you come home, this will be all over, and you will have missed the most exciting thing to happen since the USSR collapsed."

Feeling a bit better, Ionna ended the call and continued her tour. However, long before she got to California, she discovered her mother had been wrong. Not only was Russia taking over the Crimea, but they were also building up troops and bombing nearby cities. While touring the Grand Canyon, Ionna had tried Skyping with her parents but couldn't get the call to go through. She assumed it was her connection. But when she tried again later from the hotel and once again at the airport before flying to California, she began to fear the worst.

She remembered very little from her California trip,

spending most of the time looking down at her phone, trying to find out information about Ukraine. Most of what she found was old – days old – rehashing the August 24th invasion. But it was now September 3[rd,] and she was desperate for more current footage.

She had a return flight to Kiev for September 7th, and school started on the 13th. She wondered what she would be flying into. More importantly, she wondered why her parents weren't answering her calls.

One of her answers came in the form of an email from the airlines:

Dear Ms. Petrushevych,
We regret to inform you that all flights into and out of Ukraine have been halted at this time and until further notice. We would be happy to work with you to book a different flight or provide you with a refund. Please contact us at 1-800-866-1111 at your earliest convenience.

This email was followed closely by another email from CCUSA that had sent her to Camp Shenna and was signed by Sephi.

Ionna,
Because CCUSA purchased your tickets for your return flight, we were just informed that you are not currently able to enter your country. I am aware that you are touring in California, but when you find a free moment, please give me a call, and we will help you make plans.
Sincerely,
Sephi Comerly

And then, the floodgates of information lifted with a news account that brought her to her knees. The city of her birth was under siege. She saw footage of a bomb hitting the market a few blocks from her home. She heard the spattering of gunshots. She saw smoke filling the sky. Her home had become the frontline of a war with Russia.

Ionna didn't know what she was supposed to do next. Her flight to Ukraine was leaving from California, so she was stuck on the opposite side of the US from all her friends and coworkers, and she still had not heard from her parents. When she called Sephi, panic in her voice, the older woman, who had become like a big sister to her over the summer, soothed her with soft words.

"I know it looks bad, Ionna, but we are going to do what we can to help you. You don't have to worry about calling the airlines. CCUSA worked on it today, and we've gotten you a flight back to Raleigh in the morning. We've also been on the phone trying to understand the extent of the travel ban. When you arrive, you can stay with me until we get this whole mess figured out. We might be able to find smaller airlines to take you into smaller cities in central and Eastern Ukraine. Whatever it takes, we are here to help. It's going to be okay."

Ionna felt lucky to have so many people helping her. She couldn't begin to imagine the nightmare of talking with airlines and government officials over the phone with her limited English and heavy accent. "Thank you. You don't know how much this means to me."

"Shhh, now, it's okay, really."

Ionna realized she was crying again. Or still. She

wasn't sure which. "I can't find my parents. I don't know if they are dead or alive." It was the first time she had let those words fall from her lips, though they had been racing around her thoughts for days.

"Oh, darling," Sephi crooned. "I'm sure they are fine. A news story showed lots of people leaving the city when the fighting moved closer. Your parents are probably moving away from the bombing. And communication is crazy during times like these. Why, I remember when the last hurricane came through here that we couldn't reach my mama on the coast for nearly a week. But enough about me. You couldn't care less about some hurricane when you've got your parents on your mind. You just keep saying those prayers, and you'll see. You're bound to hear from them soon."

Although she wasn't sure that prayers would help, Ionna was willing to give it a try. Her parents believed it, and Babusya had believed it. If there was a God who listened, now would be an ideal time for Him to show Himself to her.

"Okay, hon, I've texted you the flight information. You stay at the hotel you already booked for your original flight and take the shuttle to the airport. I'll meet you at the airport. And hon? I promise to be there this time."

Sephi was true to her word. As Ionna came through the same tunnel into the lobby almost four months after first arriving in America, there stood Sephi with her arms held open. Ionna stepped closer and those arms came around her in an enormous bear hug. "I've got you now, child. I've got you now."

Chapter 31

September 2014

"Mama! Mama!" Ionna strained to hear her mother's voice through the staticky line. "Oh, Mama! I've been so afraid!"

Sephi came running from the other room when Ionna began shouting and speaking rapidly in Ukrainian. Ionna covered the mouthpiece and said in English, "It's Mama!" and went immediately back to her mother.

"Are you okay? Where are you? Where is Papa?" she said in one breath.

"Slow down, Ionna. Slow down. Your father and I are fine. We packed some of our things and rented a little place in Cherkasy. Far enough away from the fighting and not too close to, as your father says, 'those bloody Russians.'"

Ionna had trouble believing her mother could make jokes at a time like this. "I couldn't reach you. I didn't know if...if you...I just didn't know." She couldn't say the words again, not now that her mother was alive and well.

"Oh, baby. I'm so sorry you had to worry. We couldn't make a call. Cell service has been abysmal. In fact, I can only talk for just a minute. We wanted to tell you we are safe and away from the fighting."

"I can't come home, Mama. They won't let me come home," sobbed Ionna.

"You'll come home, baby. Soon. It will just be for a while."

Ionna sniffed. "How soon, Mama? I'm already missing school."

"Your father called university. They are aware of your situation. They've put you on an academic hold for a semester. No doubt, you'll be home long before that. Don't worry. Be good. Remember who you are. Your papa wants to hear your voice, and then we've got to hang up. There's a line for the phone. It's one of the few that has signal."

The receiver rustled in her ear before the booming voice of her father came on the line. "Ionna, my dear Ionna!"

"Oh, Papa! I love you Papa. And mama. I didn't tell Mama I loved her." She began to cry again.

"She's right here, sweetheart. She heard you. She knows you love her. We are fine. We'll call again soon. Don't worry. We are safe. We love you." And the line went dead.

Ionna turned to Sephi, and in a mixture of Ukrainian and English with a smattering of tears and hiccups, she explained her parents were not in danger. Although Sephi couldn't understand everything, she got the gist of the situation and thanked the Lord her parents were fine. Although she wouldn't have said so out loud, she had begun to wonder. Ten days was a long time to wait for news.

Sephi admonished, "Now, don't forget to say thank you to God tonight in your prayers. He's been listening to you all these nights when you needed Him, and He'll want to hear from you tonight praising His name."

Ionna went to bed early that night. The exhaustion of anxiety had caught up with her, and she wanted nothing more than to sleep the sleep of one who knew her parents were well. However, she did do what Sephi said and knelt to give her thanks.

"God, it's me, Ionna. I'm sure you are aware my mama and papa called me today. They are well. Healthy. Alive." Her voice choked. "Thank you for that. I don't think I would have been able to survive if they had died in this war. I still need them, God. Can you please continue to keep them safe for me? Thanks. Amen."

As she crawled under the covers, she thought about her relationship with God. Until her grandmother died eight years ago, she believed because her parents believed. After her death, Ionna couldn't make up her mind if God was real or just something someone believed in to make themselves feel better. She still wasn't entirely sure, but she must admit that talking to Him about her problems did make her feel better. And her parents were alive. Surely, that was a sign? "Yes," she thought as she drifted off to sleep, "The perfect sign."

———————

Unfortunately, the conflict in Ukraine didn't seem to be ending too quickly, and she couldn't go back home. But she also couldn't stay because her work visa was expiring.

CCUSA refused to send her to some other foreign country for her to wait it out. "You are our responsibility," they had told her. "We will figure something out."

In the end, due to the extenuating circumstances, they had been able to extend her Visa by three months, calling her an employee of Camp Shenna. Although she didn't do much for them, she did go into work with Sephi a few times each week, doing office chores like stuffing mailers or emptying trash. She also spent quite a bit of time with the lawyer she'd been assigned to who was working to secure a Visa extension until such a time as the fighting stopped and her parents could return to their home and their livelihood.

They had been in their temporary home for several weeks now, and since nothing was likely to change any time soon, her father had taken employment in town. He had no way to teach chemistry, but their meager savings were running out, so he worked for a local merchant, taking the shifts that others didn't want.

Ionna hated to think of her father working in a store instead of lecturing to his students, but he told her in one of their now-daily Skype calls, "It's fine, my girl. I am one of the lucky ones. I have a job. We have a home to keep us warm and dry. We have food to eat. And I've been assured by the university that once the fighting has stopped, we will all go back to teaching students."

Each evening, before she went to bed, Ionna Skyped with her parents as they started the next day. It became a routine, and Ionna looked forward to talking with them as she ended her day.

"I spoke to my lawyer again, today. She is trying to get my Visa extended, but the laws here are really difficult.

She's only got six weeks left. I don't know what I'll do if she can't help me. CCUSA can't extend my Visa again. And, though Sephi says I can stay here with her, I really can't if I'm not supposed to be in the country."

Papa gave her a smile. "It will work out. It always works out." But the smile didn't reach his eyes, and it certainly didn't reach her heart.

———————

The news was grim.

"Ionna, I'm working the system as hard as I can, but I don't see me getting this approved before the deadline. We must come up with an alternative plan. I've been trying to find another country that will accept you as a refugee until we can straighten this out here. I've not had any luck so far, but I've been told to try Romania and Poland. Both have been accepting Ukrainians fleeing from the conflict."

Ionna didn't want to go to Poland or Romania. She didn't speak the language, she had no friends, and she might not have the same access to her parents. She wanted to remain in the US, but she didn't say any of that to her lawyer. Instead, she set up an appointment for the following week, but it was an appointment she didn't intend to keep.

For several weeks, she had been cooking up a "just in case" plan because although things did work out in the end, sometimes the end was too far away to sit and wait for. Going to Poland or Romania was not a viable solution. Staying in the US wasn't a legal solution. But what if she stayed without permission?

Sephi would let her stay, but the authorities would obviously search for her at Sephi's house first. She might be able to hide for a week or so, but not much longer than that. She needed somewhere she could blend in, and that was when she thought of New York City.

While on her tour, the guide had chatted with her during one of the stops and learned that Ionna was from Ukraine. "How interesting!" she had said. "Did you know there is an entire section of the city populated with expats from Ukraine, Russia, and other Soviet bloc countries?"

"Expats?" Ionna had said.

"Oh, yes, sorry. People who once lived there but now live in Brighton Beach. If you ever visit the United States again, you might find it interesting to go there. I'd be curious to learn how much the settlement is like your home."

And then, the rest of the tour participants began to gather, and they made their way to the Statue of Liberty.

Brighton Beach would be the perfect place to disappear among the crowd. She spoke the language, so she could explain her situation to someone and find some help. At least that was the plan, and now that her lawyer made it clear getting the Visa in time was unlikely, tomorrow was the day to put the plan into action.

The next morning, after Sephi left for work, Ionna packed her things and lugged her suitcases to the front door. She pulled down a pen and paper, knowing she had to let Sephi know she was okay, but without giving her too much information. Ionna had to remain hidden.

Dear Sephi,

Thank you. Thank you for all things. Thank you for helping me when I cannot go home. I know you try hard. But Visa expiring, and I must leave here. I be

okay. No worry, please. Please tell Mama and Papa I
be okay. When I can, I see you again. I love you.
Ionna
Also, please send folded letter to lawyer.

Then she penned a quick note to her lawyer. Although she'd been told her lawyer couldn't tell anyone what was said to her in private, she wasn't sure if that was true. So, she kept that letter as short and devoid of information as her letter to Sephi, merely asking her to keep trying to obtain the Visa and that she'd be in touch.

Dear Ms. Addleton,
Thank you for help. Please keep trying. I will keep
writing you. I am safe.
Ionna

Then, without another look back, she began the three-mile walk to the bus station. Her bus would not leave the station until 8:00 pm, so she had plenty of time. Her biggest concern was that someone would find her at the bus station before she could leave town, but she intended to rent a locker for her suitcases and find a coffee shop nearby until closer to her departure time. Although there were earlier tickets, she didn't want to arrive in the city after midnight, especially since she knew no one and had no solid plans.

By noon, she was at the station, had purchased her ticket, and placed her bags into a storage locker. The clerk told her of a Starbucks a few blocks away, and she spent her afternoon and early evening nursing a latte and reading the Raleigh News and Observer from cover to cover – twice.

As she boarded the bus, she said a silent prayer despite the answer she sought not being a foregone conclusion. "God. It's me, Ionna. Please let Sephi understand. Please keep my parents from worrying when I don't call them tonight. And please help me find someone in New York that will help. Thank you. Amen."

Chapter 32

December 2014

Although she had been to New York City when she thought she eventually would be flying back to Ukraine, she had been a tourist. With the giddy anticipation of a visitor from a foreign country, she had soaked up all the brightly lit, bustling city had to offer. She spent her time seeing an Off-Broadway show, the Statue of Liberty, Times Square, and the 9/11 Memorial. She shopped in Macy's, she drank coffee in Central Park, and ate a hot dog purchased from a street vendor. She took photos, bought souvenirs, and even ate New York Style pizza. She had not assumed she would visit the city again, at least not so soon.

However, this time was different. Instead of traveling into the heart of the city with its horns and sirens and crowds, she got off the bus in Brooklyn, the closest station to Brighton Beach – still a full thirteen miles away. As she studied the bulk of her suitcases, she concluded that thirteen miles was too far to walk, so she inquired about the nearest subway station.

The Jay St – Metrotech was a short, five-minute walk. From there, she would have to wait for the F-line which would take her to Neptune Avenue. Then, she could either walk the remaining blocks or catch a bus. She figured she would walk and hoped to come up with something concrete to do, given her plan wasn't much of a plan now that she reached the city.

She realized how little information she had about the area. What she did know, however, calmed her, if only slightly. Brighton Beach was where the Russian and Soviet-bloc immigrants lived, which meant she would understand the people. It also meant she wasn't the first person to come here to hide.

As she walked toward the subway, she contemplated her situation. One: She had only a little money. She was afraid to pull her cash out to count it, but she had barely enough for one night at a less than stellar motel and potentially a cup of coffee the next morning. She was going to need to make some money so she could survive. Food and shelter would have to be priority number one, once she got to Brighton Beach.

Ionna had never held a job other than her summer employment with CCUSA. She had worked hard and believed she was an exemplary employee, but she couldn't reach out and ask for references. Not now. She considered her skill set. She could write...in Ukrainian. She could speak several languages...to some degree. She had mad arguing skills...just ask her father. She was an expert at curing homesickness...among the elementary-age crowd.

But when it came to employable skills, something valuable to those who lived in New York City, she had none. Although her thoughts created a dismal picture, she squared her shoulders and continued to enumerate her problems.

Two: Her parents had no idea where she was and would be concerned. Concerned? How about terrified? Inconsolable? She had already missed one Skype call and would surely miss more before things were settled enough for her to make contact. What would her father be doing? Calling CCUSA, no doubt. Demanding to know why they had not kept a closer eye on her. Threatening them to find her, or else.

Ionna had no doubt that Sephi shared everything with them as soon as she discovered her letter. And she was grateful, really. At least her parents didn't have to wonder whether she'd been raped and murdered or sold to a sex trafficker. Of course, they would not be happy with her decision.

But she did what she believed she had to do. She wasn't the one who started this crazy war or created the red tape for seeking asylum in another nation, but she was the one having to live with the consequences. So, she, and she alone, had to determine the best course of action. Hands down, hiding in New York among Ukrainians was far better than being shipped to Poland and living in a refugee camp. Eventually, she was sure she could convince her parents her decision was the best of two bad choices. Eventually. But she wasn't looking forward to that first conversation.

Three: She was completely alone. At this point, she had gotten on a subway crammed with people but was utterly alone. No one knew her name. No one knew why she was there. No one cared to know. Even though that was the entire point of coming here, the knowledge that if she disappeared between here and her stop, no one would notice was terrifying.

Her mother's words came back to her, "You've been away in Ukraine, Ionna. It's not the same thing. This time, you'll be far away from everyone and everything you know." How right her mama had been.

She studied her surroundings, hoping to figure out what her next steps should be. In less than thirty minutes, she would exit the subway and what? Work? But where? Sleep? In a doorway, perhaps? Eat? Food scavenged from the trash? With each question, her squared shoulders rounded a bit more until she was a tiny girl huddled over two suitcases.

It was then she heard a sound that wriggled her hopelessness a degree to the left. She abruptly realized the people around her, though strangers, had a familiarity. Gone were the narrow faces and rounded noses she had grown accustomed to in North Carolina. Instead, the subway car carried broad faces with defined cheekbones, light colored, barely slanted, deep-set eyes, full and prominent eyebrows, and sharp noses. Until this very moment, she hadn't considered the differences, but they were, without a doubt, quite distinct. Immediately, Ionna blended in, and if it had not been for the suitcases pulled in close around her, any casual observer would have said she belonged.

While she marveled at the people, familiar words floated past in both Russian and Ukrainian with a light, musical lilt, far different than the harsher sounds of

English. She let her eyelids fall shut and the sounds wash over her, almost believing she was at home. There was a conversation to her right about some new show called House of Cards. "YA lyublyu nove shou pid nazvoyu «Kartkovyy budynok». Personazhi duzhe intryhuyuchi. Vy bachyly tse na Netflix mynuloyi nochi?" Netflix hit her eardrum like a jackhammer in the midst of angels singing, bringing her squarely back to the United States and her situation. And just in time. Hers was the next stop.

She stood awkwardly, wrestling the two suitcases from between the seats and edging toward the door. A young man, older than Ionna but far younger than her father said, "May I help you with those?" His English was perfect but his accent, a Ukrainian accent, was strong.

She answered in her native tongue, "Although not necessary, it would be very helpful. Thank you."

He smiled broadly, taking the handle from the nearest case and rolled it toward the door, ushering Ionna along with him. When the doors opened, the press of people pushed her forward until she was standing on a covered, concrete platform, location signs pointing in two different directions.

"Which way," the young man asked, eager to continue to offer his services.

She hesitated. Which way, indeed. She read the signs, hoping one would give her an idea, but nothing came to her. She had no idea. Looking up at him, she wondered about his own story and what he might think of hers. Was he the kind to turn her in to the authorities, though technically, her Visa didn't expire for another three days? Or was he someone who could help her find her way in the underground of Brighton Beach?

She noted that his expression had turned from expectant to quizzical. However, he still appeared to be willing to help her, regardless of her indecision.

"I need to find a place to eat breakfast. Something inexpensive. I haven't eaten since breakfast yesterday. I'm pretty hungry, but my funds are limited. What would you suggest?" Everything she told him was the truth, and though it hinted at her story, gave nothing away.

His expression, firmly quizzical now, still contained warmth and hospitality. He considered her for a long moment, and then said, "I have two places in mind. I'll leave it up to you. The first is a quiet café about two blocks from here run by Petruso Kushnir. There, you will find all the foods from home like halusky, semolina, and syrniki. If I tell him that you are new to the area and missing home, he will let you eat your first meal free of charge. He does that for all Ukrainians relocating to Brighton Beach."

That sounded wonderful. Ionna hadn't had any semolina since leaving home. However, the young man had said he had two options. "And the second?"

He hesitated. "My name is Fadekya. I have lived in America for three years with my mama, papa, and babusya, who happens to be the best cook in all Brighton Beach – maybe even all New York. I am certain they would be happy to meet you and offer you breakfast." He tried to gauge her comfort level. "And perhaps other things you are in need of," he added.

Ionna prided herself on being a good judge of character, and she immediately liked and trusted Fadekya. On the other hand, she had heard macabre tales of men luring young women to their homes and turning them into sex slaves or worse.

He saw her hesitation. "Petruso's it is. Would you like to meet my family? I can have them come by the restaurant. I'm sure they would love some news of the home country."

Ionna smiled. "It's been seven months since I've been home, but I talk to my parents nearly every day. I would love to meet your family and share all the news."

Fodekya whipped out his cellphone and rang up his parents. "Mama, you and Papa and Babuysa need to come to Petruso's. I met a new friend. Her name is," he paused, realizing he had yet to get her name. She mouthed 'Ionna.' He continued, "Her name is Ionna, and she is newly in America with much news of Ukraine. I'm taking her by for her first meal in Brighton Beach. Can you join us?"

Within moments, it was settled that Mama and Babuysa would be along within the hour. Papa was out running errands, but she would leave him a note in case he got home before Ionna went on her way. With that, Fodekya led the way to the restaurant.

It wasn't much to look at. Simple tables and chairs covered with red vinyl clothes. Saltshakers stood sentinel on either side of the day's menu. Silverware was wrapped in a paper napkin and brought to the table as they were seated.

A young woman, known by Fodekya, came to the table. "Good morning, Mykhaila. Please, meet Ionna. This is her first day here in Brighton Beach. She has come to enjoy her first meal at Petruso's."

Mykhaila smiled widely at Ionna, "Dobryy ranok! Shcho b vy khotily na snidanok s'ohodni vrantsi?"

Ionna's spirits lifed as she was greeted in Ukrainian and given a rundown of the morning's menu. She settled on semolina with fresh fruit and varenyky filled with onions, mushrooms, potatoes, and cheese. Her mouth began to water just at the ordering of the food, though she had grown accustomed to hamburgers and baked chicken, her taste buds longed for home as much, if not more, than her heart did.

Mykhaila also brought out a glass of ryazhenka, which was a cross between an American glass of milk and a cup of yogurt. The biggest difference was that ryazhenka was served at room temperature. She brought the cup to her lips, took a long swallow, and drank in the joy of all things Ukrainian. She imagined her American friends would find this disgusting, just as she found peanut butter, and something called artificial maple flavored syrup. However, she didn't really care at the moment. She was in her own little heaven.

Fodekya said knowingly, "See? I told you. And the best is yet to come."

Moments later, Petruso himself, came out from the kitchen with her breakfast. "Hello, young lady. Welcome to Brighton Beach. Please, enjoy your meal!" He held one dish in each hand, bowed at the waist, and, with a flourish, presented her food.

"Thank you for your hospitality, Petruso. I hope to see you on a regular basis!" And with that, she picked up a spoon, filled it with semolina, and took a bite after saying, "To Ukraine."

Although she had tried to eat slowly and savor each bite, she was physically and emotionally hungry, needing both the sustenance and the comfort of home. The meal was gone almost before she knew it. She looked up sheepishly at Fodekya as she wiped her mouth with the back of her hand. He didn't seem to mind her abysmal manners. In fact, he seemed to relish the idea that he had brought her such joy.

Without asking, he motioned to the waitress, help up three fingers, and gave her a quick wink when she nodded. Almost immediately, Petruso appeared again, this time with a plate of syrniki, cheese pancakes, topped with sour cream, strawberry jam, and powdered sugar. Ionna tried to protest, not wanting to take advantage of his hospitality, but Petruso waved her concerns to the side. "Here, at Petruso's, no one ever goes away hungry. And you, Ionna, new to Brighton Beach, appear to be hungry."

He was right. She was still hungry. So, rather than argue, she picked up her fork and knife. This time, she was able to eat a bit slower and enjoy the food, chatting with Fodekya between mouthfuls. She was still unwilling to give him too much information but did let him know that she had come to America over the summer to work and was taking a semester leave from school.

Because it was innocuous enough, she told him all about her summer and the kids at camp without ever revealing which camp or its location. In detail, she expounded on her first trip to Walmart, her first time trying a s'more, her first kayaking experience beyond the small cove, and the first time the waitress at a restaurant refilled her cup of soda.

"I was so angry that she filled it to the top without asking and before I had even finished the first glass. I told the girls that it wasn't right that I would have to pay for two sodas and that I wanted to complain to the manager," she said with a lopsided smile. "I couldn't understand why the girls were laughing, and my English was not very good. It took a while before I understood refills were free. Free! Before leaving, I let the waitress refill my cup five times. And," she said slyly, "I took one to go!"

Popping the last bite into her mouth, Ionna slid the plate away, finally satisfied. "That was amazing. Although I would never say so to Mama, I think those are the best syrniki I have ever eaten." Of course, she reasoned, her mama had spent her entire life rationing food of one kind or another. It might be possible her mother's recipes would taste infinitely better if she always got all the needed ingredients without having to make interesting substitutions.

As she wiped her mouth with her napkin, coming away with a smudge of strawberry from her chin, Fodekya's mother and babuysa walked in.

"Mama! Babuysa! You made it!" He jumped up and helped the older ladies with their chairs, asking if the ladies wanted anything to eat or drink. "Let's see if Petruso is ready to make some pierogis. We'll take the mixed plate and share."

Fodekya waved to Mykhaila, put in the order, and waited for the interrogation to begin. Guilt twinged at his conscience because Ionna wouldn't leave the table without telling everything she knew about Ukraine and everything that brought her to America, but Fodekya sensed she needed someone to talk to.

"I am Kalyna, but everyone just calls me Mama. You may do the same," said Fodekya's mother. And then, gesturing toward her mother, said, "This is Nataliya."

"Hello, Kalyna," said Ionna, holding out her hand.

"Mama. Just call me Mama."

"Hello, Mama," and then she turned to Nataliya.

Before she could shake hands, Nataliya said, "And call me Babuysa. Nataliya is a name for a young woman, and, as you can see, I no longer fit that description!"

Ionna reached across the table. "Hello, Babuysa. It is nice to meet you."

At first, Mama and Babuysa let her talk at her own pace, bringing up whatever topics came to mind. Soon, however, they began interjecting a question here and there, and before long, Ionna was answering a steady stream of questions, mostly about Ukraine and what she knew of the fighting.

Because she spoke to her father daily, and because her father was always informed, Ionna was able to tell them many of the smaller details they couldn't find out from the American news sources. Ionna even began to offer her father's analysis of Russia's intent, which led both women to turn their heads to one side and pretend to spit on the floor. Ionna assumed the spit would have been real if they had been outdoors rather than in a dining establishment. It seemed that they, along with the others in the restaurant who were now listening intently, held the same opinions as her father, muttering words about the dirty Russians, many of which she could never repeat in polite company.

Ionna wondered how this 'hatred' played out in Brighton Beach, which she understood to be a conglomerate of Ukrainians, Russians, and other Soviet-bloc immigrants. However, before she could broach the subject, the conversation turned to her.

"So, Ionna, what brings you here to Brighton Beach?"

Ionna dropped her gaze, not sure what to say, and

definitely not wanting to say it with a crowd listening on.

"Just visiting," she replied vaguely.

"Oh, that's nice. Who have you come to visit? Perhaps we've met them?" said Mama.

"I...um...probably not. They are new here, too." She sought desperately to turn the conversation back to something safer, like Russian power-grabbing or nuclear war. Gratefully, now that the conversation had turned personal, the other patrons had gone back to their own meals and conversations, but Ionna wasn't sure how much to say.

Mama would have none of it. "It seems to me," she said a bit more softly, keeping her opinions at their table, "that you are being a bit vague. Could it be that there is something you are not telling us?" She caught Ionna's eyes with hers. "Come, now. Tell Mama all about it. There must be a reason a young girl arrives in Brighton Beach with two large suitcases, an empty belly, and no one to meet her at the subway station."

Still wary, Ionna started a partial story to gauge the reaction. "I was working at a summer camp in another state and decided to stay a while longer. I figured Brighton Beach was the best place to land because I would feel more at home." Everything she said was true, at least to a degree.

"I see," said Mama. "You decided to stay in America before flying back to Ukraine, but instead of enjoying the American culture, you thought you'd lose yourself in American-Ukrainian culture. Far better than going home, I'm sure." Her eyebrows arched to emphasize her sarcasm.

Mama was not slow-witted or easily fooled. Obviously, the story was whitewashed, and she wanted Ionna to know that she knew. Ionna blew out a long breath. She either had to trust this family or extricate herself from them immediately. "And then what? And go where?" she thought to herself.

Quickly, before she could change her mind, she began her saga, starting with her summer plans to work at a camp as a counselor and ending with her clandestine Greyhound bus trip to Brooklyn. "And then I met your son who helped me with my bags, brought me here to eat good food, and introduce me to his mama and babuysa. That is the whole story."

She waited expectantly for the reaction of the three strangers who now were privy to her story. "My plan has no next step. I don't know where to go or what to do next." She lifted her shoulders up a fraction of an inch and let them fall again. "I..." she went silent, wondering what would happen next.

She was still legal. They couldn't really turn her in because, as of yet, she had done nothing wrong. She hadn't missed work. She was old enough to travel without permission. There was nothing that said she couldn't visit Brighton Beach before relegating oneself to a Polish refugee camp. However, if they decided not to help her, they would likely tell others, and her chances of finding a way to stay hidden in the area would be greatly diminished.

Her eyes implored them as she said, "Please, I need help. Or at least I need no hindrance. Please..."

Chapter 33

February 2015

Ionna called to Petruso in the kitchen. "There's a lull. I'm going to take my break. Myk says she can handle anyone that comes in."

"Fine, fine, Ionna. Take the time you need. The lunch traffic will begin soon enough."

Ionna had begun working at Petruso's days after first eating at the restaurant and meeting Fodekya's family. Without hesitation, they had taken her in and given her a place to sleep, even when she explained she had no money with which to repay them.

"Bah," said Mama. "I do not want your money. You brought us word from Ukraine and delighted us with your stories. That is payment enough. We will help you get on your feet." Although she didn't say they would help her hide, it was exactly what they did.

However, hiding here wasn't exactly hiding. She went out every day and even worked. But Petruso paid her under the table and the locals didn't ask questions because they didn't care to know the answers. She assumed she was not the only person here illegally. And she was illegal, officially now for two months.

A month ago, she rented a room in an apartment with two other girls. They didn't want to know the details of her life – they simply wanted her share of the rent. She was happy to oblige. Though she was happy living with Fodekya's family, she didn't want to be a burden and worried that they might lose their legal status by harboring someone who was supposed to be in a Polish refugee camp.

Petruso allowed her to use the shop's Internet, but due to her hours and the fact that her flat was a 40-minute ride, she now called her parents at the start of her day and the end of theirs. To say they were unhappy with her decision to hide was an understatement of epic proportion. Her father had tried every trick he knew to force her to go straight back to Raleigh, apologize to the lawyer, and fly on a plane to the refugee camp. But Ionna would not consider it.

"No, Papa. It isn't what is best for me. I cannot go thousands of miles from here to sit in a tent city with limited supplies and rampant disease. It would be stupid. And, once I am out of America, what will be the hurry to approve my Visa? I won't be able to work. I won't be able to easily communicate with you and Mama. It makes no sense."

In the end, her papa realized that he could do nothing about it. He could not force her to go, and he certainly wasn't prepared to disown her for disobeying his wishes. Although he still wasn't happy, they rarely discussed it except to receive lawyer updates.

"I spoke to my lawyer yesterday," she had told them earlier this morning. Ionna kept her promise to touch base with her Raleigh lawyer who gave her the name of an excellent immigration attorney in Brooklyn. Kara was the daughter of Russian immigrants and worked to help many families in the area bring family stateside. She had agreed to help Ionna.

"She said that she thinks I might receive a temporary visa in as little as six weeks. If that happens, then I will be legally here while she attempts to secure permanent asylum for me."

She hated the thought of her parents living in Ukraine while she lived in the United States, but the outbreak of fighting had not abated and didn't appear that it would any time soon. In fact, the Russians were getting loud again and threatening to move further into Ukraine. According to her father, who was no longer trying to shield her from the truth as he had early on when he let her believe she would be coming home again before the spring semester of college, it could be years before everything was settled once again. In fact, he had confided in her that he doubted he would ever work as a professor again.

"I'm getting old, Ionna. By the time university is up and running again, I will be replaced by younger, more eager professors. And rightfully so." He tried to put a positive spin on it, but Ionna knew her father loved teaching and missed his daily lectures and contact with his young students.

"Have you and Mama considered moving closer to

another university? Perhaps finding work there?" she had asked during one conversation. He had, but the conflict had, once again, thrust Ukraine into an economic downturn, so fewer students were going to university, and no one was hiring. He felt grateful for the job he had and the food, though sparse, that they had to eat.

Ionna sat down at a table at the back of the restaurant and fished a book out of her backpack. She had begun reading a new book given to her by a regular customer. "You will love this, Ionna," the woman had said. "It is a great book full of adventure. And," she said with emphasis, "it was written by a Ukrianian-American living here in New York City!"

The woman had been right. The book was intriguing. And since she still hoped to someday be a writer, she not only read to enjoy the story, but read in a critical way, studying how and why he used the words he did. He had a delightful way of describing characters that made her feel like they were sitting in the booth with her.

Shortly before her break ended, an older gentleman walked into the restaurant. She glanced up to be sure that Myk didn't need her help. The man, though not a regular, had been here before, and she gave him a small smile and nod before dropping her eyes to the book again. She wanted to finish up the chapter before the lunch bustle began.

A shadow fell over the page, and Ionna glanced up to find the man standing there, watching her read. "Do you like the book?" he asked.

"Yes, very much. I particularly like the character development. Have you ever read anything by Yakiv Nesviatypaska?"

"Actually, I have. You see, I am Yakiv Nesviatypaska, and I'm glad you are enjoying my book."

As her lawyer had intimated, Ionna was granted a temporary Visa and given a set of instructions – rules she must follow to remain in the United States. One of those rules was to pay taxes. She had immediately asked Petruso to become a real employee on his payroll. He was more than happy to oblige.

Everyone at the restaurant loved Ionna. In fact, Petruso commented that he wondered if they were coming in for his food or her company. Although he had always been busy, the restaurant was busier than ever, with more and more people willing to eat a later breakfast and an earlier lunch just to be seated.

Petruso paid his waitresses well, but Ionna's tips were what kept her at the job. It was not unusual for her to make $200 or more in a day. She began saving her money and sending it to her parents as often as possible. At first, they had protested, saying she needed the money. But the truth was that they needed it more. The money she sent them each month was the difference between getting by and going hungry. Even with the money, finding food was not easy.

One time, when Ionna told her mother that she had put a roast in the crockpot and would eat it for supper and then as leftovers for a few days, her mother's eyes flew open wide. "Ionna! That is so extravagant. Why would you spend your money that way?"

Confused, Ionna replied, "It wasn't too much, Mama. I got it on sale for $10. I'll eat from it most of the week.

Really, it is quite reasonable."

Her mother was stunned. "Ten dollars? An entire roast for $10? We haven't found beef at the store since Russia invaded, and if we did, we would expect to pay $200 or more." Afterward, Ionna spent hours talking with her mother about all the choices she had at the store from fruits and vegetables to meats to breads and pastas. Ionna only wished she could send home food rather than just money.

As her shift neared its end, she saw a familiar face walk through the door. Ever since he caught her reading his book, Yakiv had become a regular, often seeking out Ionna to discuss Ukraine or writing or both. He encouraged her to try her hand at writing, but Ionna felt so unprepared with just one year of university under her belt.

"University is not where you learn the craft of writing. There, you only glean the concept. The true craft comes from doing. To become a writer, Ionna, you must write."

He sat down at an empty table and greeted her warmly. "Good day to you, Ionna. How have you been? Have you been writing?"

This was his standard question, and she gave him her standard answer. "I'm fine, Yakiv. And not yet. I don't know what to write about."

To which he always replied, "Write about not knowing what to write about. The point is to write!"

She laughed, as she always did, and wondered if she would ever write something just to change the banter between them.

"What can I get for you today, Yakiv? It's rather late for your lunch. Are you here for an early dinner?"

"Actually, Ionna, I have come bearing an invitation

from my wife. You've met Daniela."

Ionna nodded. Yakiv had brought her to the restaurant a few times and was quick to introduce them to each other.

"Well, my dear wife wishes to have you come for dinner some night soon. She says she is tiring of my company and needs a fresh opinion!"

Ionna laughed heartily. She couldn't imagine tiring of Yakiv, but she was more than happy to accept the invitation. "I could come by on Thursday after work. That's my short-shift day. If possible, I'd like to eat early. The subway ride home is long, and I don't really like riding too late at night.

"Yes, yes, of course! I will tell Daniela to expect you on Thursday for an early dinner. She will be so happy that you've consented to be our guest."

As Ionna counted her tips in the back room and then hid them in various places in her clothing for the subway ride home, she realized she was happy. Sure, there were things she would change if she could, but generally she was happy. She had a job she enjoyed, money enough to pay her bills and help her parents, and good friends. She had made the right choice in coming here.

Chapter 34

Summer 2015

Ionna put down her fork. "No more, Daniela! If you keep feeding me like this, I am going to have to buy all new clothes!"

Since her first dinner date at the Nesviatypaska home back in April, Ionna had become a regular guest at their table. In fact, she had a standing dinner date each Thursday where Yakiv treated her to his intelligent conversation while Daniela treated her to her delectable food.

Daniela was not Ukrainian. Her grandparents moved to New York from Poland. However, after two generations in the States, the recipes passed from grandmother to mother to child had morphed into something that was a cross between Polish and a host of other nationalities. She constantly encouraged Daniela to start a restaurant or least write a cookbook. "You would make a fortune, Daniela. Petruso is a good cook, but he can't hold a candle to you. And look how busy he is."

Daniela would just smile and shake her head. "I'm too old to be that busy. I like my quiet simple life."

"Then at least put them into a book. Life without these recipes wouldn't be worth living!"

Yakiv and Daniela married later in life and had no children. Ionna couldn't bear the thought of these generational recipes dying with Daniela. "I will write them down for you, my dear. If you choose to make them into a book, be my guest."

Now, each time Ionna came for a meal, she left with the recipes for the dishes she'd eaten. She had every intention of putting them into a book and getting it published, but in Daniela's name. The woman was so modest that she couldn't see how amazing she was.

Ionna no longer had to leave early. Yakiv had taken to riding the subway with her and then back home again. She told him it wasn't necessary, but he had insisted. "We want your company, my dear. And we would be horrified to learn that by insisting upon it, you ended up in trouble on the subway."

"But what if someone hurts you, Yakiv?" she had asked.

"No one will bother an old man who looks wealthy enough not to be a bum but poor enough not to carry anything of value. I will be fine. I've lived in this city a long time without any issues. I'll likely go to my grave that way."

Although they talked of many things, and he went to great lengths to provide specific details about his work and his time in New York, he had always been vague about his time before living in Brighton Beach.

In an early conversation, she had innocently asked, "How long have you lived in New York, Yakiv?" after learning of Daniela's heritage.

Yakiv had answered, "Many years, now" and deftly changed the subject.

Although she had poked and prodded, she never got any more out of him than he was born in Ukraine and moved to New York some years before. He never spoke of his extended family. She finally quit asking, assuming that he, like she, had come here under 'not so legal' circumstances. It didn't really matter to her. He was a good friend, and whether he shared his distant past or kept it to himself was of no concern.

———————

She had begun writing, much to Yakiv's delight, and part of their meal was spent talking about her work. Although he was complimentary, he was also willing to be critical, offering her suggestions and insights. It was like having a one-on-one writing class without having to pay the tuition.

She had begun by writing short stories of 3000 words or less but was now tackling a novel. During dinner, she asked, "Yakiv, when you write, do you ever feel like there are two of you?"

Yakiv raised his right eyebrow. "Go on," he encouraged.

She felt rather crazy, almost like she had multiple personalities. "Sometimes," she began, "I am writing something at my computer and the thoughts come so quickly that my fingers can barely type the words fast enough. At the same time, I am reading the words as they pop up on the screen." She paused, looking at him closely. "Sometimes, I can hardly believe what I am reading, as though I've never seen those words before – even though it was me that just punched the words on the keyboard."

Yakiv grinned. "You, my dear, have become a quirky writer! Yes, yes, I have experienced that same thing. It is like in the Bible where it says that the left hand shouldn't know what the right hand is doing!"

Yakiv and Daniela were of a religious mindset, often going to the Orthodox Church on Sundays. Although Ionna still wrestled with the idea of God, she had grown more comfortable with the idea of someone in charge of her life, as well as the concept of things turning out okay in the end. She knew her grandmother would be pleased with the progress.

On this particular night, after going over the most recent chapter of Ionna's novel, Yakiv said, "Have you considered going back to school, Ionna?"

When she appeared shocked by the idea, he said, "It may be a long time before you get back to Ukraine and the life you left behind. There are programs here in the States to help immigrants who speak English as a second language attend school. Would you be interested?"

Of course, she would be interested. Ionna had always loved school. But how would she fit it in with her job? And the cost? Would it be too prohibitive? And could someone on a temporary Visa go to school?

Yakiv believed she could go while on a Visa, and as for cost, said, "Ionna, I have no children. No family here at all. My career has been quite prosperous. I've been blessed in that regard." He paused and his eyes misted for a moment, as if remembering a 'regard' in which he hadn't been as blessed. The moment passed, and he went on, "I'd love to send you to school. I think you could go part time, perhaps in the evening, or some online. Even just a class or two at a time would be better than nothing at all. What do you say?"

She was incredulous. Here, a man she met by accident in the restaurant, wanted to help pay for her schooling. She could hear Babuysa's voice in her head, "There are no accidents, love." Maybe Babuysa was right. Maybe God had orchestrated her meeting with Yakiv. Maybe His plan was for her to fill a void in his life while he filled a void in hers. Who was she to throw God's will out the window?

"Yes, Yakiv. I would like that."

"Superb. We will begin looking into it immediately."

Chapter 35

February 2016

Ionna was working at the restaurant, listening to the chatter about the big blizzard prediction. The weather forecasters had been making great noises about the upcoming snow event. Ionna wasn't worried. This was her second winter in New York, and she had seen plenty of snow. The forecasters were always making mountains out of molehills.

She loved using that expression since learning it in her English class at school. She had enrolled in The State University of New York (SUNY) as an English as a second language student this past fall, with Yakiv and Daniela helping her with the tuition. As an ESL student, she was required to take a series of four English classes in addition to her other coursework.

She didn't want to quit her job at Petruso's, so she

decided to take two additional classes each semester. It would take her twice as long to graduate, but, as Yakiv said, she could always change the pace if her circumstances changed.

This semester, she had her second English ESL class, World Literature, and Intro to Fiction Writing. Now, when on break at work, rather than reading for pleasure, she read for a grade. The classes were arduous because her English was still not as fluent as she would have liked. In fact, her abilities had downgraded considerably once she moved to Brighton Beach and no longer had the need to use it as often. However, since taking these classes, she was finally seeing considerable strides.

Yakiv and Daniela's help was invaluable, especially when it came to her fiction writing class. She had creative ideas – in Ukrainian – but found it difficult to translate them into English without reverting to second grade primer material. "Jane ran. The dog ran. The cat ran" were not going to be sufficient for her professor. Each Thursday evening, the two helped her revise her work into something she felt more inclined to turn in as a finished product.

Two customers came in, bundled from the top of their snow-covered toboggans to their soggy boots, bringing in a whoosh of cold air with them. "They say it will be three feet."

"I heard four!"

Ionna shook her head. She had never seen more than 10 inches fall at any given time, but the tale of the blizzard was taking on a life of its own. She sat down at 11 o'clock and began to study *Midnight's Children* by Salman Rushdie. The readings took her a long time as she struggled with the English language, which she found even harder when reading foreign works that had been translated into English. Before her break was over, the first flakes began to fall.

By the time the lunch rush was over, there were six inches on the ground and the snow kept steadily falling. Ionna's shift didn't end until 4:30, but, unlike typical days at Petruso's, the store was virtually empty.

"Go ahead and study, Ionna," Petruso had said. "You may as well do something productive. It looks like the big blizzard has scared away my customers. If we aren't busy by 3:30, you may as well leave for home early."

Ionna sat at the back table once again, preparing to tackle Rushdie's works when the door blew inward and the abominable snowman shuffled in. It took both the snowman and Petruso to force the door closed against the howling wind. Ionna did not look forward to the walk to the subway.

As the snowman lost his layers of snow and outer clothing, none other than Yakiv appeared.

"Yakiv! Is that you under all that snow and wool? What are you doing out in this weather?" she admonished. "You are going to catch your death of a cold. Here, let me pour you a cup of coffee. You look frozen through and through."

Ionna hurried to the counter and fetched a cup of coffee, adding a splash of cool water so that Yakiv didn't have to wait to begin drinking.

"Let me bring you something warm to eat," Petruso said. But Yakiv waved him off. "I only came for a moment. I'm here to see Ionna. I have news about the storm. Daniela and I learned they are stopping the subways. The storm is going to dump two to three feet of snow. The snow is already over a foot and the storm has barely begun. We don't want you out in this mess, Ionna. Daniela asked that I bring you back to our home for the evening, and perhaps for the next several days, until the storm and its aftermath has passed.

"That's nice of you Yakiv, but I'll be okay. It's just snow."

"Don't make me go home to Daniela empty-handed," he begged in mock horror. "You know how she is!"

Ionna giggled.

"Seriously, Ionna. Come home with me. Daniela has been cooking all day. Even if we lose power, we'll have plenty to eat. I've got the fire roaring. And we can study," he pointed over to her book, "that long tome you call literature!"

She was about to protest again, when Petruso added his thoughts on the matter. "Go, Ionna. I'm closing shop to help my family finish the final preparations for this storm. It makes no sense to stay open. And you shouldn't try to ride home on the subway in this kind of weather. I'd hate to think of you getting stuck down there if the power fails."

The thought of being stuck in a dark tunnel for days was enough to change her mind. "Oh, all right. You win. Let me gather my things."

As she packed up her backpack, she remembered her morning Skype with her parents. "Yakiv? Would it be alright if I used your Internet to call Mama in the morning? I call them every morning from work. She'll be worried if she doesn't hear from me."

"Of course, my dear. You are welcome to do so."

———

It was the storm of the century. According to the newscasters, "It was a blizzard like no other." And when the power blinked several times before going out, Ionna wasn't the least bit concerned. She was safe and warm, eating some amazing soup with bits of ham and potato. "Be sure to give me this recipe," she called out to Daniela.

"I already have it printed out for you. It's sitting on the counter."

By the time the snow stopped falling around 2am, they had gotten 34 inches. The city, for the first time since Ionna's arrival, was silent. No cars, no horns, no sirens. Just peace and quiet. Shortly before dawn, Ionna woke to a bright light in her eyes. She had fallen asleep without turning the light switch off.

She glimpsed the time on her watch and decided since she was awake and the power was back on, that she would Skype her mama and papa and tell them about the snowstorm. She padded into the kitchen to the small office in the nook to the right of the island.

To her surprise, Yakiv was already awake and making coffee. "Good morning, Ionna. Did you sleep well?"

"Yes. Well until the light flashed full force in my face," she replied.

"The same happened to me. I decided to drink a cup of coffee while the world was still quiet. It won't last much longer. Any time now, the snowplows will start, then the people, and the cars. It will be New York City again before noon."

"Enjoy your solitude, my friend. You don't mind if I call Mama and Papa, do you?"

"No, no go right ahead. My house is your house." He poured his coffee and went to sit by the picture window to admire the unmarred fallen snow before it disappeared.

She got on the computer, added her username to Skype, and made her call to her mother. "Good morning, Mama! How are you today?"

"Fine, Ionna. But where are you? That doesn't look like Petruso's."

Ionna told her mother all about the night's events from the wind to the snow to the lovely invitation to spend the night. Her parents had heard a lot about Yakiv and Daniela over the months and were grateful that their daughter had someone looking out for her.

"Be sure to give them our thanks, Ionna. We are so grateful for their help keeping an eye on our daughter when we aren't able to do so."

Just then, Yakiv walked back into the kitchen. "I have something even better, Mama. Why don't you thank him yourself?"

Ionna called over her shoulder, "Yakiv, would you come here for a moment? My mother wants to meet you and thank you for your kindness."

"Gladly," said Yakiv as he walked into the room.

But instead of greeting her mama, he just stood there, staring at the computer screen like he'd seen a ghost. Ionna glanced at her mother, whose mouth was shaped like an elongated letter O and amazement filled her eyes. Before she could ask what was happening, Yakiv finally spoke.

"Yevtze? Moya dochka?" My daughter.

In return, her mother said, "Papa?"

And both wept openly.

Epilogue

2021

Ionna stood in her grandfather's kitchen, watching her Babusya Daniela busily stirring and tasting some delicious concoction that had to be prepared in the last moments before their guests arrived. Today was a day of celebration. Ionna had just received word that her manuscript was now under contract. Ionna, with a lot of hard work and a lot of help from Didus and Babusya, was soon to be a published author.

Even now, five and a half years later, she still had trouble believing she had a grandfather. Of all the places she could have ended up and of all the people she could have met, stumbling upon a grandfather thought to be dead in a country so far from home was more than miraculous. It was truly inconceivable.

Shortly after discovering Yakiv's true identity, Ionna

had taken a trip to North Carolina to visit her friend Elizabeth, whom she had reconnected with as soon as she regained legal status. She was sitting in their pale-yellow living room, talking about the man who had befriended her, the storm, her call to her mother, and the recognition by the man she knew as Yakiv of her mother.

Hannah's eyes had been wide but strewn with questions. Ionna's English was still awkward, often missing the small connector words and said with her heavy accent. Hannah's mouth moved, repeating the words she had heard silently, trying to rearrange them in some way that made sense. Finally, she said, "Are you telling me that Yakiv, the man who wrote this book" – she held up the paperback of the novel Ionna had brought her from New York – "is your grandfather? And that you didn't realize you had a grandfather in the United States? Or anywhere? That you found your grandfather, completely by accident? And that while on a Skype call, he recognized your mother – his daughter?"

Ionna nodded after each question, as Hannah's eyes cleared of questions, growing rounder and more astonished. "That's remarkable. That's unbelievable. That's got to be a movie!"

Though Ionna agreed the story was movie-worthy, it would never happen. Some of those who had wanted her grandfather dead were still alive, and certainly, the powers who wanted him dead, though no longer actively controlling the government, still existed. If they knew he had survived, there could be trouble, if not for him, then for her parents who remained in a country still torn by war, still fighting against Russian encroachment.

Didus came into the kitchen, then. "Ah, there you are,

Ionna. Your guests are arriving. They want to see the famous author."

"Well, then, Didus, what are you doing in the kitchen? Surely, they are here to see you!"

He laughed heartily. "My dear one, I am merely an old washed-up Ukrainian novelist who gets published simply because Ukrainian-Americans now recognize my name. You, on the other hand, are just beginning a promising career that will stand entirely on the feet of its writing prowess rather than its native heritage. No, they are definitely here to see you."

He ushered her into the living room, urging Daniela to finish up with the sauce and join them. "In a minute, Yakiv, in a minute."

It had now been seven years since she had seen her parents. Seven years since she had embarked on a three-month adventure that turned into a 91-month odyssey. She wished they could be here now, but it was not possible, just as it was not possible for her to go home. Her parents didn't possess the right papers to travel, and because of years of war before the Soviet takeover, and the years of political upheaval since, getting a passport for those born prior to Ukrainian freedom was difficult and expensive.

Ionna continued to send money to her parents, especially now that her father had officially retired. They had purchased a small house far from the fighting and hoped to live out their retirement in relative peace, while Ionna continued to work with officials to secure them papers so they could travel.

Although she had the freedom to travel to Ukraine, doing so was not wise. Ionna spoke regularly with her immigration lawyer. The laws were clear about holding a green card and leaving the US – anything was possible. Although the rules were laid out in neat bullet points on her attorney's website, one line kept her from taking advantage of her privilege to travel: "Your reentry into the United States is not guaranteed. Be aware of the risks of being found inadmissible or deportable upon your reentry."

As much as she missed her parents, neither she nor they wanted her to come back to Ukraine. "You have such an amazing life in the States," her father had said. "So much better than you could have here. The universities are still not operating in many cities, jobs are scarce, food is scarcer. Your opportunities would be so limited here. Do not come home, Ionna. Do not jeopardize your standing in the US for a hug."

So, today, as with other momentous days, like her graduation from SUNY with a degree in creative writing, her birthdays, and every Christmas since she left home, her parents were present only because of technology. Yakiv had set up their chat on the big screen TV and placed the camera such that they were part of the party.

After a toast with "the best vodka money could buy" and the singing of mnohaya lita, the guests began to mingle, chatting with her parents as if they were in the room and not thousands of miles away. As Ionna watched them chat, she thought of that morning five years ago, along with the hundreds of mornings like it, as her mother and grandfather, surrounded by their loving spouses and children, pieced together a story that was not supposed to be told.

The silence after the recognition, after Yevt said "Papa" was almost too quiet to bear. Ionna's gaze swiveled first to Yakiv and then to her mother, both of whom gaped at the other as if at a ghost. Finally, Ionna said, "Mama? What?"

Ionna's voice shattered the silence, confusion and heartache filling the void.

"It can't be. You are dead. You died. Mama said you died. They said you..." Yevt couldn't continue. He was in New York City. Alive. All these years without him, and he was alive. Without warning, she began to shake with rage. How could he sit there looking so happy, so pleased? When he had left them to starve and never once thought of them again.

"Ionna," she said sharply. "Pack your things. Go home this instant. Thank Yakiv for his kindness because it is the way I brought you up, and then never return. That man...that man..." she began to cry. "That man does not deserve to know you. He gave you up when he gave me up. When he gave your babusya up. He doesn't deserve you, now." She buried her head in her hands, as Ionna looked on, dazed and confused. Yakiv still hadn't moved or said a word since recognizing her mother.

Daniela, unaware of the video call, padded into the kitchen with a yawn, stopping when she saw the expression on her husband's face and the tears streaming down Ionna's cheeks.

"What has happened? Ionna? Are your parents okay? Yakiv? Yakiv!" When he didn't respond to her, she said, in a quiet voice, "Lyaksandro?"

At the utterance of his name, everyone began talking at once. Yevt pleading with Ionna to leave at once. Danya trying to get her to calm down. Ionna begging someone to explain what was happening. Daniela sternly shaking her husband, asking him to tell her what was going on. Yakiv saying, "Bozhe miy, oh my God," over and over again.

Finally, Danya got Ionna's attention. "I don't know what is going on there, Ionna. I'm going to log out for now and try to get your mother to make sense. See if you can do the same. Call me in an hour. Can you do that?"

Ionna nodded numbly and the screen went dark. Now, the only sound was Yakiv mumbling "Bozhe miy" and Daniela's quiet "Shhh, shhh. It's going to be okay. Shhh, now."

"What is going on? Why did you call my mother your daughter? Why did she call you Papa? My didus died. A long time ago. When she was a child. We were told he died in the bed of his lover. How do you know my mother?"

Daniela, who had finally gotten Yakiv to sit down, where he held his face in both hands, rocking slowly toward his knees and back again, said, "I think it is time to tell you a story, a story that, until today, was one without a happy ending."

She quickly told Ionna what she had been told of Yakiv's past. "Long ago, Yakiv was known as Lyaksandro Hadeon Rosmakha." At the pronounciation of her babusya's surname, Ionna flinched as if someone had slapped her hard across the face.

Daniela reached out to hold Ionna's hand, understanding this story with the unhappy ending had been her story as well. "He was spying for the rebellion and was nearly caught. But the British organization that was sponsoring him, whisked him out of Ukraine to save his life." She hesitated. This was the part of the story which was new to her.

"When he insisted upon taking his wife and daughter, your babusya and mama, they told him no. They would kill him first. And later, when he insisted again that they bring his family to him, they said...they said..." Then in a barely audible whisper, "They told him his wife and daughter were dead. Killed by the KDB."

Ionna shook her head violently. "But it's not true. My babusya died when I was 12. And my mama. I talk to her every day. It was didus who died. Who was killed by an angry lover. My mama still has the ring. The wedding ring they pulled from the finger of the man found in the remains from the fire. The ring that identified him. He was unfaithful and died and left my babusya and mother to starve, except for the kindness of others." She glared at Yakiv with a mixture of hatred and confusion.

"I understand that is what you were told, Ionna. But he was not cheating on his wife. He was passing information to the British. I guess they created a story so your mama and babusya would be safe."

"But he never came back! He didn't try to find them. My babusya was never the same. Never."

"I don't understand that part, Ionna. I know he tried. He begged them to bring his wife and daughter. And they told him his family had been captured by the KDB and killed. He went quite crazy with grief. It was years before he began living again. Even now, today, he has times that haunt him. I'm the only person who knows who he is, and even I only know what he has been willing to share."

Over the next several months, more of the story was told from both sides of the world, with Yakiv and her mama vacillating between excitement at getting to know one another, sadness at time lost, and anger at those who meddled in their family.

In one of these conversations, Yakiv explained his new name. "I could no longer be Lyaksandro Hadeon Rosomakha. The Brits had given me a new name when they flew me to England, but I demanded to choose my own name.

"Your need for information killed my family. You took me from my home country. You have given me a life I no longer wish to lead. Certainly, for all that, you can allow me to pick a name of my own."

They had consented, and Lyaksandro wrote his new name for them, "YAKIV PAVLO NESVIATYPASKA."

"Do you know why it was so important to me, Yetti?" She had shaken her head no, and Ionna, who was sitting at the computer with Yakiv, did the same.

"My papa named me. The name he gave me was a name to be proud of. It was a name which would guide me through my life. But I..." His voice broke into shreds as he struggled to gain composure. He bowed his head, and then squared his shoulders, ready to confess. "But I dishonored that name. I chose the cowardly way out and ran. I no longer deserved a name like Lyaksandro. My new name is perfect for a man like me. Yakiv means supplanter. Pavlo means small. Nesviatypaska means do not get blessed. If I had been able to find a word for coward and weak, I would have chosen them instead."

———

Now, they were united again. In this room. On this day. Differently, but united, nonetheless.

Lyaksandro still insisted on remaining Yakiv, even to his family, saying regardless of the outcome or the lies, he no longer deserved his birth name. Her mother, for her part, forgave him, having always believed that her father was a decent and loyal man regardless of the papers she had seen stating otherwise.

And Ionna? She had inherited her grandfather's ability and desire to write, though not, as her grandfather did, 'to ward off the demons that threatened to swallow him.' She wrote because, though young, she had seen how God or perhaps the hand of her grandmother, had guided her to this place at this time. She wrote because she finally had something to say.

Author Note

My experiences writing this story were both extremely ordinary and highly irregular. Generally, the sparks of inspiration for my works of fiction occur when doing ordinary, everyday things like listening to the lyrics of a song, laughing over a social media meme, or recalling a family story. Some instinctive intuition resonates with these sparks, fanning them into stories burning to be told. Before my rational side has a chance to take control of the process with character development and detailed outlines, my creative side urges me to the keyboard where I watch the first draft of Chapter One emerge.

Sunflowers Beneath the Snow, however, did not start with a spark, but rather a red-hot coal. During a conversation with a Ukrainian family friend, goosebumps raced up my arms, and even my rational side clearly recognized a story begging for a voice. Unlike other tales I have created, however, this one did not jump spontaneously onto the page. Instead, it took me three years to figure out how to stay true to her experiences, while at the same time, staying true to the craft of fiction writing.

Although names have been changed and circumstances are of my own creation, the basic premise of the story is true. This is, without a doubt, a case where truth is far more powerful than fiction.

About Atmosphere Press

Atmosphere Press is an independent, full-service publisher for excellent books in all genres and for all audiences. Learn more about what we do at atmospherepress.com.

We encourage you to check out some of Atmosphere's latest releases, which are available at Amazon.com and via order from your local bookstore:

Ann's War, a novel by Pat Jones

1963: Hitchhiking Across America, a novel by Daniel Robinson

Around the Edges: Book I, by Wyatt Parr

A Curse in Ash, anovel by Julie Zantopoulos

Her Neighbor, a novel by D. A. Olivier

We Have Something to Say!, a novel by Sonia Myers

Among the Alcoves, a novel by Andrew Mitin

Family Crystals, a novel by Amber Vonda

The Truth About Elves, a novel by Ekta R. Garg

How to be Dead–A Love Story, by Laurel Schmidt

About the Author

Born in Athens, Greece as an Air Force brat, Teri M Brown came into this world with an imagination full of stories to tell. She now calls the North Carolina coast home, and the peaceful nature of the sea has been a great source of inspiration for her creativity.

Not letting 2020 get the best of her, Teri chose to go on an adventure that changed her outlook on life. She and her husband, Bruce, rode a tandem bicycle across the United States from Astoria, Oregon to Washington DC, successfully raising money for Toys for Tots. She learned she is stronger than she realized and capable of anything she sets her mind to.

Teri is a wife, mother, grandmother, and author who loves word games, reading, bumming on the beach, taking photos, singing in the shower, hunting for bargains, ballroom dancing, playing bridge, and mentoring others.